THE HERETICS BIBLE

A James Acton Thriller

Also by J. Robert Kennedy

James Acton Thrillers

The Protocol
Brass Monkey
Broken Dove
The Templar's Relic
Flags of Sin
The Arab Fall
The Circle of Eight
The Venice Code
Pompeii's Ghosts
Amazon Burning
The Riddle
Blood Relics
Sins of the Titanic
Saint Peter's Soldiers
The Thirteenth Legion
Raging Sun
Wages of Sin
Wrath of the Gods
The Templar's Revenge
The Nazi's Engineer
Atlantis Lost
The Cylon Curse
The Viking Deception
Keepers of the Lost Ark
The Tomb of Genghis Khan
The Manila Deception
The Fourth Bible
Embassy of the Empire
Armageddon
No Good Deed
The Last Soviet
Lake of Bones
Fatal Reunion
The Resurrection Tablet
The Antarctica Incident
The Ghosts of Paris
No More Secrets
The Curse of Imhotep
The Sword of Doom
The Heretics Bible

Dylan Kane Thrillers

Rogue Operator
Containment Failure
Cold Warriors
Death to America
Black Widow
The Agenda
Retribution
State Sanctioned
Extraordinary Rendition
Red Eagle
The Messenger
The Defector
The Mole
The Arsenal

Just Jack Thrillers

You Don't Know Jack

Templar Detective Thrillers

The Templar Detective
The Parisian Adulteress
The Sergeant's Secret
The Unholy Exorcist
The Code Breaker
The Black Scourge
The Lost Children
The Satanic Whisper

Kriminalinspektor Wolfgang Vogel Mysteries

The Colonel's Wife
Sins of the Child

Delta Force Unleashed Thrillers

Payback
Infidels
The Lazarus Moment
Kill Chain
Forgotten
The Cuban Incident
Rampage
Inside the Wire
Charlie Foxtrot

Detective Shakespeare Mysteries

Depraved Difference
Tick Tock
The Redeemer

Zander Varga, Vampire Detective

The Turned

THE HERETICS BIBLE

A James Acton Thriller

J. ROBERT KENNEDY

This is a work of fiction. Names, characters, places, and incidents are products of the author's imagination. Any resemblance to actual persons, living or dead, is entirely coincidental.

ISBN: 9781998005871

First Edition

For Alfie Macleod.

You don’t need feet to stand tall.

THE HERETICS BIBLE

A James Acton Thriller

"How much longer can this deception last?"

Frederick II, commenting on the sight of a priest on his way to administer the last rites.
Circa AD 1235

"Frederick II, this pestilent king, a scorpion spitting out poison from the stinger of his tail, has notably and openly stated that—in his own words—the whole world has been fooled by three imposters, Jesus Christ, Moses, and Muhammad, two of whom died honorably, while Jesus himself died on the cross. Moreover, he has dared to affirm, or rather, he has fraudulently claimed, that all those who believe that a virgin could give birth to the god who created nature, and all the rest, were fools. And Fredrick has aggravated the heresy by this insane assertion, according to which no one can be born without having been conceived by the prior intercourse of a man and woman; he also claims that people ought to believe nothing that cannot be proven by the strength and reason of nature."

Pope Gregory IX
AD 1239

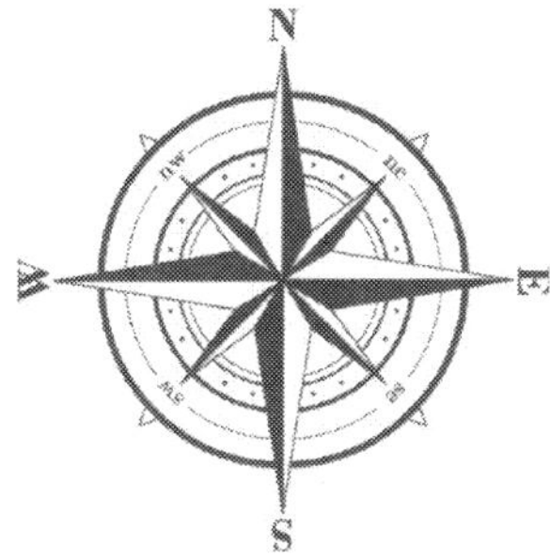

PREFACE

It is hard to imagine, almost a millennium later, the power struggle taking place within Christendom over who should control Christianity. Today, the undisputed and unchallenged leader of the Roman Catholic Church is the pope in Rome, and he is chosen by the College of Cardinals upon the previous pope's death or abdication.

In 1239, things reached a boil with a war of words between Pope Gregory IX and Holy Roman Emperor Frederick II that led to accusations of heresy and blasphemy, and a furor in the courts of Christendom.

When Pope Gregory IX accused the Holy Roman Emperor of being a heretic, it was the latest, but most significant, salvo in a long feud between Frederick II and the Papacy in Rome. Frederick, who held land in Sicily to Rome's south, and other territories in Italy that surrounded the Papal States, was believed to be motivated by the desire to unite his holdings and control all of Italy.

It didn't help that he was a known skeptic when it came to the Church's teachings.

So, when a document was delivered to His Holiness, penned in the emperor's own hand, so blasphemous it couldn't be ignored, it triggered a series of events whose repercussions changed history.

And today, almost 800 years later, the long-rumored document, never before seen, has been discovered.

Once again threatening to embroil Europe in conflict.

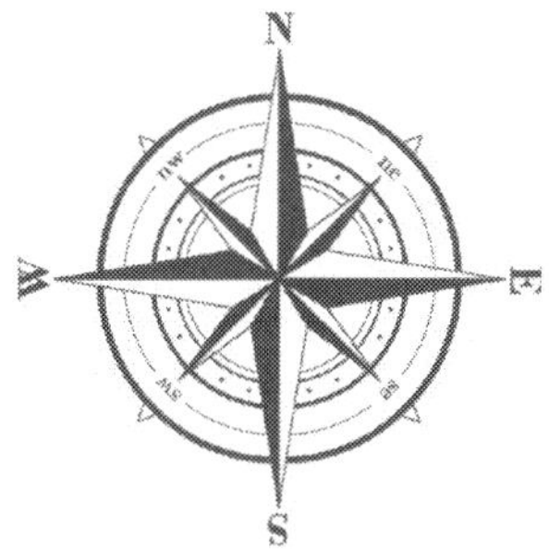

North of Sipicciano, Italy

Present Day

Archaeology Professor Laura Palmer cringed at the sound of gunfire behind her and she checked to make sure her husband, Archaeology Professor James Acton, was still with her. The gunfire was far enough away that it didn't concern her.

It was the enraged mob that was chasing them through the trees that had her heart hammering.

"Was that gunfire?"

The question was asked by Command Sergeant Major Burt "Big Dog" Dawson, a friend, and more importantly, a member of 1st Special Forces Operational Detachment–Delta. The Delta Force member had reached out by phone when he had seen them on live TV, the story spreading across Italy.

"Yes! It's back at the dig! Can you help us?"

"A few of us have liberty. We're at a beach near Rome and already heading your way."

She glanced over her shoulder at the approaching mob and her beloved James shook his head, signaling his assessment of their situation. They were about to be overtaken, and if they were shooting people back at the dig, they weren't going to survive this.

She just prayed Tommy and Mai escaped.

"Unless you're going to be here in the next two minutes, it's already too late."

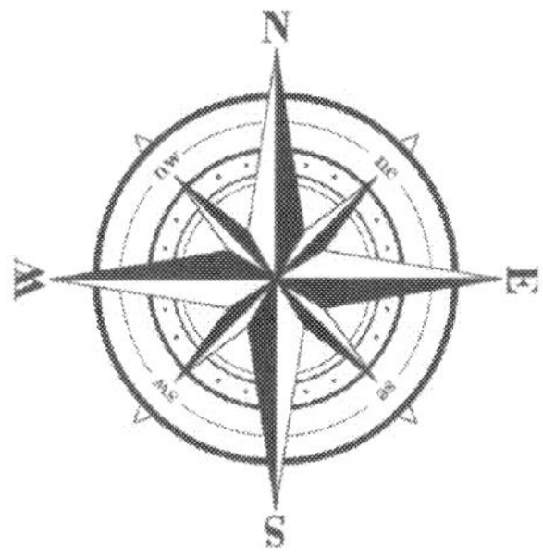

The Vatican

AD 1239

Father Francis stood in silence, his hands clasped in front of him, his head slightly bowed as he listened to the briefing provided by Cardinal Simon de Cantimpré to His Holiness Pope Gregory IX. Francis could only recall seeing the pontiff this agitated twice before, and both those times involved similar briefings, the subject matter always the Holy Roman Emperor.

"He's proposing what?"

Cardinal Simon took an involuntary step back at the harshness with which the question was snapped. "He's proposing that *all* cardinals and bishops be appointed by him and the other prince-electors of Christendom."

"That's ridiculous! It's already ridiculous how much say they have in who leads the Church. The papacy should be supreme in all these matters. Saint Peter must be spinning in his grave knowing what has happened to this holy institution."

Simon grimaced. "I'm afraid there's more."

His Holiness sighed heavily, throwing a hand in the air. "What more could the man possibly want?"

"The emperor is proposing that it should be the prince-electors of Christendom that name your successor, not the College of Cardinals."

His Holiness sprang from his chair, his face red. "Unacceptable! Unholy! Unchristian!" He growled. "Unbelievable! He must be stopped. Otherwise, we might as well burn this place to the ground for it will have lost all its meaning!"

Francis gasped at the words spoken in anger, and the pontiff turned, raising a hand. "You know I, of course, mean that figuratively. This place has stood for almost a thousand years and will stand for another thousand, long after we and the emperor are gone and forgotten. He must be stopped, however, otherwise, the credibility of the Church will be compromised. There's already enough politics involved in the appointment of cardinals and bishops. If we leave it to princes, those that now occupy these exalted positions may be the last pious men to do so." He returned to his chair and clasped his hands in front of him, closing his eyes, his lips moving as a silent prayer was delivered. He regarded Simon. "I have no doubt you've spoken to the other cardinals about this at the congress. What do they think?"

"Most think as I do, and I, of course, agree with you."

"And what course of action would they recommend?"

"The emperor has too much power at the moment. We have no leverage over him. And the princes like what he proposes because it gives them more power. If they get to choose the cardinals and bishops on their lands and the pope that sits in Rome, they can eliminate their critics. The Church has long been a thorn in the side of those who believe they rule by divine right."

His Holiness frowned. "What possible leverage could we have over him?" He shook his head vehemently. "No, it's unchristian. I cannot partake in anything akin to blackmail or extortion. Those are the tools of the Devil."

Simon cleared his throat, shifting uncomfortably, and His Holiness regarded him.

"What is it?"

"Well, Your Holiness, what if the tools of the Devil were used against the Devil himself?"

Francis' heart pounded, his eyes widening. He hadn't heard the Evil One mentioned so frequently in this holy office. His Holiness appeared surprised at the words as well.

"Explain yourself."

Simon reached under his robes and withdrew a folded sheaf of papers. "While at the emperor's court in Padua, I came into possession of this document. It is…" He paused, struggling for the words. "It is disturbing, to say the least."

"What is it?"

"The person who gave it to me, a man I trust and a man who would have access to it, claims it is a treatise penned by the Holy Roman Emperor himself."

"A treatise? On what subject?"

"On his true beliefs, Your Holiness." Simon handed the document over. "And if this is how he truly feels about God and our faith, then a man such as this can never be allowed to not only choose cardinals and bishops, but the very head of the Church itself. For if he were to choose your successor, then the dominion of God could be guided by the hand of Lucifer himself."

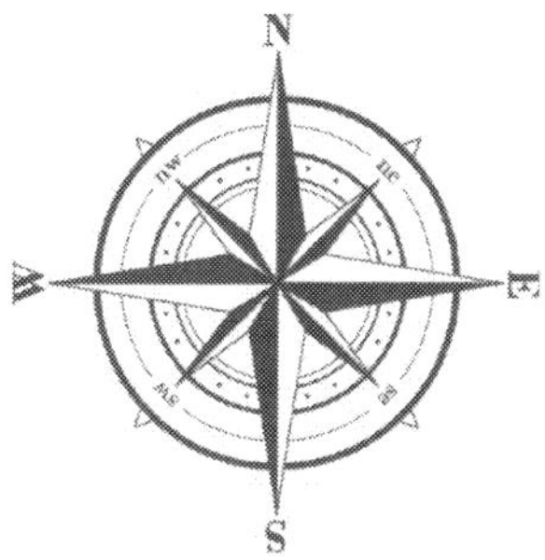

Rest Stop off Highway A1

Italy

Present Day, Two Days Earlier

Matteo sprinted through the trees, giggling as his older brother chased him. School was out, summer vacation had started, and the family was heading to the beaches in the south. He couldn't wait to get in the water and play in the sand. Last year was the first time he had ever experienced it, and he had thought of almost nothing but since. It had affected his performance at school. But he didn't care. School was boring. School was where he was picked on. School was the last place he wanted to be.

They were at a rest stop, his father ordering them all to the bathroom, everyone given fifteen minutes to stretch their legs. He didn't need to pee and had instead decided to explore. The rest stop was large with lots of parking for trucks and cars alike. There was a main building with restaurant facilities and, of course, the gas pumps and charging stations, but he didn't care about any of that. He loved nature. He would rather be outside whenever given the opportunity.

He had headed straight for the trees, checking his watch.

"Keep an eye on your brother!" his father had called, and Romeo had followed him into the forest that lined the highway on either side. Matteo was certain his brother didn't mind. Romeo loved the outdoors as much as he did, and as they raced deeper into the trees, his delight grew as his brother pretended to chase him down. Romeo was five years older than him. There was no way he couldn't catch him if he tried, but he was happy he didn't.

He rounded another tree, twisting to see where his brother was when the ground below him gave out and he fell into a pit of darkness. He hit the ground hard then covered his head as debris fell in on him from above.

"Romeo, help me!" he cried, gripping his ankle, a blinding pain overwhelming him.

"Where are you?"

"I fell in a hole!" He could hear his brother pushing through the underbrush above.

"Where are you?"

"I'm over here!"

"Just a second! I hear you!"

The sounds of his brother got closer and Matteo gently tested his foot, inhaling sharply at the jolt of pain. He fell backward and extended his arm out to brace himself when it touched something, something creepily strange. He twisted his head to look behind him, the slivers of sunlight from above barely allowing him to see. He squinted into the darkness, then gasped at what he saw.

And a blood-curdling scream pierced the calm of the forest.

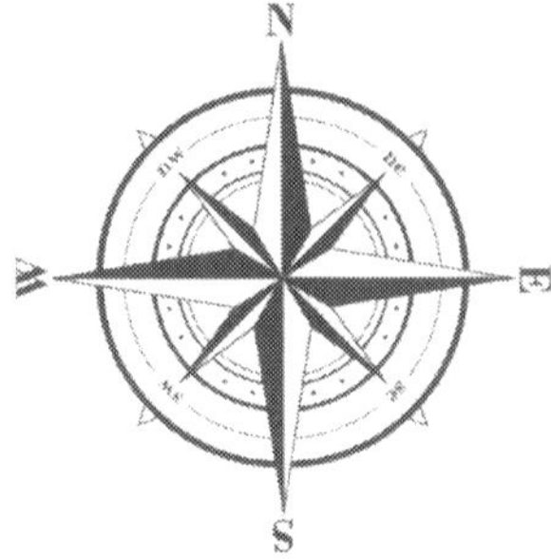

The Vatican

AD 1239

A service bell rang and Father Francis glanced up to see it was from Pope Gregory IX's office. He rose, checked his robes, then stepped over to the large intricately carved doors that separated the inner office from the outer. He rapped twice, pressing an ear to the door.

"Come in."

He opened the door and entered, closing it behind him before bowing. "How may I be of assistance, Your Holiness?"

The pontiff sat behind his desk, as he had been when Francis had last seen him at the conclusion of the briefing by Cardinal Simon. The blasphemous document still sat in front of the man, but a freshly penned letter sat beside it. "You've had time to dwell on what you heard. What's your opinion of this?"

Francis gulped. He was an aide to the pope, yet he had never been asked for his opinion on something like this. His Holiness had read aloud the contents of the document so those in the room would know everything he did and it could be properly debated. Francis had remained out of the discussion. He was a mere priest, the others in attendance cardinals and bishops, and of course the head of the Church himself.

But now they were alone.

His Holiness regarded him then gave him a reassuring smile. "Speak freely, Father. There are no ears to hear your opinions."

Francis drew a deep breath, holding it for a moment as he stood in front of the pontiff's desk, his hands clasped in front of him. "Your Holiness, several assumptions need to be made before a proper course of action can be decided upon. One is whether this document is genuine."

The pope tapped it. "It sits here before me."

"Yes, of course, Your Holiness. Someone has obviously penned it, but did they do so because this was their true beliefs, or is it created for some nefarious purpose?"

His Holiness regarded him. "You mean to implicate Emperor Frederick?"

"Yes."

"To what end?"

Francis shrugged. "I'm not sure. However, the timing is rather convenient."

"You mean this power grab by the emperor over the papacy?"

"Exactly."

"That had occurred to me as well. However, I compared several letters written in the emperor's own hand to this document, and they do appear to match."

"Some forgeries are called clever for a reason."

His Holiness frowned, leaning back. "Yes, this has occurred to me as well. If we assume it is fake, then we should do nothing with it, wouldn't you agree?"

Francis got the sense His Holiness was seeking an answer other than the expected. He took a moment to carefully craft his words. "If we were absolutely certain that the document was a forgery, then yes, we should do nothing with it. Whoever perpetrated this hoax should not be rewarded. But is there any way we can be certain? We have a document, its contents blasphemous, written in what appears to be the emperor's own hand, provided to us by Cardinal Simon, a man we trust, who in turn was provided it by someone he trusted within the emperor's own court. I guess the question is, do we dare ignore it? The implications…" Francis struggled to find the words to express how severe the implications truly were.

"The implications are monumental," finished His Holiness. He tapped the document in question. "If these are indeed the words of Emperor Frederick, then it would explain much of what he has been trying to accomplish. If he is indeed a blasphemer, a pagan who doesn't believe in the God Almighty, who doesn't believe in the Abrahamic religions, then he cannot be allowed to choose who heads the Church. It could mean the end of everything our Lord and his apostles built. And should darkness fall upon Christendom, I fear Satan's minions could swarm those left without a leader to guide them in their faith, and God's creation could be lost to the denizens of Hell itself."

Tingling ran up and down Francis' spine as a cold sweat broke out on his forehead and upper lip. He felt nauseous, his stomach turning at the terrifying words. Could the Holy Roman Emperor truly have penned this document? And if he had, what was his motivation? Simple control, or something far worse such as the destruction of the Roman Catholic Church? And should Christianity lose its shining beacon the Vatican provided, could Christianity stand on its own, or would the faith falter? He finally rediscovered his ability to speak. "Your Holiness, if that is indeed his motivation, he must be stopped."

The pontiff's head bobbed in agreement. "Even if we are uncertain as to the legitimacy of this document, if there is even the remotest possibility, I agree, he must be stopped."

"But how?"

His Holiness tapped the freshly penned letter. "The Electoral College is meeting at the emperor's behest at his palace in Padua. I've written to them, describing the contents of this document and demanding action be taken to stop the emperor's efforts."

"Will they believe you? I mean, even we have our doubts."

"Which is why I've only referred to the contents of the document in general terms, and that it appears to be in the emperor's hand."

"But surely they'll want to see it."

"And they will." His Holiness picked up the document and held it out in front of him. "I want four copies made. Put our best scribes on it. Their replicas should appear exactly as this does. It must appear to be in his emperor's hand, not to deceive, but merely to prove how genuine the original appeared."

Francis took the document with a trembling hand. "The monks will be quite disturbed by the contents of this."

"As they should be. Have their master choose two of the most trustworthy, and explain to them the importance of what they're doing, and the need for absolute secrecy. And tell them that their orders come directly from me, and that what I ask of them is the will of God, so their adherence to my directive is absolute."

"It will take some time."

"As soon as the first is ready, have it brought to me. It must be sent to the Electoral College."

"You're sending them a copy? What of the original?"

"It will be placed in the Vault where all such things go."

Francis hid his surprise at the mention of the Vault, a secret archive hidden under the Vatican grounds that only a handful were aware of. It was used to store documents and items considered a threat to the existence of the Church, whether they be evil or heretical. "Understood."

The pope handed him the letter. "Have this sent by Templar messenger immediately."

"But it will arrive long before the proof."

"Exactly. Without a copy of the document, they will be forced to speculate as to its contents, and to whether it is genuine. It will be enough to cause a furor within the court and the college, and the emperor will be forced to address the accusation."

"But won't he just deny it?"

"Of course he will. Otherwise, he'd find himself drawn and quartered. But days of speculation followed up by the delivery of the document in question could be enough to foil his plans to gain control over the papacy. If all that comes of this is that, then we will have succeeded in saving the Church."

"And should we fail?"

"Then I fear war will tear Christendom apart."

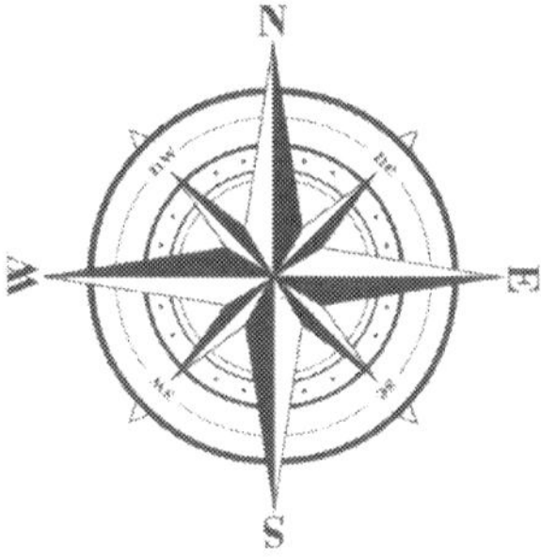

St. Paul's University

St. Paul, Maryland

Present Day

Tommy Granger aimed his phone's camera at the open textbook sitting on the desk in Professor James Acton's classroom. He tapped at the screen to take a photo, everything he did mirrored on the large projection screen at the front of the class. "Okay, now I have this photo from this old textbook I uploaded into my app. Now I already know it's in Spanish, so I'll make life a little bit easier for my software." He tapped several options indicating the source language as Spanish. "And now we want to translate it into English." He tapped again, and moments later, the English text appeared. "So, as you can see, it only takes a few seconds to do the translation, and, of course, it's going to be fairly rough. What my software does is accurately pull the actual text from the source material far better than most other software does, then, using Google APIs, harnesses their translation capabilities to convert the text. I'm in the middle of an upgrade to use AI to improve the output, but as you can see, it's already pretty good."

James Acton agreed as he read the English translation. He stepped forward, pointing at the original text on the left of the screen. "So, for those of you who don't read Spanish, rest assured the translation is quite accurate. This is better for academic texts rather than literature. A computer-generated translation obviously can't capture the nuances of the original without it being gone over by a human who's also a talented writer."

Tommy raised a finger. "I'm hoping the AI is gonna address quite a bit of that."

Acton gave his young friend a look. "I'll be the judge of that."

"Yes, sir."

Acton laughed. "You'll have to forgive Tommy. He loves technology so much, when he's watching The Terminator, he's cheering for the robots." Laughter rippled through the classroom. "So, you've all seen translation tools similar to what Tommy has here, and you might be wondering why I asked him here today to demo his app. Well, what Google won't do for you and what his app will do is take ancient languages and translate them. Why don't you show them?"

Tommy wagged his phone. "Now, this is a work in progress. I've got alpha versions of all kinds of languages people like you have discovered over the years, including Sumerian and Cuneiform. The Latin is nearly complete, and of course, as soon as I was satisfied with it, Google rolled out its own. But I like to think mine's better." He opened another textbook and took a photo, again activating the translation, the English version of the Latin text appearing a moment later.

"What's neat about this," said Acton, "is that the software looks for similar forms. So, let's say we have an ancient language that we've never encountered before. It will look for common elements from other languages."

"Exactly," continued Tommy. "We know from history that a lot of languages are inherited from others, elements taken from one or another, others are root languages of scores of others. If the software can't identify what it's looking at, it'll automatically begin to parse things out and see if it can find any matches in other languages that it's already been programmed with."

Acton faced his class. "The ultimate goal here is to be able to be at a dig site, take a photo of something that you've discovered, and then the software will translate it for you on the fly if it recognizes the language. And if it can't, it will attempt to provide you with possible meanings, and then, of course, as context is added, the user can update the translation themselves."

Tommy grinned and Acton knew this was what he was most proud of. "It allows us to crowdsource the translation of ancient languages. If we discover something new, the software will attempt to find commonalities with other languages, and as more are discovered, it can attempt to identify the alphabet used or the symbology. The users of the app can suggest possible meanings for words, and as the software learns and the community contributes more, it can translate the text more completely and eventually, perhaps, put together a fairly complete vocabulary, at least enough for us to be able to get the context of whatever it is we're looking at."

Somebody raised their hand, somebody Acton didn't recognize, the room jampacked. "Everything you've shown us are things you were already prepared for. How do we know it actually works?"

"Well, the app is actually live. These new features are in development and haven't been shared, but all the standard translation stuff is live and people around the world are using it right now."

"But we only have your word for it."

Acton frowned. "Mr. Granger didn't come here to be accused of being a fraud."

"I'm not saying he is, but today so many things on the Internet claim to do something, but they rarely do."

Tommy's cheeks flushed and Acton felt a twinge of guilt. This was exactly what his young friend was afraid of. "I can prove it," blurted Tommy. He took a deep breath. "I can prove it," he repeated, this time in a more controlled manner. "There are two versions of the app, paid and free. Anything you do with the paid app is confidential, but anything you do with the free app is uploaded to our servers so that we can improve the software."

The skeptic raised an eyebrow. "Is that legal?"

"It's in the terms and conditions you accept when you install the software."

Acton smirked. "This is why you should always read the 5000-page terms and conditions that we all skip over."

Tommy stepped over to his laptop as the gathered students laughed. "We had a few dozen people overnight translate documents. Oh, here's one. This could be interesting. It's a Latin translation into Italian." He brought it up on the main screen. "I don't read Italian, so I'm gonna change the target language to English." A few taps of his keyboard and the Italian was quickly replaced.

But Acton was way ahead of it, already reading the Latin. "Holy shit!"

Everyone in the room turned their attention to him.

"What is it, Professor?" asked Tommy.

"This is a letter from the pope, dated 1239 AD."

"What's The Treatise of the Three Imposters?" asked someone in the room, obviously reading the English translation.

Acton pursed his lips, still in disbelief. "It's a rumor. It was always thought to be fake." He scratched at his chin. "But this, this suggests it's real. What you're witnessing here, right now, could change history as we know it."

Phones were held up throughout the room, photos snapped, videos taken, and Acton stepped over to Tommy as excitement rippled through the gathered archaeology students. "Can you find out where this was taken?"

Tommy worked his laptop then gave a thumbs-up. "I've got GPS coordinates embedded in the photo they uploaded."

"Who are they?"

"I don't know. They took the free version of the program, but it was installed a few minutes after the photo was taken. My guess is they found this letter, Googled how to translate it, found my app, installed it, translated it, and now here we are."

"I need you to figure out some way to reach them."

"Why?"

"Because they might have stumbled upon an incredibly important piece of history, something that could answer a question almost eight hundred years old."

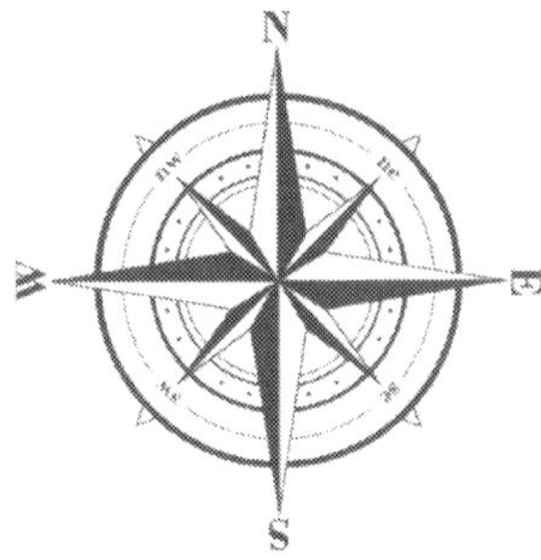

Santa Maria del Priorato, Templar Headquarters for Rome

Rome, The Papal States

AD 1239

Father Francis stepped into the office of the Templar Master for the region. Sir Enrico Teutonico rose and bowed. "Father Francis, this is an unexpected pleasure. How may I be of assistance?"

Francis closed the door to give them some privacy. While everyone here should be loyal to the Church, he couldn't take any chances, not with what was going on. He had had more time alone with his thoughts on the matter since he had made arrangements for copies to be made of the treatise, and he had serious concerns. The emperor was powerful, and the prince-electors of Christendom had sworn their loyalty to him after electing him. If his power were challenged, would their support falter, or might they instead unite behind their emperor and declare the papacy an enemy? By challenging the emperor in the hopes of protecting the Church, they might just bring its downfall.

And then, of course, there was the question of whether the document was genuine, something he had serious doubts about. Why would anyone in the emperor's position be foolish enough to write down thoughts such as these?

He held up the sealed letter the pope had penned earlier. "I need this sent as quickly as possible through your network to the leader of the Electoral College now meeting in Padua."

Sir Enrico took the letter. "Consider it done. Is there anything else?"

"Yes." Francis stepped closer, lowering his voice. "I have something else that must also be delivered to the College, but it is of a delicate nature. The fewer hands that carry it the better."

Enrico regarded him for a moment. "This item is important?"

"Yes."

"Will the messenger be at risk?"

"If it becomes known he has it, potentially."

"Then it must be delivered outside of the network. I recommend one man, a knight."

Francis agreed. "He must be of the utmost integrity."

"I have the perfect man in mind."

"Excellent." Francis removed a piece of paper from his pocket and slid it across the desk with a single finger. "These are his instructions for the meeting. He must be given orders to follow them, and any other instructions provided at the meeting, to the letter."

"He will be so instructed."

"Very well. Speak of this to no one. I was only here to have that message"—he indicated the letter from His Holiness—"delivered, and nothing more."

Enrico bowed. "It shall be so."

"I pray your brother has a safe journey, for if he fails…" Francis' voice drifted off and Enrico regarded him curiously.

"Father?"

Francis pursed his lips. "Then God help us all."

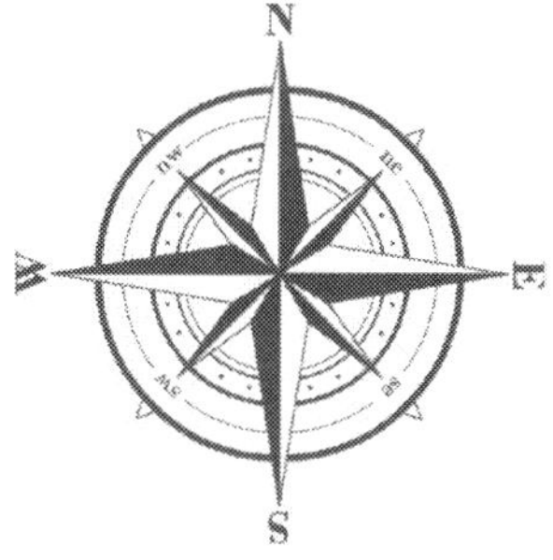

Acton/Palmer Residence, Overlook Village Gated Community

St. Paul, Maryland

Present Day

James Acton watched in appreciation as his gorgeous wife, Laura Palmer, darted from one side of the room to the other in nothing but her bra and panties. She caught him staring and stopped.

"Shouldn't you be helping?"

He jerked his chin toward his carry-on bag sitting near the door. "I finished while you were in the shower."

She turned to see the bag and growled. "Men. Let me guess, two pants, four shirts, and a fist full of underwear?"

"Don't forget the socks, and I'll have you know there are two fistfuls of underwear, just in case."

"Toiletries?"

"Done."

"Passport?"

"Done."

She continued packing her own bag. "Chargers?"

"Every length and type and all that nonsense. Don't worry, if we forget anything, Mario can complete our kit."

She stopped and gave him a look. "Mario Giasson is the Inspector General of the Vatican Police. He is *not* going to pop out to the local store to pick up what you forgot."

"He doesn't have to. People actually live at the Vatican, you know. If I need more clothes, I'll just ask for a set of robes. I like those red ones."

"You mean the ones the cardinals wear?"

"Yeah. They really bring out my figure."

"You wore one once to a costume party and somebody said you had a nice ass. And he was drunk."

Acton gave her a toothy grin. "It still counts."

She leaned back and stretched, and Acton's grin spread. She caught him. "Should I just take these things off?"

"What a wonderful idea."

She stabbed a finger at him as he rose from his chair. "Don't you dare move, mister. I'm still packing. Plenty of time for that later."

He tapped his watch. "Not really. Our flight leaves in an hour."

"You didn't leave us much time to get ready. You're sure this is the real thing?"

"I'm not sure about anything. As soon as I saw the letter, I didn't know what to think. You read it, what's your opinion?"

She zipped up her suitcase in triumph. "I wouldn't be scrambling to pack a bag and fly to Europe if I didn't think there was something to it."

She took a moment and stared at him. "The Treatise of the Three Impostors. I had always just assumed it was fake."

Acton agreed. "It's interesting that academia has dismissed it as fake. The early copies that started to appear in the eighteenth century were obviously bullshit, but all of it was based on an accusation made by the pope in 1239. The accusation was real, the reference to the Treatise of the Three Impostors was real. The only thing that was in question was whether this treatise ever actually existed because no one ever found a copy. And back then, with the hatred between the pope and the Holy Roman Emperor and those surrounding them, anything's possible."

He rose and picked up her bag from the bed, placing it next to his by the door. He faced her and pulled off his underwear, the only thing he was wearing, and she smiled.

"Somebody's happy to see me."

He shrugged. "Could be you, could be the excitement of a new archaeological discovery."

She reached back and undid her bra, revealing the twins. "Are you sure?"

He grinned like a Cheshire Cat. "Sorry, I just forgot my name."

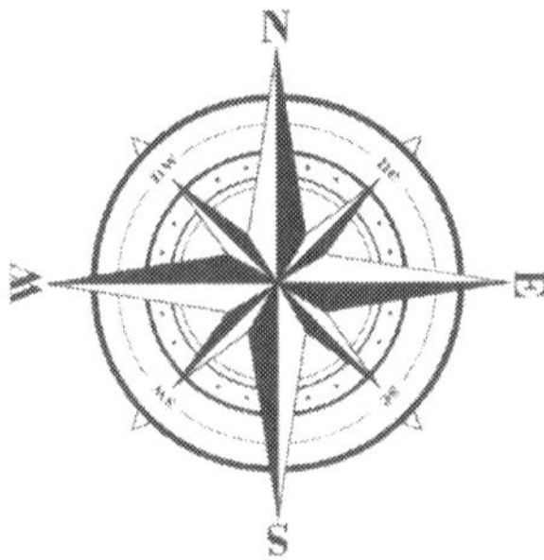

South of the Vatican

Rome, The Papal States

AD 1239

Sir Ricardo Gabillone, knight of the Poor Fellow-Soldiers of Christ and of the Temple of Solomon, known to the citizens of Christendom as the Knights Templar, stood on the wet cobblestone, a light rain having just finished, leaving the road slick. To his right was a bakery, to his left a butcher shop, and in front of him an alleyway between the two. This was where he had been told the meeting would take place, a meeting he knew nothing about. As a Templar Knight, he had gone on countless missions in his over twenty years of service, and managed to survive them all, though just barely on occasion. His right leg, just above the knee, ached as it always did when the weather changed, a constant reminder of the Saracen that had almost bested him a decade ago. Right now, his old injury was telling him the light rain they had just received was merely a taste of the storm yet to come. He shivered. He had left the hot and arid

Holy Land behind three years ago, and was still unaccustomed to the constant chill of an Italian winter.

Church bells chimed in the distance, marking the top of the hour. He stepped into the inky black darkness of the alleyway, torches lighting the street casting long shadows, his own stretching out before him then lost. He steadied his breathing. He wasn't scared. He didn't expect to be accosted here, yet he was always cautious. His hand gripped the hilt of his sword, a blade that had served him well in battle, and it, combined with the crisp white cloak with the red Maltese cross emblazoned on it, were usually enough to send most who unwisely challenged him scurrying.

He cocked an ear, listening for any sign that the person he was to meet was somewhere in the dark, but heard nothing. He continued forward. This was the location. This was the appointed hour.

"That's far enough," echoed a voice ahead.

Ricardo stopped, his grip tightening. "The moon shines dim on a cloudy night."

"But the sun will quickly burn those clouds away in the morning."

Ricardo relaxed, the response to his challenge properly returned. A foot scraped on the cobblestone directly ahead. He could barely make out the figure approaching. The creak of shutters on a lantern opening was followed by a dull orange glow revealing their immediate surroundings. Before him stood a man in the cloak of a monk, his head hooded, though not so much as to hide his face.

The monk's eyes widened slightly. "I wasn't expecting a Templar."

"Nor was I expecting a monk."

The man bit his lip for a moment. "I suppose it makes sense, and that you can be trusted."

Ricardo regarded his counterpart. "Trusted with what?"

The man reached under his cloak and produced a leather folio, tied tightly with cord. He held it out in both hands, almost reverently. "With this."

Ricardo took it and made to open it when the man stopped him.

"No, you must not open it."

"What's in it?"

"I cannot say. It's not for you to know."

Ricardo frowned slightly. "Can I at least know the nature of what it is? Is it a document?"

"Why would you need to know?"

"If I end up having to choose between using a road or wading across a river, I need to know if water could damage the contents, or if it must be shielded from a heavy rain like we're about to get? Details are important."

"It's a document."

"And I assume it's an important one if all of this"—he waved a hand at their situation—"is necessary?"

"Of the utmost importance. It's critical that this be delivered to the leader of the Electoral College now meeting in Padua as quickly as possible."

Ricardo cocked an eyebrow. "Padua?"

"Yes."

"Isn't that where the Holy Roman Emperor holds court?"

"Yes, but it is essential *he* not intercept this message. It must be delivered to the head of the Electoral College."

"Interesting, considering here we stand in Rome, with the glow of the Vatican visible from the street where the pope, the emperor's greatest challenger, holds court."

"Like I said, you're not to concern yourself with such things."

"But I'm a Templar Knight sworn to protect the Church and its leadership."

"By delivering this, you'll be protecting not only the Church, but the Papacy. If I could explain why, I would, but secrecy is of the utmost importance. You must never look at the document."

Ricardo frowned. His gut told him something was wrong here, that there was more going on than so far revealed. Yet he had his orders. The Templar Master himself had issued them, though he had been told it was a simple messenger job. The Order had an extensive network throughout Christendom that could swiftly deliver messages and goods from one corner to the other, for a fee, of course. It was one of the ways the Order funded its operation.

Normally, however, knights weren't assigned such tasks. This would be outside of the network, a personal delivery, not the traditional route of one messenger delivering to the next outpost, where a fresh rider and horse would be waiting to continue the journey. It made sense if the document contained within this folio was so important.

The fewer hands it passed through, the better.

He held up the folio. "Your words and demeanor suggest that should someone know I possess this, they might attempt to take it from me."

The man's head rapidly bobbed. "Yes. No one must know what you possess. No one, not even the members of your order."

Ricardo's eyebrows rose. "My brothers can be trusted."

The man dismissed his assertion, pointing at the folio. "Not with this. If they caught wind of what this contains, even your own brothers would kill you where you stand."

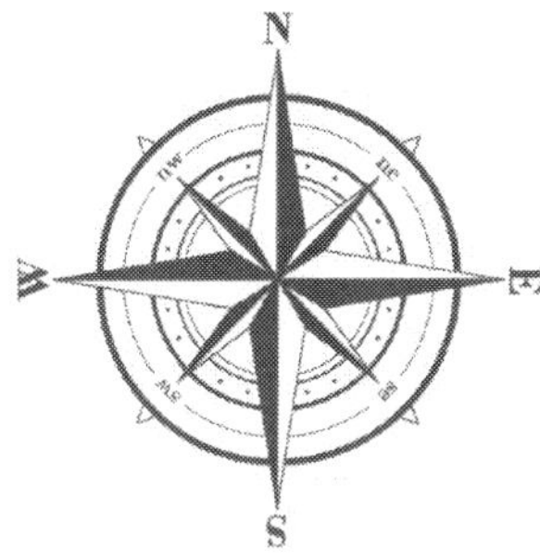

Clearview Private Airport, Maryland

Present Day

"Sorry we're late," apologized Laura Palmer as she stepped inside the private jet, part of the lease-share network of which they were members. "Somebody decided to take his time."

Acton smirked at his wife. "I thought you liked it when I took my time."

Her cheeks flushed. "Keep talking like that and there won't be a next time."

Acton grinned at the flight attendant. "I think I'm in trouble."

"You would be if you were my husband."

Acton laughed and slapped the man on the back as he followed Laura deeper into the cabin. Mai Trinh and Tommy Granger rose to greet them, both leaping at the opportunity for a chance to visit Italy.

"So good of you to invite us," gushed Mai as she gave Laura and him a hug. The young woman, exiled from her native Vietnam after helping them evade Vietnamese and Russian authorities several years ago, was a recent American citizen and, now that she had that prized passport, was seeing more of the world than she had ever dreamed. With her family back in Vietnam, she was like a surrogate daughter to them, and by extension, Tommy was like their son-in-law. They were very close, and he would die for them both, as would Laura, though he doubted that would be a problem on this trip. All they were doing was heading to Italy to examine a document.

That was it.

Everyone took their seats and they were in the air a few minutes later. He had grown up middle class, the life his parents had provided comfortable, and though his career as an academic didn't allow for much of a savings account, it still kept him with a roof over his head and fed. After meeting Laura, however, things had changed dramatically. She was filthy stinking rich thanks to an inheritance from her brother when he had died, or rather, supposedly died. They now wanted for nothing and were slowly indulging a little more in her extreme wealth, though he still wore the same style clothes, still enjoyed a good steak on the barbecue or a lowly hamburger, and usually drank domestic beer. Life was definitely good, and one of the pleasures they both took in the money was helping out friends.

"Did you reach Hugh?"

Laura shook her head. "I didn't even try. It's after his bedtime. I sent him an email. He'll get it in the morning. I let Mary know that he might be calling her to come join us."

"I hope he does." Mai cuddled up with Tommy. "I like him. He's kind of like, I don't know, a grandfather."

Acton chuckled. "Don't let him hear you say that. I think the first time he wants to be called a grandfather is if his son happens to have a child, because then it's factually true. You saying it just means he's old."

Laura snickered. "He's not old."

Acton cocked an eyebrow. "I have a sneaky suspicion that when you're his age, you won't agree. I'm younger than him and I'm already starting to feel the pains."

Tommy regarded him. "It might help if you stopped getting yourself shot, stabbed, and beat up."

"Don't forget blown up," added Mai.

"Right!"

Acton wagged a finger. "Wait a minute, of the two of us, who was the last one to get shot?"

Tommy rolled his shoulder. "I don't know. You get shot so often I've lost track."

Laura giggled. "I should talk to Cameron and see if there's some sort of civilian body armor that we could wear when we're out and about."

Acton grunted. "We'd have to wear it 24/7. We've been attacked in our own home and, unless it feels like regular clothing, I don't want to wear it."

Tommy leaned forward. "Actually, there are some interesting developments in that area. You might be surprised at what's available for the uber-rich."

Laura pulled out her phone. "I'm going to send him a message now before I forget. 'Tommy says there's magic clothing that can protect us from bullets and missiles. Can you look into it please?'"

Tommy's jaw dropped. "I never said that!"

She shrugged as she put her phone away. "I just misinterpreted the headline and didn't bother to read the article. Isn't that what your generation does?"

Tommy squirmed. "Sometimes I hate the year I was born in."

Acton laughed. "I don't think it really matters anymore in this post-fact world. Some teenager called me a boomer the other day. Are you kidding me? My father was a boomer. I'm Gen X. If you're gonna insult someone, don't make yourself sound like an absolute moron while doing it."

Laura rolled her eyes. "There you go. You got him started."

Mai attempted to change the subject. "So, what can you tell us about this document we're going to look at?"

"Very little and a whole lot," replied Acton, to which Tommy cocked an eyebrow.

"Huh?"

Acton laughed. "Well, what prompted this trip was the letter that your app translated for a user in Italy this morning. I called Mario at the Vatican and he was able to find out that a young boy was playing in the woods and fell into a hole—"

Mai gasped. "Is he all right?"

"He broke his ankle but he'll be fine."

"Oh, thank God."

"I should say, he'll be fine physically. Mentally, he could be effed up for life."

"James!" admonished Laura.

"Hey, I said effed up. I didn't say—"

"James!"

He grinned and continued. "He found a body in the hole. Looks like it's been there for centuries. And if the document that was found on the body is genuine, then it looks like he's been there for almost eight hundred years. The letter, it turns out, was from Pope Gregory IX and it was a letter to the head of the electoral college."

Tommy cocked an eyebrow. "Electoral college? You mean like we have?"

"Sort of. It's where we got the term from, certainly. It was a group of princes from Europe that would choose the next Holy Roman Emperor after the current one died or was otherwise unable to fulfill his duties. It appears to be a cover letter that refers to another letter sent the same day this was penned, indicating that what accompanied it was the promised copy of the Treatise of the Three Impostors as penned in Holy Roman Emperor Frederick II's own hand, proving he is a heretic."

"Is that important?" asked Tommy.

Mai nodded, her education in history and anthropology. "Very much so. There could be no more serious an accusation in those days."

"Exactly," agreed Laura. "What was different this time was that Frederick was known to be a bit of a skeptic, quite often challenging the teachings of the Church, questioning why things were the way they were. But this document, this Treatise of the Three Impostors that accompanied the accusation of heresy, was unique. Never before had someone in such a position been accused of such a thing with only alleged proof."

Tommy raised a finger. "Alleged. Whenever I hear that, it raises flags."

"And it should," said Acton. "See, the problem is the accusation was made by the pope claiming that the emperor had written this document outlining his true beliefs, but the document was never produced. Frederick denied writing any such thing and the treatise was lost to history, though it did lead to the eventual decline of Frederick's power and eventually his family line."

Tommy wagged his phone. "But I don't get it. I did some googling on the way here and you can buy the treatise on Amazon."

"All fakes."

Tommy's eyebrows rose. "Does Amazon know?"

Laura laughed. "Amazon doesn't care, nor should they. We're talking about centuries-old fakes that started to appear in Europe in the eighteenth century. They all covered the premise of what we know the treatise was supposed to be, but it was quite evident from examining them that they were forgeries."

"I'm a little confused. A treatise is an academic paper, right? Sort of like an essay?"

"Yes."

"Then what or who are the three impostors? What's this referring to?"

Acton turned on teacher mode. "Well, let's look at it this way. We know claims of heresy were made because of it."

"So it has to deal with religion."

"Exactly. So, what are impostors?"

"People who pretend to be something they're not?" replied Mai, uncertainty in her voice.

"Exactly." Acton pointed at her. "And don't doubt yourself. Answer with confidence even if you might be wrong. More than half the time, you'll come off looking like a genius."

Laura groaned. "Please don't take my husband's advice."

He stuck his tongue out at her. "Fine, don't look like a genius like I do."

"'Look like' being the important qualifier here."

"Man, you're just going after me today, aren't you? And after I took my time and everything with you."

She opened her mouth to deliver a retort but he cut her off, continuing with his little lesson.

"So, we have three people who pretend to be who they're not. We know it deals with religion. So, what do you think the treatise deals with?"

"Well, they'd have to be important," said Mai. "If it were just three priests or three princes, it certainly wouldn't be enough to bring down an emperor."

Tommy's eyes widened. "Isn't that a key thing? If the emperor believed that these three people were impostors, why would anyone care even if they were important? He's claiming they're impostors. Big deal. If he's right, then people should be concerned that they are. And if he's wrong, it doesn't really matter. He's the emperor. He can pretty much say whatever he wants."

"You're getting warmer. So, let's operate under the premise that these three people that the emperor believes are impostors are important, extremely important, and related to religion. Who could they possibly be?"

Tommy shrugged. "I don't know. The only important people I can think of in Christianity would be Jesus and his apostles."

Acton tapped his nose. "You got one of them."

Tommy's eyes widened. "Wait a minute. Jesus is one of the three impostors?"

"Yes. And if Jesus is one of them, who are the other two?"

Mai's eyes bulged. "You don't mean…wow. You mean like Moses, Jesus, and Muhammad, the founders of the three Abrahamic religions?"

"There you go. You figured it out."

"So just what are you saying?"

"What I'm saying is that the pope at the time accused the emperor of writing an academic essay on why he believed Moses, Jesus, and Muhammad were all impostors who lied about everything they said, meaning there is no God and therefore Judaism, Christianity, and Islam are all fake religions."

"Wow!" exclaimed Tommy, leaning back. "That's the kind of shit that'll get you killed today. I can just imagine what the reaction must have been back then."

"Exactly. What made it worse was it was an accusation without proof. No one ever saw the treatise or whoever did see it never came forward to claim they had. Most historians believe that Pope Gregory IX made it up in order to discredit Frederick II, whom he was in a dispute with."

Mai shook her head. "It's hard to believe what was going on back then with the Church."

"Well, remember, the Church is a creation of man and anything created by man is fallible. And back then, these people with absolute power, they'd get away with almost anything. Definitely different times."

Mai paled slightly. "Are you sure this isn't dangerous? I mean, don't you two know firsthand what can happen when Muslim fanatics get upset?"

Acton chuckled. "We do that. But on those occasions, we were dealing with religious artifacts, not a document written by a Christian that, until today, everyone thought was fake. Remember, you can order this on Amazon and nobody's tried to burn down their headquarters yet."

Tommy chewed his cheek as if he were uncertain as to what to say.

"Speak," said Acton, and Tommy sighed.

"Well, with all due respect, if everyone knew what Amazon was selling, then they'd have no reason to burn it down. What we're saying is that this could be the real thing. Doesn't that mean there are three religions out there who might not want it to see the light of day?"

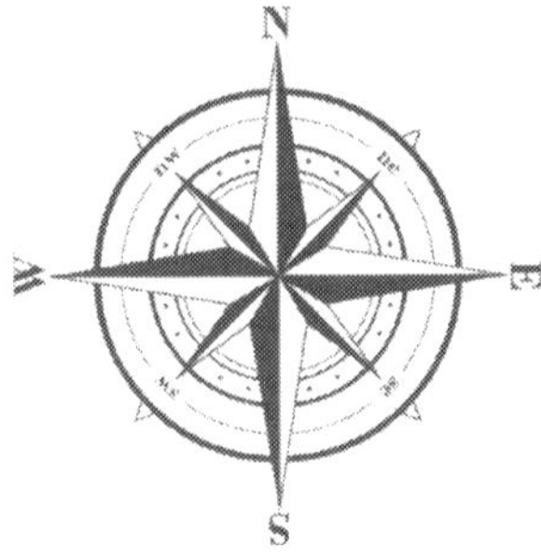

North of the Vatican

Rome, The Papal States

AD 1239

Sir Ricardo didn't believe for a moment what the monk had warned him about was true. The very idea that his Templar brothers would kill him for what he now carried was ridiculous. Yet the earnestness in the man's voice, in his eyes, certainly indicated the monk believed it was true. His orders from his Templar Master were to do whatever was asked of him at the prearranged meeting, and if the monk wanted complete discretion, then that's what he would get.

Ricardo hadn't returned to the garrison after the meeting had concluded, instead waiting outside a local stable where he would equip himself for the journey ahead with some of the coins in the generous purse the monk had handed him at the conclusion of their meeting.

Templars were only allowed to carry four *dinars* on their person, except under special circumstances. The amount of currency he now held was more than he had ever possessed on his person since joining the

Order. Templars were monks, all of whom had taken a vow of poverty, any worldly goods they had before joining the Order forfeit.

Those like him were already knights before joining. One didn't join the Order then become a knight. The Order didn't have the power to grant that. That was reserved for nobility. He was nobility, as had been generations of his family, but the Holy Land had beckoned, and the stories of Saracens accosting the pilgrims had infuriated him. When his wife had died giving birth to a stillborn child, he had made a decision and marched into the nearest Templar commandery, signing the papers that day to join.

It was the best decision he had ever made. They had given him a purpose, serving God, serving his fellow man, protecting the innocent, protecting the weak. The trappings of wealth were something he didn't miss. He preferred hard work. Being doted upon by servants had never held any appeal, though life in the Order as a knight still had its privileges. Sergeants obeyed his orders, as did the countless squires and others who served in lesser capacities.

Everything was provided. Food, drink, shelter, even the horse he rode upon and the clothes he wore. He wanted for nothing, including companionship. The brotherhood he had found in the Order had filled the void left behind by the death of his wife and the abandoning of the only home he had ever known. So, when the monk had insisted he make the journey alone, it had been disappointing, though understandable. A sergeant and several squires would have provided him with happy company and additional security, but it would also draw attention.

He stared down at his cloak.

Speaking of drawing attention.

He unhooked it from his shoulders then rolled it up, stuffing it in a saddle bag as sounds of life from the home attached to the stables could be heard even above the heavy rain that now pounded the ancient city. He lifted his foot off the ground, bending his knee, wincing slightly, and hoped that the Saracen responsible was burning in Hell for the lifelong suffering he had caused.

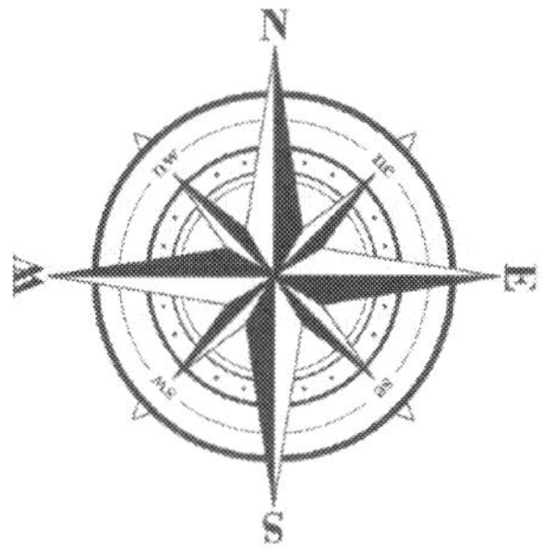

Minsk, Belarus

Present Day

Former Spetsnaz Colonel Alexie Tankov groaned in ecstasy as the young blond Belarusian woman worked her magic fingers all over his back. He figured he still had at least a good decade left in him as an active participant in his group's activities, but he was suffering the aches and pains of age more with each mission. He was getting tired of the game and was thinking of retirement, but he needed one last score, something huge.

His last attempt had been foiled by Professor Acton and his friends. In fact, his last two major attempts. He wanted something big that he could take his cut and disappear. New face, new identity. The only decisions he wanted to make were what he wanted for dinner, what wine he wanted paired with that, and who he had for dessert, without worrying about who might be around the next corner waiting to take him out.

There was a knock at the door and he frowned. He wasn't to be disturbed during these sessions that always ended happily, but since his men knew that, and there was only one who would dare violate that order, it could be good news. "Come in, Arseny."

Arseny Utkin, his second-in-command, opened the door and Tankov turned his head toward him. "How'd you know it was me?"

"Because you're the only one with balls enough to interrupt my massage hour."

"Well, I figured I was safe to come in during the first half."

Tankov grunted. "It better be good."

"It is. You know how you've been after that one last big score."

Tankov pushed up on his elbows and glanced at the girl. "Out, but don't go far. We're not done here."

She scurried from the room, the door closing behind her, and Tankov swung his legs around so he was sitting on the massage table, his towel covering the start of a raging erection. "What have you got?"

Utkin wagged his tablet. "What I think most of our competitors are going to ignore because they don't know any better. Ever heard of The Treatise of the Three Impostors?"

"Can't say I have."

"Brief history. Back in 1239, Pope Gregory IX accused Holy Roman Emperor Frederick II of being a heretic for penning a document called The Treatise of the Three Impostors in which he claimed that Moses, Jesus, and Muhammad were all lying to their flocks, meaning the only conclusion one could draw is that Judaism, Christianity, and Islam are all fake religions created by liars."

Tankov whistled. "All right. So, what's new? That's eight hundred years ago."

"What's *old* is that no one ever found the actual document that the pope accused the emperor of writing. A few hundred years ago, fakes started to appear, but everybody knew that's what they were. Fakes. But what's *new* is that earlier today, it looks like they might have actually found the original."

Tankov whistled louder. "Now, I can think of a few people who'd really like to get their hands on that."

"Exactly. We have Jewish, Christian, and Muslim buyers who would love to make sure this never saw the light of day."

Tankov smiled. "This Atheist smells a bidding war."

"Exactly what I was thinking."

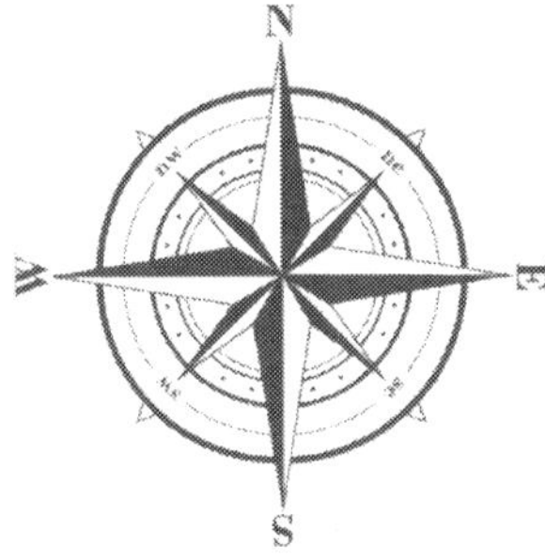

Reading Residence

Whitehall, London, England

Interpol Agent Hugh Reading woke with a start. It was still dark, and he glanced over at his clock and cursed. It was hours before his alarm was supposed to go off. He adjusted his CPAP mask then paused, his hand darting to his chest. Something was wrong, but he wasn't sure what. There was no pain, but he just felt off, and with his recent history of heart troubles, he immediately feared the worst.

He turned off his CPAP and tore the mask from his face as he swung his legs out of bed and sat upright. He felt weak and his breathing was slightly labored, yet still, there was no pain, no tightness, no typical signs of a heart attack. But something was definitely wrong. He didn't feel himself.

He opened his nightstand and retrieved the box containing the KardiaMobile ECG monitor Laura had given him. He pulled it out and launched the app on his phone then pressed his fingers on the device. Thirty seconds later he had the answer, and it was terrifying

So much so, it had to be bullshit.

His heart rate was 235 beats per minute. How was that even possible? Wouldn't his heart explode? He tried again, pressing his fingers a little harder, certain it had to be a mistake. 238. He had no desire to go to A&E. The wait times were insane. But this was his heart and he had no choice. He didn't scare easily, and never in his wildest dreams would he have ever thought he would be terrified in his own home, but he was, and he was all alone.

He needed help.

He called his son, the only person he could think of to call, but it went directly to voicemail. His phone was either off or set to Do Not Disturb, and if he weren't so scared, he might have been heartbroken to realize his son hadn't set his phone number as one of those allowed to ring no matter what.

If only I lived with Jim and Laura.

He cursed, staring at his phone, then sniffed hard as he thought of another possibility. He dialed his partner at Interpol, Michelle Humphrey, and she answered on the second ring.

"You do realize some of us are trying to get our beauty sleep? We don't all want to end up looking like you when we get to your age."

His shoulders shook as he struggled to maintain control. Someone had cared enough to answer, and the thought led to an uncharacteristic tidal wave of emotions.

"Hugh, are you all right?" asked Michelle, her concern obvious.

He finally managed to strangle out some words. "No, something's wrong with my heart."

"Where are you?"

"Home."

"I'm coming right over. I want you to hang up right now and call 999."

"Tell my son I love him and that I'm sorry for having missed out on so much of his life."

"You'll tell him yourself. Now hang up and call 999. I'm on my way."

She ended the call and he wiped away the lone tear that had escaped. This wasn't him. He was a tough guy. He wasn't supposed to have emotions like this. But dying alone, uselessly, was one of his greatest fears, yet how else had he expected to die? He had hoped on the job, but Interpol wasn't exactly a dangerous vocation. His friends were more likely to get him killed.

You're not dead yet.

He dialed 999, finally thinking clearly, then prayed that the afterlife he might soon be visiting wasn't a load of bullshit made up by a bunch of con artists to control their minions.

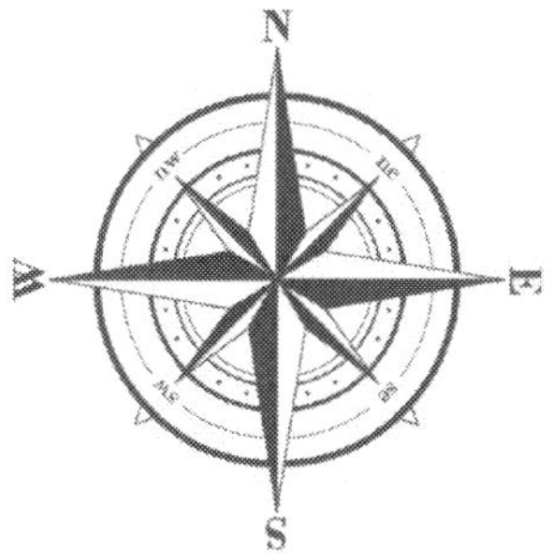

The Vatican

AD 1239

Father Francis pressed a hand against his uneasy stomach. Ever since he had arranged for the pope's letter and a copy of the treatise to be delivered, he had been unsettled, unable to eat, a sense of impending doom weighing heavily on his shoulders. This entire endeavor was unworthy of the papal office. They should put their fate in God's hands. After all, surely He would protect the Church from any threat the emperor might pose, and should He not, then perhaps it was God's will that the Holy Roman Emperor be the office that decided who was to be God's voice on earth.

By doing what they were doing, were they meddling in His affairs? He feared nothing good could come of this, yet it wasn't his place to express this opinion unless asked. To do so unprompted, especially when it went against His Holiness' decision, would be overstepping his bounds.

He headed swiftly down the corridor toward the doors that led to a team of monks whose duty it was, day in and day out, to make copies of the Bible so perfect, so beautiful, they were fit for royalty and the leaders of the Church. Few in Christendom possessed a Bible, for few could read, and even fewer could read Latin. The clergy of the Church and the nobility that ruled were the only ones entitled to copies. Yet that still provided enough work for the monasteries scattered across Christendom to continue their work without pause.

He entered to find two of the monks at their tables and their abbot behind his desk, none of them here last night when he had picked up the first copy readied by their most talented scribe.

The abbot rose. "Father Francis. Fortuitous timing." He picked up a sheaf of papers separated into two bundles. "I have your first two copies here."

Francis stepped forward, extending a hand when he froze. "*First* two? What do you mean, *first* two?"

"Father?"

"I was informed that the first copy was ready last night."

"Indeed, it was, Father. Brother Bernadino is quite skilled and was able to produce the first copy in exquisite detail."

"Yes, I saw it myself when I came to pick it up last night."

The abbot's eyes narrowed. "I think there's been some confusion, Father. What you picked up last night was the original, not the copy."

Francis inhaled sharply, taking an involuntary step backward. "You mean…" He was at a loss for words. If he had been given the original, then what the Templar was delivering to the Electoral College was the only true copy. And if it were intercepted or destroyed, there would be no proof to back up the claims made by His Holiness in his letter that would be arriving at the Electoral College shortly. "This is a disaster," he murmured.

"Father?"

Francis snatched the two copies from the abbot's hands before storming out of the room, replaying the conversation he had had with the monk who had completed the first copy. Unfortunately, he couldn't remember exactly what was said. He had been tired, stressed, and worse, in a hurry. Yet who was at fault was irrelevant. The mistake had been made. And if he were being truthful with himself, it was made by him. The question now was what to do about it? He would have to inform His Holiness of the error and it would be up to him to decide what to do, though he feared it was already too late.

His error could undermine the very papacy they were attempting to save.

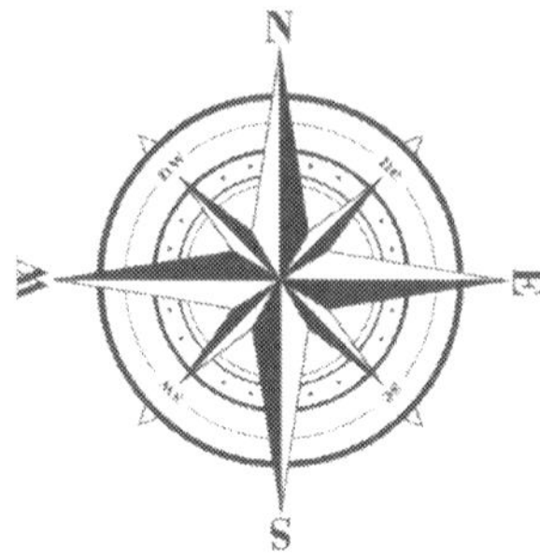

Giasson Residence

Via Nicolò III, Rome, Italy

Present Day

Inspector General Mario Giasson of the Corps of Gendarmerie of Vatican City State finished his coffee then wiped his mouth with a napkin. He was up early today, and it wasn't exactly by choice. Two troublesome academics were coming into town because of a possible archaeological find that one of them, James Acton, claimed could be of significant importance historically to the Church. He was looking forward to seeing Acton and his wife. He considered the couple friends, though not close friends. He couldn't recall the last time they had ever just socialized. Their interactions always had something to do with his job or some trouble they were in, yet they were good people, people he would always make time for.

And fortunately for him, people His Holiness respected and liked.

Their flight was arriving in a couple of hours, so he had set the alarm early so he could greet them in person at the airport. The household was still asleep. His wife had offered to get up and make him breakfast, but he had refused. Her mother was coming for a visit today, which was always a stress on both of them, especially him. She wasn't a fan, but he had come to terms with that, deciding he simply didn't care what the woman thought, and he was secretly hoping that whatever the professors had in store for him would keep him away, ideally for three days and two nights.

He smirked. "That would be perfect."

"What's that, dear?"

He flinched at his wife, Marie-Claude, entering the kitchen. "Nothing, just talking to myself. What are you doing up?"

"Oh, you know how I have a hard time sleeping when you're not in the bed." She leaned in and gave him a kiss on the top of his bald head.

He smiled up at her. "Please tell me you don't have any lipstick on. The last thing I need is to go through my day with your territory marked."

She giggled. "Don't worry." She leaned in and polished the top of his head with her elbow, making a squeaky-squeaky sound as she did so.

"Ha-ha."

She headed to the counter to pour her own cup of coffee. "When are Jim and Laura arriving?"

He checked his watch. "Less than two hours. I'm going to head into the office for a few minutes then pick them up."

"What time do you think you'll be home?"

"I'm not sure. What time is your mother arriving?"

She regarded him. "Now why would that have any bearing on when you're coming home?"

He tensed. It was a rookie move, something a man who had only been married one or two years might make. "It doesn't. Depending on the time, I might be able to be here to greet her."

His wife brightened at his response. "Her train gets in at three. We should be home around three-thirty."

Giasson grimaced in delight. "Sorry, that's just too early for me to get away. Hopefully, I'll be home my usual time, though anything's possible when Jim and Laura are in town."

She sighed. "Those two are always trouble."

"Tell me about it."

"But how much trouble could they actually get into this time? I thought we were talking about some document that was found."

"Yes. The Treatise of the Three Imposters."

"Sounds like a boring crime novel."

He chuckled. "It does, doesn't it?" He indicated his laptop sitting open beside him. "I had my team pull some info and Rizzo sent me a reply last night. The poor guy was up past midnight putting it together."

"He's Gerard's replacement, isn't he?"

Giasson frowned at the mention of the man who had been at his right hand for years. He had betrayed him, secretly working for a group known as the Keepers of the One Truth. He had fired the traitor the day he had discovered the truth, and it still hurt. He had had multiple encounters with the Keepers over the years. They claimed to be a brotherhood sworn to protect the Vatican from its enemies, founded by Saint Peter himself, and he had no reason to doubt that. Yet they were answerable to no one, not even His Holiness, and that always made him nervous, for not only did they have their own agenda, their tentacles reached deep within the Vatican.

So deep, it was impossible to know whom he could trust.

"Mario?"

He flinched. "What?"

"Where were you?"

"Sorry, just thinking of Gerard."

"You still miss him, don't you?"

"Every day. But yes, Rizzo is his replacement. A good man." He tapped the screen. "This report he put together is interesting. By the looks of it, everybody thought this treatise was a hoax made up by Pope Gregory IX in the thirteenth century."

Marie-Claude cocked an eyebrow. "The pope made it up? I find that hard to believe."

Giasson grunted. "Things were different back then. But if what was discovered yesterday is real, it could mean he wasn't a liar at all, that it wasn't a hoax."

"And just what is this treatise?"

"Basically, it's an essay by the Holy Roman Emperor Frederick II claiming that Moses, Jesus, and Muhammad were all liars who made up everything they said and that there is no God, no virgin birth, et cetera, et cetera. It basically poo-poos on Judaism, Christianity, and Islam."

Marie-Claude sat across from him, stirring her coffee, 'black' never a word that could be used to describe her preferred cup. "That's going to piss a few people off."

Giasson chewed his cheek for a moment. "Yeah." His mind drifted to a few years ago when an ancient relic had been found on the body of a Templar Knight, and the chaos that had followed.

Her spoon froze in midair. "You don't think there could be trouble like before?"

"I hadn't thought there would be, but it might be best if we put a lid on this."

"It's not too late?"

"I don't think so. Not a lot of people know about it, and even if they did, hardly anyone knows what this treatise is. Last time it was a piece of the Koran so everybody understood what that meant." He picked up his phone and dialed the office, hoping to head off a problem before it started.

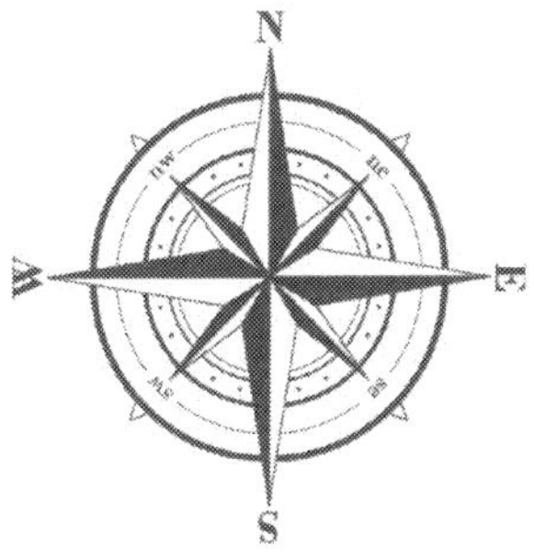

Reading Residence

Whitehall, London, England

"Supraventricular Tachycardia. SVT for short. It means your heart is racing out of control and we need to reset the electrical impulses to fix it."

Reading frowned at the paramedic that had arrived with her partner only minutes ago. He didn't like the sound of what he had just been told. "Is it going to kill me?"

The paramedic smiled. "Now that we're here, no. But if you let this go for too long, yes, it can damage the heart and kill you." An IV was placed in his left arm. "I'm going to give you an injection. It might not work the first time, so I might need to give you a second one."

"What's it going to do?"

"It will slow your heart and give it a chance to reset."

"What does it feel like?"

The woman smiled at him. "I've never done it to myself. They won't let us."

"Yeah, the bosses are no fun," laughed her partner. "Some patients have described it as feeling like a freight train coming at you, but it only lasts a couple of seconds."

"Bloody hell," muttered Reading. "Just get it over with."

The apartment door opened and he glanced over his shoulder to see his partner, Michelle Humphrey, rushing in, shock registering as she took in the scene.

"Bet you never thought you'd see me in my knickers."

She rushed to his side and took his free hand. "Is he going to be all right?"

"He will be." The paramedic looked at him. "You ready?"

"Yeah."

She pushed the plunger in and Reading braced for whatever the hell a freight train was supposed to feel like, but nothing happened. The paramedic glanced over at the monitor, his heart rate at 245.

This was when Michelle noticed it for the first time. "Bloody hell!"

"Exactly what I was thinking when I first saw it."

The paramedic smiled at him. "All right, that didn't work."

"No shit."

"I'm going to give you a second injection. This one usually does the trick."

"Usually? If it doesn't?"

"You can count to three, can't you?"

"Every fiber of my being is resisting the urge to tell you to sod off."

The paramedic laughed. "Ready?"

Reading nodded. "Do it."

Again, the plunger was pushed, and once again he expected nothing, but then, holy shit. He wasn't sure how to describe it, but impending doom might have been a better comparison than a freight train. Fear overtook him as his racing heart rapidly slowed, and as he stared at the monitor, the out-of-control beeping dropped off a cliff and then he could swear he heard it flatline.

Michelle gasped, squeezing his hand hard as his life flashed before his eyes filling him with nothing but regrets at things left undone.

And then the machine beeped, and it beeped again.

Nice, normal, slow.

"There we go. Told you it was nothing."

Reading took a cautious breath. "What the hell just happened?"

"Well, I don't know if you technically were dead, but what the drug does is it stops your heart, then your body automatically restarts it, in theory resetting the electrical impulses that have gone haywire."

"Bloody hell! Why didn't you tell me that?"

"Would you have let me do it if I did?"

Reading grunted. "Perhaps not."

"Which is exactly why we don't tell you what it's actually doing."

"What now?" asked Michelle.

"Now we take him to the hospital. They're going to do some tests, see if there was any damage to the heart muscle, and monitor him for a little while."

"But he's out of danger?"

The paramedics began to pack up. "Immediate danger, yes. The SVT attack is finished. But like I said, they need to do some testing to see if there's any permanent damage. Hopefully, we got it in time and he'll be fine, but unfortunately, there's no way for me to be able to tell from here."

"How do you feel?" asked Michelle.

"I feel like I just ran a marathon in lead shoes."

The paramedic slapped him on the shoulder. "That's about the best description I've ever heard. You're going to be wiped for a few days, but you'll be back to normal eventually, and you'll have one hell of a story to tell your mates."

Reading smiled up at Michelle. "Hey, did you hear about the time I died?"

"You mean the time you died in nothing but your knickers?"

He frowned. "I think we're going to have to make a few revisions to the story."

The door to the apartment burst open and Reading turned to see his son, Spencer, rushing in, wearing his police constable's uniform. "Dad, are you all right?" Michelle stepped back and Spencer kneeled beside his father.

"Apparently, I just died."

Spencer paled.

"Hugh, don't joke about something like that with your own son!" admonished Michelle.

"You're no fun. Fine. I didn't die, I had some sort of super-duper track meet attack that caused my heart to race. These fine people gave me a couple of shots, brought everything back to normal. Now I have to go to the hospital for some tests." Reading eyed him. "What are you doing here? How'd you find out?"

"I was on duty. Night shift." Spencer jerked his chin at Michelle. "She called dispatch and they passed the message on to me. I got here as soon as I could." He gripped Reading's wrist. "I'm sorry I couldn't be here."

Reading patted the lad's hand. "You're here now. That's all that matters."

"All right, Mr. Reading, it's time to get you to the hospital."

Michelle cleared her throat. "Does he have time to put some clothes on? Those knickers aren't leaving much to the imagination right now."

Reading glanced down and cursed at the sight of one of his boys on full display. He made no effort to correct the situation and instead gave Michelle a look. "I'm not going to ask why you were looking down there."

She shrugged. "I guess I'm a little hard up as of late. I'll go get you some clothes." She darted from the room and Reading grinned at his son.

"I've still got it."

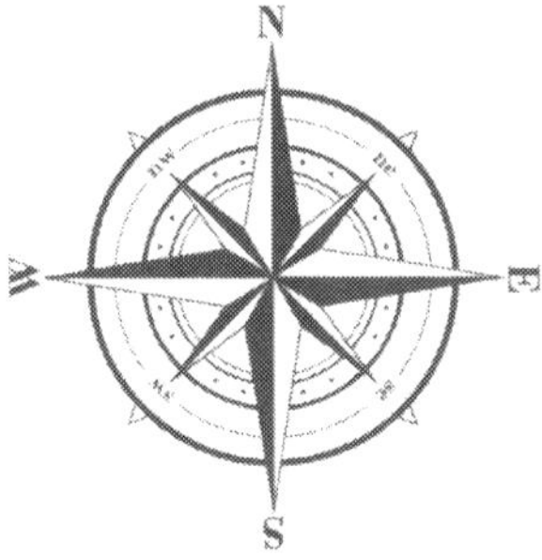

Alberto's Residence

Rome, The Papal States

AD 1239

Brother Alberto's heart continued to pound despite the fact his meeting with the Templar Knight had taken place hours ago. His job was finished, the document now out of his hands. As a member of the Keepers of the One Truth, he had led a double life since becoming a man. Established by Saint Peter over a thousand years ago, the Keepers were sworn to protect the Church from all enemies, including those who resided within its walls.

It was a double life made more complicated by the turmoil in the Roman Catholic faith going on for over a hundred years. With the pope and the Holy Roman Emperor at odds, it had divided loyalties across Christendom, the battle between the two offices unchristian. Even his own brotherhood struggled, though most stood by their traditional allegiance to the pope. Unfortunately, there were a few who made the argument that their allegiance was to whoever occupied the Vatican, and some believed it should be the Holy Roman Emperor holding court within those hallowed walls rather than His Holiness.

He had never bought into the argument that the Keepers were there to defend the Vatican. It was nonsense. They were sworn to protect the Church. If the Vatican were destroyed tomorrow, wiped off the face of the earth by the forces of evil, would the brotherhood disband? Of course not. It would continue, for its duty was to Christianity as a whole, not the structures built by man. If a church burned to the ground, did the flock scatter and give up their faith? No. They rallied together and rebuilt, for their souls and their faith would remain intact, and the community that had worshipped together would prove why their belief in the teachings of the Church made them stronger.

There was a knock at his door and he spun toward it, visitors at this hour unheard of. The sun had just cracked the horizon, the roosters were announcing the beginning of the day, and the first signs of humanity could be heard on the street. Yet just because the city was awakening did not mean visitors should be expected.

It had to be urgent business with the Keepers.

He put his faith in God and opened the door without questioning who was there, and was surprised to see Father Francis. Alberto's eyes shot wide. "Father Francis, what brings you here at this hour?"

Francis stepped inside without being invited. Alberto said nothing, instead closing the door, waiting for an explanation from the pope's senior aide. "You carried out the task you were assigned last night?"

Alberto's eyes narrowed. "Father?"

"Answer the question!"

Alberto took an involuntary step back at Francis' harsh tone. "Yes, of course. I did exactly as you asked. Why?"

Francis cursed, spinning on his heel and pacing the narrow confines as he tugged his beard.

"Father, what is it that vexes thee so much?"

Francis spun toward him. "Do you realize what you've done?"

"Of course. I did as you instructed me. I handed over a document to a man I would meet in an alleyway."

"And do you know what that document was?"

"Of course not. You didn't tell me. All you said was that it was an extremely important document that had to be delivered directly into the hands of the leader of the Electoral College, and that it was critical that no one saw what the document contained."

"And do you believe you convinced the man you met of the importance of this document?"

"I believe so." Alberto smiled slightly. "As you're aware, in my youth I did a little theater. I merely pretended I knew what the document contained and that it terrified me. I think I successfully passed that fear on to him."

Francis cursed again, the two instances of profanity more than Alberto had ever heard uttered by the man. "Fool! You were supposed to deliver it into his hands, tell him never to look at it, and to be aware that if anyone found out he had it, he could be in danger."

Alberto eyed him. "And that's what I did."

"No, you went beyond your instructions." Francis resumed his pacing.

Alberto tensed. "What's going on here? What aren't you telling me?"

Francis regarded him for a moment. "You truly don't know what you've done, do you?"

Alberto's pulse pounded in his ears and he shook his head. "I don't understand any of this. I merely followed orders. *Your* orders."

"But you far exceeded them. The question is, why?"

"What do you mean, why? The man I met was a Templar Knight. Telling a man like that, who had clearly seen battle in the Holy Land, he would be in danger because of some papers he was carrying would hold no weight. I doubt he'd be concerned at all, but by implying the document was dangerous and that even I was afraid of it, I convinced him that he should take the warning seriously."

"And if you succeeded, then no one will see this Templar Knight until he delivers the document."

"I don't understand. Isn't that a good thing?"

Francis growled in frustration, pulling at his long hair. "Fool! What are we going to do?"

Alberto's fear was quickly replaced with frustration. He had been given orders by Francis and had executed them brilliantly, as far as he was concerned. Yet here stood a man he knew and respected, who he had known since childhood, implying he had done something horribly wrong.

And it angered him.

Francis opened his mouth and Alberto jabbed a finger at him, cutting him off. "Enough of this! Either tell me what's actually happening or leave."

Francis glared at him, his nostrils flaring as he sucked in rapid, angry breaths. He closed his eyes, his shoulders visibly relaxing, and he stepped closer, staring into Alberto's eyes, lowering his voice. "The document that you were given to be delivered by the Templar…"

"Yes? What is it?"

"It's called the Treatise of the Three Impostors."

The blood drained from Alberto's face as he stumbled backward in shock. "It can't be!"

Francis' jaw dropped as he stared at him. "Wait, you've heard of it? How is this possible?"

Alberto's heart slammed as he realized his mistake. He wasn't supposed to know. He couldn't know. Yet the Keepers knew. Cardinal Simon was a member and had briefed them on it before he had even met with the pope. But Francis wasn't a member. He likely had no idea the Keepers even existed. His mind raced, searching for a response. "Everyone knows."

Francis clutched his chest. "That can't be!"

"Well, perhaps not everyone, but many do."

"Who told you?"

Alberto vehemently shook his head. "No, I cannot say. I overheard a conversation, a conversation I wasn't supposed to hear while I had business at the Vatican."

Francis stared at him blankly for a moment before finally muttering, "How could this get any worse?"

Alberto stepped closer, lowering his voice. "What is wrong, Father?"

Francis sighed. "Thanks to you…" He held up a hand and took a breath. "Thanks to *me*, the only proof of an accusation His Holiness has put in writing against the emperor is no longer in our hands, and I fear what the repercussions will be should it fall into those of our enemies."

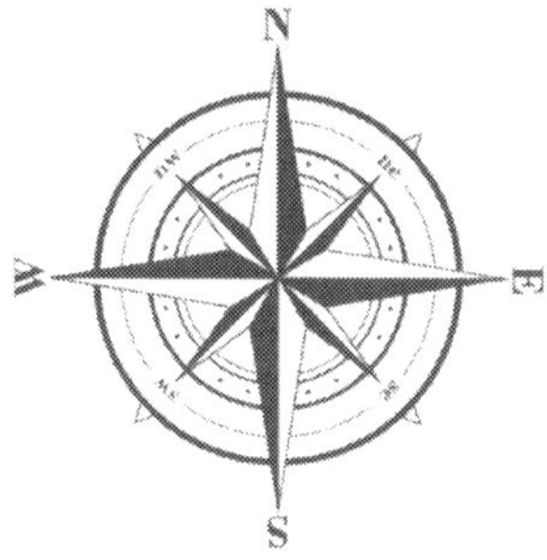

Café Roma

Rome, Italy

Present Day

Lorenzo Bruno wiped down the table when the door to his small café chimed. He looked over to greet his new customer but instead found one of his brothers entering, concern on his face.

"I need to speak with you," said Francesco Russo, one of the Keepers of the One Truth embedded inside the Gendarmerie of Vatican City.

Bruno turned to his wife. "Can you handle things for a few minutes?"

She gave him the eye. "Considering I handle things every time you're not here, which is most of the time, I think I'll be fine."

He gave her an exaggerated grin. "What would I do without you?"

"Go bankrupt."

"This is true." He beckoned Russo to follow him. He led him into the rear of the tiny café in his family for three generations, and would have been for far more if the original family business hundreds of years old hadn't been destroyed by Allied bombing during the war. A small price to pay for freedom from the fascist regime of Mussolini.

He closed the door of an even tinier office then faced the young man who was twelfth generation Keepers, the firstborn son of each member given the first opportunity to join when they came of age. Many did, but too many these days were more self-absorbed, unwilling to make the commitment being a member of the Keepers demanded. Membership in the brotherhood didn't mean giving up your life. His family had been in this business for centuries. It simply meant that when you were called upon, you had to act, you had to stop whatever it was you were doing and answer the call, as had young Russo.

"What is it? What's going on?"

"I'm not sure. Something's come up and I don't know if we need to care about it or not."

Bruno perched on the edge of his desk. "Oh? Why don't you tell me what you know and maybe we can decide together."

Russo leaned against the door, folding his arms. "Here's what I know. Yesterday, a body was found near a highway rest stop a few hours north of here."

Bruno's head bobbed. "Yeah, I think I remember hearing something about that on the news last night. Didn't some kid fall in a hole or something?"

"Yeah, and they found a body in that hole that they think was there for centuries."

"Yes, that's the report I heard on the late news."

"Right, but what they didn't tell you was what they found on that body."

This piqued Bruno's interest. "What did they find?"

"They found a letter from Pope Gregory IX dated 1239 AD."

Bruno's eyes bulged slightly. "1239?"

"I thought that might catch your attention."

"What did the letter say?"

"I can't remember it word for word, but basically it says that the messenger is carrying a copy of the Treatise of the Three Imposters as promised, that proves Holy Roman Emperor Frederick II is a heretic."

Bruno pushed to his feet, his heart racing. "Wait a minute. The letter said the messenger was carrying the treatise. Was it actually found on his body?"

Russo shrugged. "I don't know. Because it involved a pope, we were able to get the site shut down and secured by the local authorities. We've got a team going in today to examine the find."

"Who's being sent in?"

"Father Esposito and his team, but professors James Acton and Laura Palmer are going to be arriving any minute now to join them. Somehow, they're the ones who discovered the find."

"How did they manage that?"

"I don't know. Something about an app they're involved with that was used by someone at the site. I don't have a lot of information. I'm not senior enough to be privy to everything. All I do know is this treatise is something I remember reading about in the history of the brotherhood that I was given when I first swore the oath. I seem to remember it wasn't good."

"Yes, it was a dark time where our brotherhood was almost exposed. If the treatise is real, which throughout our history we had assumed it must not be, that it was simply part of a hoax gone wrong, but if this is indeed real, it's a very dangerous document."

"Dangerous? How so?"

"It's blasphemous. It posits that Moses, Jesus, and Muhammad were all fakes, were all liars, and that God isn't real, and therefore Judaism, Christianity, and Islam are all false religions, that anyone who believes in the virgin birth of our Lord and Savior is a fool. Such blasphemy cannot be allowed to exist."

Russo shifted uncomfortably. "But the Internet is filled with such things."

"The Internet is a cesspool of lies that is taken seriously by too many simpletons. This is a written document, eight hundred years old, purported to be written by an emperor who was supposed to lead Christendom, and confirmed as genuine by a pope who led the faith. If the wrong people get their hands on it first, they could publish it, and due to its pedigree, it could be taken seriously by too many people. Certainly, it would be used to discredit the Christian faith, and we both know there's too much of that going on these days. Atheists would have a field day with it."

"So then, this is important."

"Absolutely. I need you to get back to your post. Keep me informed of everything. I'm going to call the leadership and see if they want to try to get a hold of this first before anyone else. If it falls into the wrong hands, who knows the damage it could do to our faith."

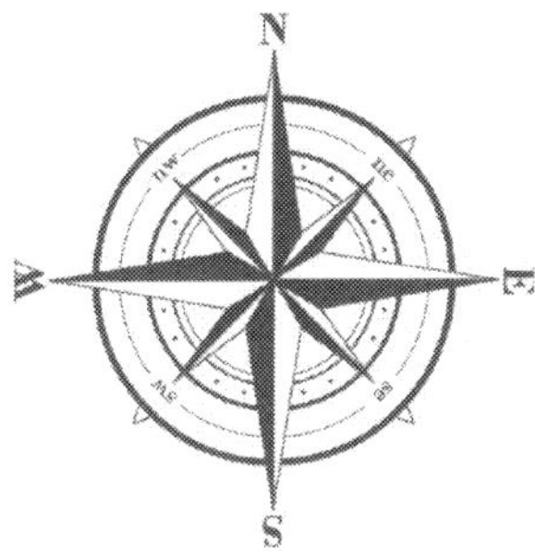

En Route to Rome, Italy

Acton noticed Laura frowning at her phone as the plane descended into Rome. "What's wrong?"

"Probably nothing, but I still haven't heard back from Hugh."

Acton checked his watch. "It's coming up on seven AM here, so that makes it six in London. He's probably still in bed. I wouldn't worry about it."

"No, I suppose you're right. It's just that it's a weekday, so he's normally up getting ready for work by now."

"He could be busy dropping a deuce. I wouldn't worry about it."

She grimaced. "Disgusting imagery aside, you and I both know that he answers his morning messages on the throne."

Acton struck a seated superhero pose. "As do all men."

Tommy snickered, elbowing Mai. "It's true."

She frowned. "I don't mind when you do that, just don't take my calls."

Laura leaned over so she could see Mai. "Does he do that to you too?"

"It's gotta be a guy thing."

Laura sat back. "Men are pigs."

Acton eyed her. "You're just discovering this now?" The tires chirped as they hit the runway, changing the subject for them as excitement set in at what the day would bring. Were they about to see the Treatise of the Three Imposters, or was it just another fake? Giasson had arranged to have the site sealed as a favor to the Vatican since the letter was from a pope, therefore technically Vatican property. Before the day was out, they could be the first people in 800 years to lay their eyes on what could very well be the most controversial document ever written about the Abrahamic religions.

He shivered with excitement. This is what he loved about his job, seeing things lost to history, forgotten by time, to be the first to see an artifact, a document, a building, something from centuries or millennia ago. There was no greater thrill. And seeing that excitement on Tommy and Mai's faces gave him tremendous satisfaction. Passing on the sense of wonder, the thrill of discovery to the younger generation was his favorite part of teaching.

Laura pointed out the window. "There's Mario." She waved as the plane came to a halt. Acton unbuckled his seat belt and rose, stretching his back. While a private jet was far more comfortable than a regular commercial airliner, it was still flying for over eight hours. None of them had managed to catch more than a couple of hours' sleep, everyone too excited, and with the time difference having most of their flight taking place in what felt like late evening, it would be an ass-dragger of a day. But he had a sense they would all be running on adrenaline before they knew it.

The pilot announced they were clear to leave the airplane and the flight attendant opened the door, extending the steps. Acton helped Laura out of her seat, Tommy doing the same for Mai, then he followed them down the aisle. They thanked the flight crew then descended into a cool Rome morning. Giasson stood by the passenger door of a Vatican-flagged SUV with a smile. Laura gave him a hug, then Acton and Giasson exchanged a manly embrace involving double-cheek kisses, the man's Swiss heritage and Italian mannerisms quite different than what Acton was used to in America. If he were to extend a fist bump to the man he would be aghast, and he wondered what their friend, steeped in tradition, would do with an elaborate slap-slap, tap-tap, boom greeting.

He snorted.

Giasson cocked an eyebrow. "Something funny?"

Acton shook his head. "Sorry, I'm a little punchy. Didn't get much sleep on the airplane." The private terminal staff brought over their luggage and they headed inside to clear customs. Within minutes, they were loaded into the SUV and on their way to the tiny city state.

Giasson twisted in his seat so he could see them. "It's about a three-hour drive north to where the dig is, so you'll all have time to sleep, and then I have a funny feeling you won't have any problems staying awake for the rest of the day."

Laura grinned. "That's what I'm hoping. What can you tell us? Anything new?"

"Just that the site has been secured and that our team is ready to depart as soon as we arrive at the Vatican. I'll give you a few minutes to settle into your rooms when we get there." Giasson gave Tommy and Mai a look. "Separate rooms for you two. It is, after all, the Vatican."

Tommy's cheeks flushed and Mai demurely looked away. Acton reached back and smacked Tommy on the shoulder. "Don't worry, they don't lock the doors from the outside. You can still visit her for some brown-chicken-brown-cow action."

"James!"

Tommy snickered and Mai's jaw dropped as Laura smacked her husband on the shoulder.

"Sorry."

Giasson rolled his eyes. "Things would be so much easier if we didn't allow any guests."

"Maybe if you made everyone sign an agreement not to do the deed lest they be condemned to Hell, you might not have to worry about it."

Giasson eyed him. "I just always assumed it was implied."

Acton's eyebrows shot up and Giasson laughed.

"Don't worry, professors, what you two do as a married couple is between you and God, and I'm sure he's got more important things to do than concern himself with such things." He turned to Tommy. "You two, on the other hand—"

Acton grinned. "No hanky-panky for you, lest ye be judged." He turned to Giasson. "You wouldn't happen to have any chastity belts available?"

Laura swatted him again but snickered, and Giasson shrugged. "We just might."

Tommy gulped. "For me or for her?"

Acton laughed. "You better hope for her. Because if it's for you, I think they put the little guy in a cage and clamp it shut."

Tommy paled. "For the love of God!"

"Exactly."

Giasson snickered and Laura shook her head. "Don't worry, Tommy. If anyone's going to Hell, it's my husband for tormenting you."

"I doubt I'm going to Hell for that. I've done far worse things than tormenting my fellow man."

Giasson regarded him, his face serious. "Let us hope your good deeds outweigh your bad."

Acton frowned, a heavy weight pressing down on him as he thought of what he had done over the past several years, how many people he had killed, how many people he had saved, the lies he had told, the crimes he had committed. He told himself that everything he did was to help others, part of God's grand plan. But was that enough? Was violating commandments that were supposed to be absolute forgivable if the intent was good in the end? He had to think so.

But then again, maybe none of it mattered. He was a scientist, yet he always had faith. A belief in God or religion didn't require proof. That was the very definition of faith, the belief in something without proof. He had faith. He had to. Too many friends and loved ones were dead that if it were all a lie, it meant he would never see them again. He thought of his mother. He thought of his students massacred in Peru, lives taken far too soon, none of them out of their twenties. This couldn't be it. There had to be more.

"Are you all right?" asked Giasson as Laura squeezed his arm.

Acton gave his head a shake. "Sorry, just thinking of my own mortality, and whether everything we've been taught to believe is real."

Giasson sighed. "It's this Treatise of the Three Imposters. Just the very notion it exists is troubling."

"Surely a man such as yourself can't be troubled by this," said Laura.

"No, I'm not questioning my faith just because of an old document. But our faith is always challenged by events in our lives, by events occurring worldwide. How can God exist when terrorists rape, burn, behead, and murder over a thousand people, then the victims are blamed for defending themselves? How can God exist when one nation can invade another, or when children are swept away in raging rivers? When homes are destroyed, people burned alive in forest fires? Every day we see stories, we hear tales that make us question our faith. How could God allow such things if he's supposed to be all-loving, all-knowing, all-caring? And we tell ourselves He has a plan, that those innocents who lost their lives lost them for a reason, that in the end it will all be balanced out with something good that we can't see right now. My faith is never shaken by such things, but it never hurts to reaffirm it."

Acton sighed. "Man, did this conversation ever take a turn." He glanced over his shoulder at their young companions in the rear row. "I blame your sex lives."

Tommy's eyes widened and he shifted uncomfortably. "Umm, are we there yet?"

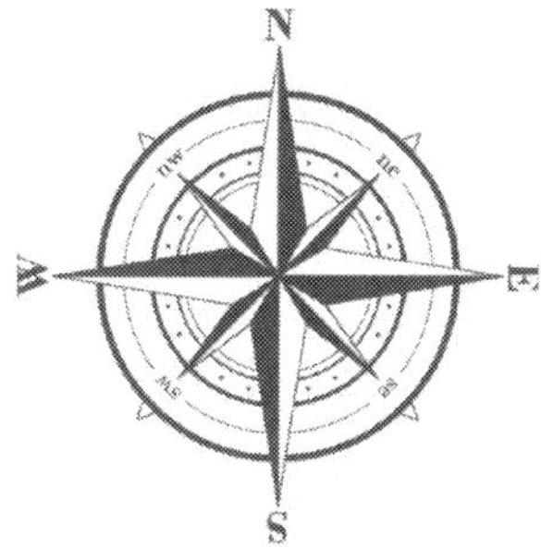

Amine Residence

Viterbo, Italy

Jihad Amine's eyebrows continued to climb his forehead as he read up on what his alerts had discovered overnight. Posts were appearing from a lecture given in the United States yesterday that included photographic evidence and a translation in both English and Italian, claiming that a letter from the pope in 1239 had been discovered near where he lived. Normally, he wouldn't have paid it much mind. His alerts were set up to find examples of Islamophobia, and as much as he hated Christians and the pope, little came out of the Vatican that could be considered anti-Muslim, beyond the fact they didn't outright condemn Jews and Israel.

His father, an imam at a local mosque, was active in the community, constantly speaking out against Muslim discrimination, encouraging his worshippers to report all instances to the proper authorities. Things were getting worse and it made him angry, more so each day with each new report he read about something being done to one of his brothers or sisters around the world. He blamed the Jews. They controlled the media, the press, they were the ones spreading lies about Islam, and they had to be stopped.

His family called Italy home, but it didn't feel like home. Anti-immigrant sentiment was growing and he no longer felt comfortable in the country in which he had been born. As soon as he turned eighteen, he intended to return to his family's native Lebanon and join the fight. He wanted to take up the cause, drive the Jews out of the Palestinian homeland and into the sea. They all deserved to die for what they had done to his people.

Unfortunately, his father disagreed, something he found stunning. How could a man so wise, so learned, not recognize the Jewish people for the threat they were? He could perhaps understand not blaming every Jew worldwide, but certainly those who resided within the borders of the Israeli colony could be blamed and should be blamed. He had lost count of how many heated arguments he had had with his father over the past couple of years. All the evidence was out there on the Internet. All his father had to do was look, but he refused, claiming that the Internet was the Devil's playground and that it was filled with lies and hate.

While he agreed with his father that there was much of what he said on the Internet, it was mostly lies about Islam and how wonderful and peaceful Judeo-Christian society was. It was so tainted, so slanted against Islam, it disgusted him. Didn't all those Jews and Christians realize that the ultimate goal of Islam was peace? A global caliphate that would rule the entire world under the banner of Islam. Once all were converted or subjugated, peace would reign. None would want for anything.

But his father refused to listen, which is why he no longer sought the man's guidance on spiritual matters. He had found a cleric, a Syrian refugee, who had embraced him online and encouraged him to continue seeking the truth. The truth his father, for some reason, wanted to keep from him.

Truth like what he was looking at right now—a letter from the pope who was supposed to be a peaceful, pious man, who simply wanted to live in harmony with everyone, referring to a document called the Treatise of the Three Impostors, purporting to claim that Moses, Jesus, and Muhammad were frauds.

Rage boiled in his stomach as his chest tightened and his fists clenched. It didn't matter if the pope hadn't written the document himself. Merely possessing it, merely allowing it to exist, was offense enough. And if this document had truly been discovered yesterday, like these posts he was reading claimed, he had to act.

And he had to act now.

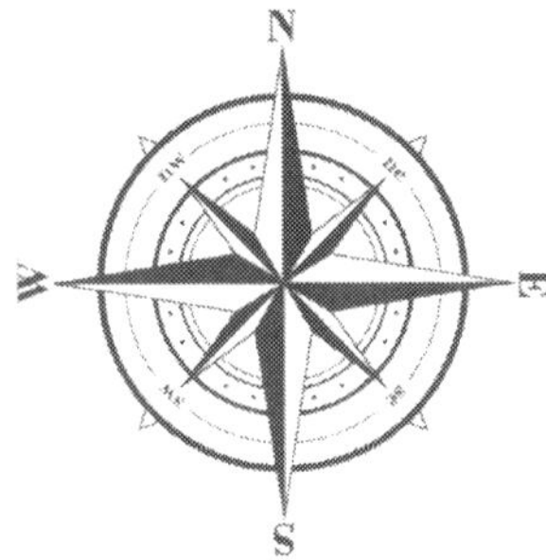

Levi Residence

Bagnaia, Italy

Davide Levi sat at the breakfast table, his phone in one hand, his spoon in the other as he ate his breakfast in silence. His head continued to shake at the Reddit thread he had been reading all morning.

"What troubles you, my son?"

He glanced up at his father and flipped the screen around on his phone for a brief moment. "Just something I'm reading. Have you ever heard of the Treatise of the Three Impostors?"

His father, a devoutly religious man, nodded. "Of course. It's a hoax. It makes the claim that our religion, as well as Christianity and Islam, are all based on lies told by Moses, Jesus, and Muhammad." His father eyed him. "Now why would you be asking me about that? Have they made a video game or a comic book of it?"

Davide rolled his eyes. "Graphic novel, Dad. Graphic novel."

His father chuckled. "Sorry. Graphic novel. But that doesn't answer the question."

Davide wagged his phone. "Apparently, they found it yesterday."

His father's eyes widened. "Really? That can't be. It's not supposed to actually exist. It was just made up centuries ago, some conflict between the pope and the emperor. I'm not very familiar with it. Ask me about Jewish history and I can tell you anything, but Christianity and Islam, not my specialties I'm afraid."

"Don't worry, Dad. Everything's on the Internet."

"Everything on the Internet isn't true."

"I realize that, but there's actually a photo of a letter from Pope Gregory IX."

"You know, photos can be faked. Pretty much anything can be faked nowadays."

"Well, this seems legit. Looks like it came from an archaeology class in the US yesterday. There was some sort of accidental discovery during a presentation of a translation app."

"Where was it found?"

"Here in Italy. Not too far from here, actually. Remember that report that was on the news last night about the kid breaking his ankle and finding a body?"

"Oh, I remember watching that," said his mother. "The poor little dear. It's going to take him a long time to get over that."

"If he ever does," agreed his father. "But what does that have to do with some ancient document?"

"I'm not sure. The going theory is that the document was found on the body."

"They did say they thought the body was quite old," commented his mother. "Not some recent murder victim. I think they said some archaeologists from the Vatican were going there today."

"Can we go, Dad? It's not far from here. Half an hour, an hour at most."

His father dismissed the request. "I'm too busy and you have your studies."

"But it's summer break."

"You still have your studies."

"I'll do them tonight."

His mother patted his father's hand. "Let him go, dear. Once he gets something on his mind, you know he won't be able to concentrate."

His father frowned. "Fine, go, but just stay out of their way. Last thing they need is some teenager bothering them."

"Can I take the car?"

His father firmly shook his head. "No, I need it."

Davide growled. "See? This is why I keep saying we need two cars."

"Get a job, then you can get a car."

Davide's face brightened. "I can get a job?"

"No, you've got your studies."

He growled again. "You're so frustrating."

"That's *my* job."

"Mom!"

"Listen to your father. He only has your best interests at heart. Focus on your studies. You'll get into a good school, get a top-notch education, then a good-paying job. You'll be working the rest of your life. Be thankful for these times."

He sighed. "I'll call Zaccaria. He's got a car."

His father regarded him. "Zaccaria? I don't like that boy. He's always getting into trouble."

"No, he's not. He's just opinionated. And you don't like the fact that some of his opinions don't agree with yours."

"I don't have opinions. I have facts. If he doesn't agree with my facts, then he's an idiot."

Davide stared at his father, his eyes bulging at the arrogance, and his mother snickered. "He's teasing you, son. Go with your friends, have fun. Be back for dinner."

His father sipped his coffee. "And stay out of their way."

Davide leaped to his feet and rushed into his bedroom, already texting a group chat he had set up with his two best friends.

Road trip!

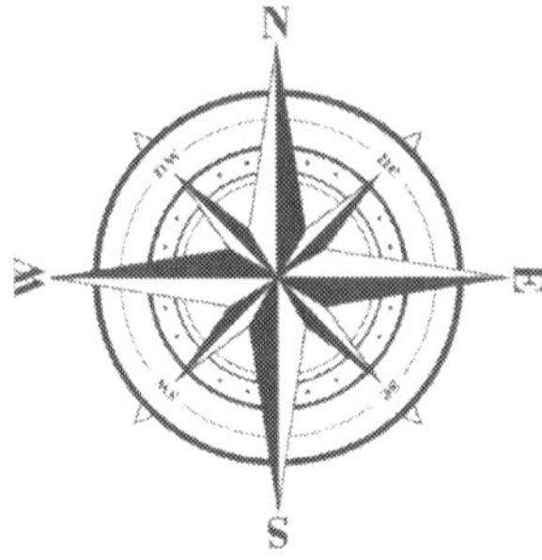

Santa Maria del Priorato, Templar Headquarters for Rome

Rome, The Papal States

AD 1239

The pope's rage had been brief, though since it was so uncharacteristic, Francis doubted he would forget it for as long as he lived. He had screwed up in a major way. His orders were to fix it, though he was certain His Holiness was fully aware the chances of accomplishing that were slim.

Yet he had to try.

He was shown into Sir Enrico's office and the man rose, smiling broadly.

"Two days in a row, Father. What have I done to merit such treatment?" The man's smile faded rapidly as he regarded his guest. He rounded his desk and closed the door, directing Francis into a chair before sitting opposite him. "Something troubles you. What is it?"

Francis searched for the words he had rehearsed but now forgotten. He opened his mouth, but nothing came out.

"Does it concern the letter from His Holiness that you had us deliver?"

Francis nodded.

"If your concern is whether it will be delivered in a timely manner, I've had no reports of any interference with our network. It should be there on time."

Francis finally found the words, or at least some. "It's not the letter. It's the other package."

"Oh. What concerns do you have? Perhaps I can allay them."

Francis shifted uncomfortably in the hard wooden chair. "The wrong document was provided to your messenger."

Enrico leaned back, his eyebrows climbing. "I see. That's most unusual. Should this incorrect document be delivered, it would be—"

"It would be unfortunate," interrupted Francis. "Most unfortunate. A great embarrassment to His Holiness." He squeezed his eyes shut, pinching the bridge of his nose. "It could damage the Church irreparably."

Enrico's jaw dropped for a moment before it snapped shut. "And you still cannot tell me the nature of this document?"

"No, unfortunately, I cannot. It is simply too delicate a matter."

"Yet this mix-up could cause harm to the Church."

"Absolutely. It's essential we get back the document your messenger has and replace it with the proper document."

Enrico tugged at his long beard, grayed from age and the stress of his position. "Give me a moment." He rose and opened the door. "Sergeant, would you join us, please?"

"Yes, sir."

Footfalls rapidly echoed through the corridor on the other side of the door before a grizzled sergeant, his uniform impeccable, his black tunic with red cross signaling his rank unwrinkled and unfrayed, the only thing detracting from his tidy appearance a jagged scar that ran down his left cheek from his eye to his lip, no doubt earned in battle.

Enrico beckoned him inside then closed the door. "Sergeant, has there been any word on Sir Ricardo?"

"No, sir. He wasn't present for roll call this morning, though my understanding is he wasn't expected."

"No, he wasn't. He's on a mission that will take him out of the city for weeks."

"Then, unfortunately, I don't think we'll hear from him until he's completed that mission."

"Have messages sent to all of our outposts between here and Padua. See if he's checked in for lodging or supplies, and leave word at all of them that he is to immediately return here without delay. His previous orders are rescinded."

The sergeant shifted his weight from his left foot to his right, his eyes darting toward Francis.

"What is it, Sergeant?"

"Well, sir, if you remember, the orders you gave me to issue to Sir Ricardo were coded non contramand."

Enrico cursed and Francis stared at both men, his chest tight. "What does that mean?"

Enrico held up a finger, turning to his sergeant. "Send those messages. We need to find him."

"And if he resists? Your orders?"

Francis stared at the Templar Master. "It must not reach Padua."

Enrico frowned. "Arrest him."

The sergeant gulped. "Yes, sir." He left the room, closing the door behind him.

Francis rose, again asking, "What do you mean by non contramand?"

Enrico tugged at his beard yet again, harder this time. "When we met yesterday, you indicated that this was an extremely important document that must reach its destination, and that should it be known that my knight was in possession of it, someone might try to stop him. Out of concern for my man's safety and for the success of the mission, I labeled his orders 'non contramand.' No countermand. It means that any subsequent orders he received that contradicted the mission are to be ignored."

"So, if you do manage to get him his new orders…"

"He will automatically assume he's been compromised and will do whatever it takes to succeed in his mission."

"Is there anything that can be done?"

Enrico frowned. "Unfortunately, the only way to countermand his orders is for me to do it in person."

"But he has half a day's head start. Is there any way you can reach him before he arrives?"

Enrico sighed. "All I do know is that if I don't at least try, there's no chance at all to intercept him."

"I would like to accompany you."

Enrico firmly dismissed the idea. "No. With all due respect, Father, you'll only slow me down. I need experienced riders on the best horses. It'll be a long, fast, hard ride if we have any hope of catching him. I suggest you return to the Holy See. I will have word sent each day as to our progress." He paused, tapping his chin. "Perhaps with this change in circumstances, you might consider sending the correct document through our messenger network. While it will exchange many hands, it will in all likelihood arrive before Sir Ricardo delivers the incorrect one."

Francis sighed, his eyes closing. He reached inside his robes and produced the copy that was supposed to have been sent, brought with him for just such a circumstance. "It is essential that nobody, and I mean nobody, looks at this."

"You have my word. No Templar eyes will ever be set upon this document."

"Good. For should someone betray their oath to your order and to the Church, they will be condemned to the fiery pits of Hell for the rest of eternity. Of that, I can assure you."

Enrico regarded him. "They will not betray their oaths, but I must ask, if the consequences of this document getting into the wrong hands are so dire, is it really worth the risk of sending it?"

Francis paused, his mind racing. In his hand was a copy of the document, an exact duplicate of what the messenger carried. If this copy reached the college first, did it make a difference? The words were the same, the effect would be the same. Putting a second copy out there might not be the wisest of things.

He sighed. “Perhaps you are right.”

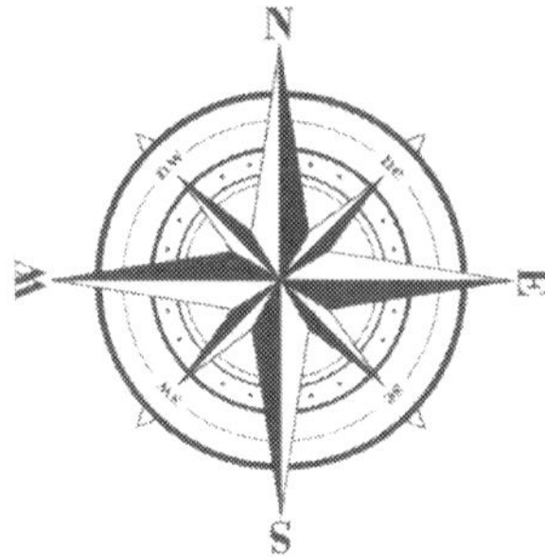

En Route to Discovery Site

Highway A1, Italy

Present Day

They drove in relative silence, everyone exhausted from the flight and the time change. Acton sat in the middle row, his eyes closed, enjoying the vibration of the SUV on the pavement. Laura was curled up beside him and he had his arm around her. Her breathing was gentle and steady, indicating she was sound asleep. He yawned and kept his eyes closed, waiting for the driver's conversation that had woken him to end. It sounded personal and heated, and Acton wished he spoke Italian.

"Puttana!" The word was spat, followed by a string of what had to be curses that had everyone waking as the driver ended his call.

"What's wrong?" mumbled Laura, sitting up and rubbing her eyes.

Their driver, Matteo Lombardi, glanced in the rearview mirror. "I apologize. I shouldn't have taken that call."

"Don't worry about it," said Acton. "Everything all right?"

Lombardi tossed his head back and growled. "My ex. She's demanding I pay to repair the car she got in the divorce. That's not my responsibility! We've been divorced for three years! Why should I have to pay for anything on that?"

Acton had to agree, but decided it was best to keep his nose out of other people's personal lives. "Hopefully it all works out for you." He changed the subject. "How much farther?"

Lombardi gestured at the GPS. "I was just about to wake you. We're making good time. Should be there in about ten minutes."

"Did we lose anyone?" asked Acton, referring to the other vehicles from the Vatican that had left at the same time.

"No. We're all still together."

Laura sighed, her hands gripping her phone dropping into her lap.

Acton regarded her. "What's wrong?"

"Still nothing from Hugh. I'm starting to get worried."

"Did Mary hear from him?"

Laura's phone pinged and she read the message, shaking her head, holding up the reply from Mary to a question she had already thought to ask. "No, nothing."

Acton pursed his lips. This was unusual for their friend. It was approaching 11:00 AM here, which meant 10:00 AM in London. Reading could be at work right now and busy, but there was no reason for him to have not responded to Laura's earlier message when he woke. "Try him again."

"I don't want to nag."

"It's not nagging. He's our friend and we're concerned. He might have forgotten to check his messages this morning or to charge his phone overnight. There are all kinds of possibilities."

"You're right." She sent him another text then rested her head against the seat back. "I hope he's all right."

"I'm sure he is. He's a tough old bastard."

"He's definitely that. I just worry about his heart."

Acton gave her a squeeze around the shoulders. "So do I."

"That's why I wish he'd move in with us."

"He'll never leave Spencer and I can't blame him. They were estranged for so long."

"Too bad we couldn't convince Spencer to move to the States."

"Oh, he'd never do that. He's just starting his career. There's only one thing that would make a man move across the ocean at his age."

"What's that?"

Acton tilted his head back. "Tommy?"

"Strange."

Laura's eyes narrowed. "Strange?"

Acton chuckled. "It's slang. Politely put, sex."

She laughed. "I suppose I could see that. After all, I did."

"That's because it's so good with me."

She patted his chest. "Don't get too full of yourself, dear."

Tommy snickered and Acton gave him the stink-eye. "I may be twenty years older than you, young man, but I've forgotten more about sex than you'll ever know."

"I've heard early onset Alzheimer's runs in families," replied Tommy, deadpan. "Does your father have it?"

Laura roared with laughter as did everyone else including Lombardi as Acton's cheeks burned, his head bobbing in appreciation. "Okay, you got me on that one. Everybody back to sleep."

"We're here," announced Lombardi and Acton grinned.

"Saved by the bell."

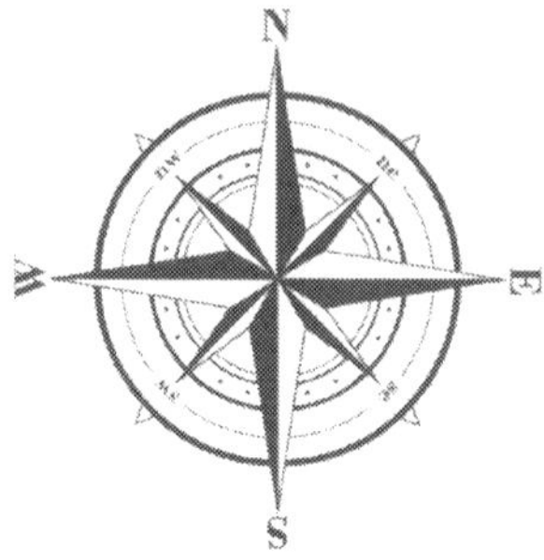

Café Roma

Rome, Italy

"So, what's our duty here?" asked Lorenzo Bruno of a screen filled with three other Keepers, all having just been briefed by him on the possible discovery of the Treatise of the Three Imposters, a dark stain on the history of their brotherhood.

"It must be secured," said Salvatore Greco.

"Well, the Vatican has a team en route now to examine the document."

"Who has jurisdiction over it? It was discovered on Italian soil, right?"

"Yes, but by treaty, anything involving the Vatican that's discovered on Italian soil belongs to the Vatican."

"While I would agree the letter, since it was penned by a pope, belongs to the Vatican, who owns the treatise? It was supposedly written by Frederick II, and while he was Holy Roman Emperor, he was also king of Sicily and died in northern Italy, where he had set up his court in his final years as emperor. Neither of those jurisdictions, then or today, were under the Church's control."

"True. But since the messenger was sent by the pope to deliver a document that the pope had in his possession, couldn't it be argued that by extension, it belonged to him?"

Alessio Conti dismissed the idea. "If the treatise was indeed penned by Frederick, there's no way he gave it over willingly. That means it had to have been stolen. It'd be like you arguing that because the stolen television was in your car, the television belongs to you. And besides, it's been eight hundred years. If Rome decides to make an issue of it, it'll be seized and held by the court until a ruling is made, which could be weeks, months, perhaps even years from now. And during all that time, this blasphemous document will be out in the open."

Greco agreed. "Yes, and I can guarantee you countless copies will be made in the meantime."

Bruno ran his fingers through his hair in frustration. "Then again, I ask, what is our duty? Is it to retrieve the document and destroy it, retrieve it and hide it ourselves, or make certain it gets back to the Vatican so that it can be properly secured in the Vault?"

Greco scratched his chin. "I would think the latter. Our job isn't to destroy something or keep it hidden ourselves. This is a blasphemous, dangerous document. Protocol dictates that once it comes into the pope's possession, he should secure it within the Vault."

"Then should we do nothing?" asked Bruno.

Conti shook his head. "No, like I said, if Rome decides to make a claim, then it might never make it within the walls of the Vatican. It's up to us to make certain that the document reaches the Vatican so that the pope can properly deal with it. If we're lucky, no one will ever know we were there because no action will be needed on our part."

Bruno chewed his cheek for a moment. "If action is required, you realize we'll be committing a crime."

"That's never stopped us before."

"No, but it means we'll have to be armed."

Conti shrugged. "Again, that's never stopped us before."

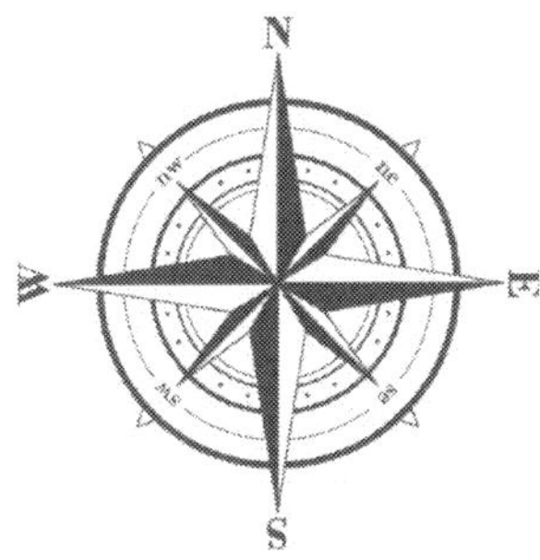

St. Thomas' Hospital

London, England

Reading lay in the hospital bed, more wires coming out of him than an old telephone switchboard. Monitors beeped, and every fifteen minutes, his blood pressure cuff inflated automatically, making a mockery out of the nurse's suggestion to get some rest. How the hell did you sleep with that infernal machine strangling the hell out of your limb?

He had sent Michelle back to work. There was no need for her to be here. Spencer had already been given the day off by his supervisor and sat quietly nearby in a chair, texting back and forth with someone who kept bringing a smile to the lad.

It had to be a girl.

"Someone special?"

Spencer looked up. "Huh?"

"Who are you texting?"

His cheeks flushed. "Just someone I met a few weeks ago."

"What's her name?"

"Caroline."

"Is it serious?"

Spencer shrugged. "Could be. I don't know. I don't think it'll work out."

"Why's that?"

"She's from Glasgow."

Reading cocked an eyebrow. "Glasgow? How'd you meet her?"

"She was in town a few weeks ago. I met her at a bar. We hit it off. We went out a few times while she was here and then have kept in touch since. She wants me to come up and visit her this weekend."

"I think you should."

Spencer gave him a look. "If you think I'm leaving town after what happened this morning, they should be checking you for brain damage, not heart damage."

"I'll be fine. You heard the doctors. Besides, you have to go back to work tomorrow regardless."

"I've got vacation time built up."

Reading dismissed the idea. "I don't want you wasting those days on me. Waste them on a girl."

Another message appeared on Spencer's phone.

"Do you kids even talk anymore?"

"Huh?"

"Talk, you know, like use your mouths to make sounds, and your ears to listen to sounds?"

"Yeah, I suppose. It's just inefficient."

"Are you kidding me? In one minute, I can have a conversation with somebody that would take you and your friend half an hour to do by text. Where did you get this idea that it's more efficient?"

"I don't know."

"And when it comes to matters of the heart, nothing beats hearing the voice of the woman you love. Call her."

Spencer shifted in his seat. "You think I should?"

"Absolutely." Reading jerked his chin toward the door. "Go, call her. Talk to her for a minimum of five minutes. You'll be amazed at how much your relationship progresses."

Spencer pushed to his feet. "I think I'm going to. Thanks, Dad." He left the room, leaving Reading alone with his thoughts, which wasn't necessarily a good thing. He was depressed. He had felt helpless this morning, and even though he was sure things would be fine in the end, it showed just how vulnerable he was all alone.

An alarm sounded and staff rushed past his door. The loud warning sound stopped, replaced by a heart monitor beeping rapidly then flatlining. The distinct thump of a defibrillator had him flinching, and he glanced over at his own monitor, staring at the numbers, attempting to make sense of everything it showed him as the staff in the next room continued the battle to save someone's life. And what was remarkable about it all was how unlike the portrayal on television it was. There was no shouting, no panic, just calm. Orders given, results reported.

Another jolt failed to restart a stranger's heart, and Reading's mind raced. Who was it? A man, a woman? Elderly, young? Did they have a history of heart problems, or did this come out of the blue? Did they have family here, or were they all alone?

And was this his future?

He wasn't a very religious man. In fact, he didn't consider himself religious at all. He wasn't sure what he believed. He liked to think there was something, but how could anyone be sure? He didn't have time for organized religion. That was just something created by man. Was there a God? Was there a Jesus? He didn't know, and he didn't really care, or at least he hadn't. There are no atheists in foxholes, and right now he was in one, right next to someone losing the battle.

He thought of his family. His parents were gone. He had no siblings. He was divorced, and all he had was his son whom he rarely saw. They were reestablishing their relationship, torn apart by his horrid ex-wife telling lies about him. Things were dramatically better than they were just a couple of years ago, and he was so proud that his son had followed him into policing. But here the boy was at a hospital, attending to his father rather than out on the job advancing his career. And worse, he was passing up the opportunity at a relationship because he was concerned about his father's health.

His son needed his space to become the man Reading knew he could be. And worrying about his old man would just get in the way of that. But wasn't that what family was all about? He sighed, closing his eyes as his chest tightened, the horror next door continuing, the staff refusing to give up. It had him thinking that it must be somebody who wasn't supposed to die now, somebody young, somebody who was supposed to have a full life ahead of them, not an old man like him already in the winter of life.

Yet he had friends that he wanted to spend time with that often needed his help. Unfortunately, most of his friends were on the other side of the Atlantic. His best friend for years, his partner, Martin Chaney, was dead, and he had left everyone from Scotland Yard behind. He had kept in touch for the first few months, but as people rotated in and out, as they had new experiences together that he wasn't part of, he quickly felt like the outsider and stopped joining them for drinks at the pub after work, and they had stopped calling to invite him. Those days were behind him and so were those people. And Interpol was different. There just wasn't the camaraderie there. He hated to admit it, but he was happiest when he was with Jim and Laura.

He felt like a bad father for thinking it.

He blasted air through his closed mouth, puffing out his lips. He wasn't sure how much time he had left. At the moment, he was feeling very mortal, not only from what had happened this morning to himself, but from what was happening to the stranger next door. He might have a year left. He might have twenty years left. And he didn't want to waste it. Perhaps it was time to embrace his friends' offer. They had built him a suite in their new home with the offer for him to stay there as often as he wanted or to simply move there. They were rich, incredibly rich, ridiculously generous to a fault. And if they were willing, he should accept their offer while he could.

What was it Laura had said to him recently? "Retire and we'll pay your pension." If he did move to the States and live with his friends, he had no doubt they would pay for him to fly back and visit his son whenever he wanted, and pay for his son to visit him. It would allow him to spend time with his friends, enjoy life, and get out of the way of his son who had his own life to live.

The sounds from the room next door stopped, the battle over, a life lost, and tears flowed. What dreams had gone unfulfilled? Who had been left behind?

And were they in a better place?

Oh God, let it be real.

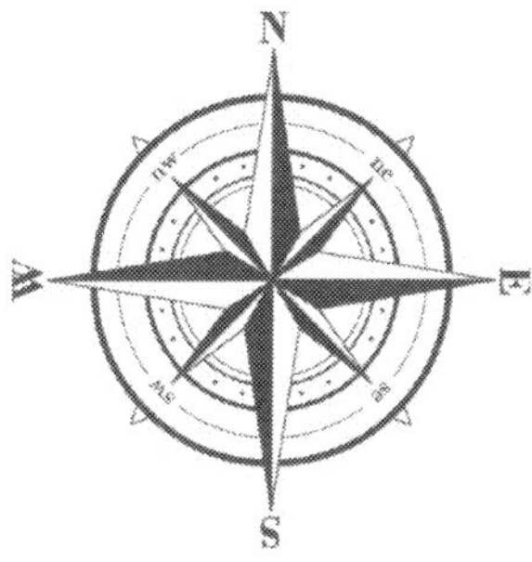

North of Rome, The Papal States

AD 1239

Sir Ricardo had cleared the city limits hours ago atop a fine steed, fully equipped for several days' ride, though his journey would take much longer. He was anticipating two weeks, assuming the weather cooperated, and he ran into no trouble along the way. The slim leather folio handed over by the monk was slung over his neck and tucked inside his cloak, pressed against his chest. He was dying to know its contents, but he had sworn an oath. What document it contained was none of his concern. It wasn't the mission. The mission was to deliver it, unopened, to Padua.

This was the first time he would be traveling to Padua where the Holy Roman Emperor held court. The Templars were aligned with the pope, and he wasn't certain how welcome he would be if he arrived wearing the markings of the Order, but if he attempted to enter the court as a mere messenger, he was quite certain he would never fulfill his mission. The mysterious man had insisted the document be delivered directly into the hands of the leader of the Electoral College meeting in Padua, and while a Templar might be expected to achieve such a thing anywhere else, it was an entirely different matter when it came to the emperor's palace.

But that was a problem for another day. For now, he had a long journey ahead, one he expected to be boring without his usual complement of brothers. Serving the Order, serving the Church, serving God, brought him a difficult-to-explain joy. He had been lost before he swore the oath of poverty and rid himself of all his worldly goods, giving himself completely to the brotherhood.

Being a member of the nobility had been misery. It was all politics and power struggles laden with salacious gossip. While that life had been adored by his late mother and father, he had hated it. Then when his wife had died giving birth, he had used his grief as an excuse to escape a life that held no meaning to him. He had seen things most mortals could only imagine and had been blessed to visit Jerusalem, Bethlehem, the lands spoken of in the Holy Bible.

And if he died today, he would die a content man.

He figured he still had a good ten years of service in him. Templars that lived past their prime were given less taxing jobs. Today, he was a messenger. In a decade he might be in charge of a commandery somewhere. A job behind a desk. Nothing but paperwork day in and day out. It held no appeal to him, even less than the life he had left behind. He had always assumed he would die fighting the Saracens, defending an innocent, some worthy death long before this. But here he stood, decades later, still alive to do God's bidding. He must have a plan for him. What that was, he had no clue, though somehow he doubted it was this mission that he had been kept alive for.

Several galloping horses behind him had him turning in his saddle. Half a dozen Templar messengers raced toward him, and he was about to hail them when he caught himself. He wasn't in uniform and he was traveling incognito. Interacting with Templars, even if mere messengers, could draw undue attention. They blasted past him, two splitting off at an intersection ahead, and it had him wondering what was amiss.

Messengers always traveled at high speed. That wasn't what had drawn his attention. It was the fact there were six of them together. Typically, when a message needed to be dispatched, it was handed to the next available messenger who then left immediately. The only time he had ever seen something like he had witnessed today was when there was a bulk dispatch, the same message sent to multiple locations.

Something urgent was afoot.

He pressed his hand against his chest, the document suddenly heavy. Could the urgent business involve him and this document? And if it did, and the Order was so concerned, did it mean he was on the wrong side of good? He wasn't exactly certain what to do, though he couldn't risk his mission simply because he had witnessed six messengers carrying dispatches that might have nothing to do with him. Yet if it did, was it to find him to warn him of something, or to warn others that if they found him, he should be stopped?

He continued forward, bracing against the chill, the hour still early, the sun's warmth yet to be noticed by his skin. He had some thinking to do, and fortunately, he had the time to do it.

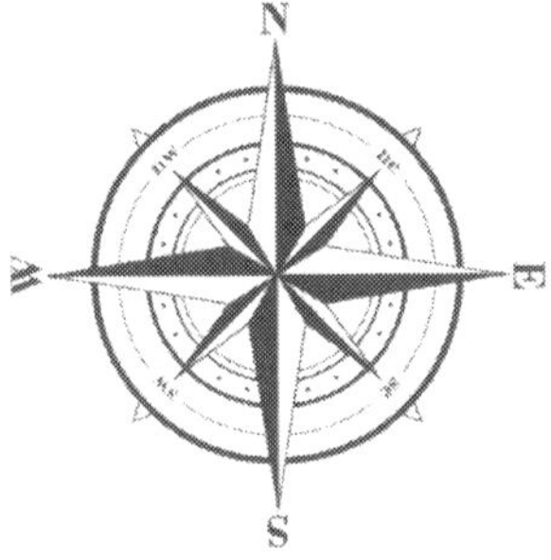

Discovery Site

North of Sipicciano, Italy

Present Day

While there as guests of the expedition, if it could be called that, Acton was never one to sit back and watch others work. He tapped in the stake holding in place his corner of the tarp covering the site, then tossed the mallet to Laura who secured her corner. He tightened a loose tie then stepped back and stretched. The site was now covered by a tarp suspended eight feet overhead, protecting it from the elements, which included the bright sun baking down on them.

The immediate area was taped off, and despite the discovery being deep into the trees near a highway rest stop, a crowd of curious onlookers had gathered. It didn't bother him. What was happening here wasn't a secret. This was Italy, a civilized, peaceful country, so he didn't expect the crowd to become unruly. He had been at several digs during his career in Third World countries where the local populations were so desperate, if they thought there was something of value, they could quickly overrun the site and loot it.

There were two squad cars at the rest stop and four officers providing crowd control around the dig, but so far, everyone simply seemed curious as to what was going on. Anything to get people excited about archaeology was fine by him. This field didn't pay well. It could mean a lot of time on your hands and knees digging in the dirt. It was usually a career path that when announced at the kitchen table with Mom and Dad resulted in disappointed reactions. Fortunately, his parents had supported his choice, though insisted he say aloud that he understood he wasn't training to become Indiana Jones.

Boy were they wrong.

Laura joined him, taking his hand. "This is exciting, isn't it?"

He agreed, giving her hand a squeeze. "There's just something about this. We already know what's in the hole. We already know what we'll find. It's the fact we might be able to prove something thought not to exist actually did that has me almost giddy."

Tommy and Mai joined them, having finished helping set up a large tent where the find would be initially examined. "This is so exciting!" gushed Mai, hopping up and down. "I can't wait to see it. How do you guys feel about it? I mean, it challenges your entire belief system."

Acton shrugged. "I've never really been one for organized religion. And remember, this is one man's opinion, and everyone's entitled to their opinions." He waved a hand at the leader of the expedition. "Why don't you ask Father Esposito?"

"Ask me what?" asked the man, walking over.

"Miss Trinh was wondering how we felt knowing the nature of the document we're about to retrieve."

"Oh, you mean with respect to it challenging my beliefs?"

"Yes. As a Buddhist, I have no skin in the game, I think is the way Americans say it." She glanced over at Tommy who gave her a reassuring nod. "But I have to assume your beliefs are strong considering where you work. Does it make you uncomfortable?"

"Not at all. I have faith, and my beliefs can't be challenged by a document written by a man who was a known skeptic. There are more people alive on this planet that don't share my beliefs than do and that doesn't bother me. Being threatened by other people's beliefs or going to war because someone doesn't believe the same thing you do is ridiculous and should be something relegated to the past. Unfortunately, as we all know, some simply can't accept that others don't share their beliefs.

"What people seem to forget is that all religions are a variation on a theme. Monotheistic religions, like Judaism, Christianity, and Islam, believe in a single god, a single all-powerful being. Polytheists believe in multiple gods, but they all believe that there's something greater than us, something bigger than the individual, something more to life than this mere brief existence we have on this planet. Everyone is just looking for meaning."

"What about atheists?"

Esposito smirked. "I'm hardly qualified to comment, but I would think atheism is a belief in itself. If there is no God, if there is no afterlife and you're comfortable with that, then isn't that a belief in itself? Doesn't that make mankind its own god? We're answerable to ourselves and our community. We do the right thing because it's what's best for everyone, as opposed to what we think God would want us to do. Like someone once said, we don't all have to believe in the same thing, but we all have to believe in something. So, I guess to answer your question, I'm excited to see what we're about to see because it could fill in a big gap in the history of the Church, but I'm quite certain at the end of the day, none of us will feel any different than we did when we woke up this morning. Now, Professor Acton, Professor Palmer, the two of you have the most experience here by far. I hope it's not too much of an imposition to ask that you retrieve the document."

Acton exchanged a grin with Laura. "Just try to stop us."

Davide Levi elbowed his best friend, Salamone, then pointed. "Look, they're going in."

He held up his phone, recording everything. This was the most exciting thing he had ever seen. There was a body in the hole covered by the newly erected temporary shelter, and on that body could be a document 800 years old that questioned his Jewish faith, in fact, challenged the validity of the beliefs of billions. He didn't care about the implications. As far as he was concerned, there were none. He had his beliefs, and most in the world disagreed with them. In fact, most in the world discriminated against him for those beliefs.

He glanced around. With the exception of him and his friends, there wasn't a yamaka in sight. There was a time when he would remove it, too self-conscious to risk the stares, and things were far worse now in Italy than they had been when he was a child. The influx of Muslims during the refugee crisis had made things far more dangerous for the Jewish community. Italians were predominantly Roman Catholic and accustomed to seeing Jews among them. Yes, there was antisemitism, but it was relatively rare. Now, with thousands upon thousands of refugees bringing the Muslim population to almost three million, raised to hate people like him, unaccustomed to seeing Jews walking among them, life was difficult.

But now he wore the yamaka, not only with pride, but as a symbol of defiance. He was sick and tired of being made uncomfortable in his own country. His family had been here for generations and he wasn't letting ignorance and bigotry change the way he lived or worshipped.

"She's hot!" Zaccaria zoomed in on the woman now climbing down a ladder.

Davide eyed his friend. "She's like twice your age. She could be your mother."

Zaccaria shrugged. "My mother doesn't look like that."

Salamone snorted. "Otherwise, apparently you'd want to mount her."

Zaccaria punched Salamone in the shoulder. "You're sick."

"I don't know. I think you're the sick one."

"Hey, all I said was she was hot. You're the one who brought mothers into it."

Davide held up a finger. "Actually, I think that was me."

"Then you're the sick one." Zaccaria grinned. "But since we're on the subject, your mother *is* hot."

It was Zaccaria's turn to get punched. He rubbed his shoulder. "So, how are things between your mom and dad?"

Salamone snickered and Zaccaria dodged another punch when one of the police officers sauntered over. "Settle down, boys."

Everyone came to order.

"Yes, sir," murmured Davide.

"You're on summer break and you choose to spend it here?"

Davide shrugged. "Don't you find it interesting?"

The police officer glanced over his shoulder as a man climbed into the hole. "I suppose it is. It's nice that it's not a fresh body for a change."

Salamone's eyes bulged. "Have you seen many dead people?"

"Too many, and trust me, it's not as cool as you think, especially when it's a kid like one of you guys. Aww shit, here comes trouble."

Davide peered over at what the officer was looking at, and the blood drained from his face and his knees became weak at the sight of four boys around his age joining the crowd, all with thick beards and the distinctive black and white Palestinian keffiyeh wrapped around their necks.

Suddenly his yamaka felt ten times heavier.

Acton activated a fourth light, redirecting the beam. "How's that?"

"That's good right there," said Laura as she kneeled over the body. She fished out her phone again, taking photographs of their surroundings then of the corpse itself.

Acton took a knee. "The clothing's rather nondescript. If he were carrying something this important, you'd think he'd be in more formal attire."

Laura agreed. "Considering the year and the situation in Italy at the time, I would've thought they would use the Templar network. They must have had their reasons not to, or perhaps they did and he was in disguise."

Acton's head bobbed. "Definite possibility, though unless we find something specific on the body, I doubt we'll ever know."

Laura gently moved what was left of his cloak aside, revealing the leather folio that the letter had been found inside. Apparently, one of the police officers called to the scene initially had opened the folio in an attempt to identify who the victim could be and had removed the letter. Thankfully, after reading the translation provided by Tommy's app, he had quickly realized he was dealing with something historical rather than modern and stopped anyone else from touching anything, returning the folio to where he had found it. It meant that what they hoped was inside the folio was not only still there, but untouched for 800 years.

"Ready?"

Laura nodded.

Acton repositioned, holding his phone up, live streaming what was about to happen to the team above and to his class back home, if they had managed to get up early enough. She gently slid the folio out from under the man's tunic, the flesh long since lost to time, allowing it to slide out smoothly. When he was alive, it was likely tight against his chest, secured by a now broken strap. "Interesting that he kept it hidden under his clothes. He must have known that what he was carrying was important and potentially dangerous. God, I'd love to know who this was."

"So would I," agreed Laura. She handed him the folio and they both rose.

"We've got it!" called Acton, peering up the ladder.

Father Esposito leaned over. "Excellent. Is it intact?"

"Yes. It looks like the officer put it right back where he found it. As far as we can tell, there's no damage. We won't know for sure until we get it up there."

"Then come on, man! We're all dying of suspense up here!"

Acton chuckled. "How good a catch are you? I can save us a couple of minutes."

Esposito laughed. "Don't you dare!"

"Fine. We'll do it the slow way."

Jihad gestured toward the group of Zionists standing across from them. He shoulder-bumped his best friend Haasim. "Do you see what I see?"

"You mean the Jewish pigs?"

"Yes. They have the nerve to wear their symbols of hate. I think before we leave, we should grab those little hats of theirs and add them to the collection. We'll deal with them later. Look." Jihad jabbed a finger toward where the action was occurring. The man and woman who had gone into the hole were now emerging, something dark and rectangular having been carefully handed up moments ago, taken by those who had remained above. It was obviously what they were here for.

"So just exactly what is this thing?" asked Haasim.

"It's called the Treatise of the Three Impostors. It's a blasphemous document that claims that Muhammad, peace be upon him, was a fraud and that our faith is a lie."

Haasim's nostrils flared. "Are you kidding me? How dare they!"

"Who wrote it?" asked Ziad.

"Some Christian emperor eight hundred years ago. Apparently, the pope at the time got his hands on it."

Haasim sniffed hard, his fists clenched. "And now another pope is going to have it and you just know the way these people are. They're going to make all kinds of copies of it and spread lies about the prophet, peace be upon him, and our religion."

Jihad agreed. "We need to get our hands on it and destroy it."

Ziad eyed him. "And just how the hell do you propose we do that?"

Jihad eyed the area. There were only four police officers, but they were fully grown men and armed. If they managed to snatch the document, he would only need a minute or two to destroy it, to tear it into pieces, and he couldn't see the police shooting him over paper. Then again, once they saw his keffiyeh, they would know he was Muslim, so would likely fire freely. He didn't want to die, but if he did, fighting for his religion, he was guaranteed entry into Jannah, where he would spend eternity in paradise with 72 virgins as his reward for his sacrifice.

I wonder why it's 72.

It seemed a rather specific number. He would ask his cleric the next time he spoke to him, though if things got out of control today, he could just ask the virgins himself. Tonight. A shiver ran through his entire body, a mixture of fear and excitement. To think he could become a martyr this very day was thrilling. In Italy, he never expected to find the opportunity, which was why he intended to move to Lebanon so he could perhaps join Hezbollah and become a martyr for the cause while taking the lives of as many Zionists as he could.

He watched as the group of scientists carried what they had found to a large tent nearby where he lost sight of them, any hope of snatching it gone.

He pulled out his phone and turned to the others. "Reach out to everyone you know. We need reinforcements. And tell them to bring weapons if they've got them. Today, we fight for the prophet, peace be upon him, and the truth he shared!"

The tent was large but crowded, though no one complained. The excitement among the archaeological team was palpable and Acton was pleased to see Tommy and Mai were just as excited. Tommy, an experienced podcaster with a large following, had his phone out, recording the proceedings, quietly commenting on what was happening, his broadcast shared with Acton's class back home and, hopefully, hundreds if not thousands of others. Unfortunately, since this was science, he would be surprised if even a dozen people were tuned in. A celebrity could get millions of views because they posted an eight-second video of them shaking their ta-tas while chewing a piece of gum, proving with pride they could do two things at once, but the important things in life went unnoticed, uncelebrated.

Father Esposito spoke in English for the benefit of his guests. He listed off the dimensions for the record then put the measuring tape aside. "I'm now going to open the cover of the folio. It appears to be made of leather. It appears dry though not brittle. Our working theory is that the location was an old root cellar, obviously abandoned at the time, otherwise, our subject would have been found in his own era rather than ours."

The leather cover was gently flipped open. Several people leaned in, taking photos and video, and Esposito reached up, adjusting several of the lamps shining down on his workspace. He leaned over and peered inside, the interior of the folio now visible with the cover flap out of the way.

He stepped back, smiling at the others. "There appears to be something inside."

Acton exchanged an excited glance with Laura, hopping up and down on her toes.

"I'm going to open the case slightly wider, though I'm not going to attempt to remove the contents. I just want to see if I can get a better sense of the condition of what's inside." He gently lifted the top of the exposed folio, and as he leaned over, he smiled.

"It's unfortunately sticking to the leather, but it definitely appears to be a document of some type, multiple pages folded together." He stood back, excited. "We definitely have something here, people. And as much as I'd like to extract the document now and confirm what we believe it is, I think you'll all agree that would be the wrong thing to do. We need to proceed at the proper facilities to preserve the integrity of the find. Agreed?"

Everyone in the tent agreed, including Acton and Laura. The man was right. Too many things had been destroyed over the years by giving in to the excitement of the moment. Disciplined archaeologists would delay their gratification to make certain they didn't destroy that which they had discovered.

Esposito pointed to a case in the corner. "Grab that for me, would you?"

One of the other Vatican scientists retrieved the case and positioned it on the table. Esposito opened it then carefully placed the folio inside before sealing it shut. He turned to the others. "Now, I know we're all eager to see exactly what this document is, but we have another find here. Who was our messenger? Why don't we go see what we can discover?"

Davide watched as the scientists emerged from the large tent, unable to contain his excitement. "What did you find?" he shouted, and one of the scientists turned, smiling broadly.

"We found a leather folio on our messenger friend, and inside, we've confirmed there are several pages folded together."

"Is it the Treatise?"

"Too early to say. We'll open it in a lab under proper conditions, otherwise, we could destroy the pages."

"They should be destroyed anyway!" shouted someone, and the gathered crowd gasped.

The man answering the questions turned toward the voice. "And why is that?"

One of the Muslims wearing the kaffiyeh that Davide had noticed earlier, stepped forward. "It's a blasphemous document, an insult to Islam, and it should be destroyed!"

"It's a piece of history that is a danger to no one."

"You call yourselves men of God, yet you do nothing! You will all pay for your sins! That, I promise you!"

The police officer they had spoken with earlier sauntered over, his demeanor the same as earlier as he attempted to maintain calm. "Everybody just settle down. There's no need for trouble here. Just let the scientists do their jobs."

"It's a free country! I'm allowed to say what I want!"

The officer smiled. "That's not exactly true. You just threatened all these people."

"I did no such thing. I merely said they'd pay for their sins."

"Oh, I think we all know what you really meant and because you chose your words carefully, it's the only reason you're not under arrest. So, if you want to stick around and watch what's going on, then keep your mouth shut or I will have you removed for disturbing the peace."

"You mean you'll have us removed for being Muslim!"

"Son, I couldn't care less what religion you are. Now, are you going to behave or am I having you removed?"

The teenager sneered at him then turned on his heel, beckoning his friends to follow, and Davide breathed a relieved sigh as they disappeared into the trees, heading back toward the rest stop.

Salamone stared at him, wide-eyed. "That was intense!"

Davide agreed. "Tell me about it. You just knew they were going to be troublemakers. Imagine, showing up with those terrorist colors. I can understand wearing them at a protest, but to come to a place like this? It just means you want trouble. Good thing there are only four of them and that the police are here, otherwise, there could be trouble."

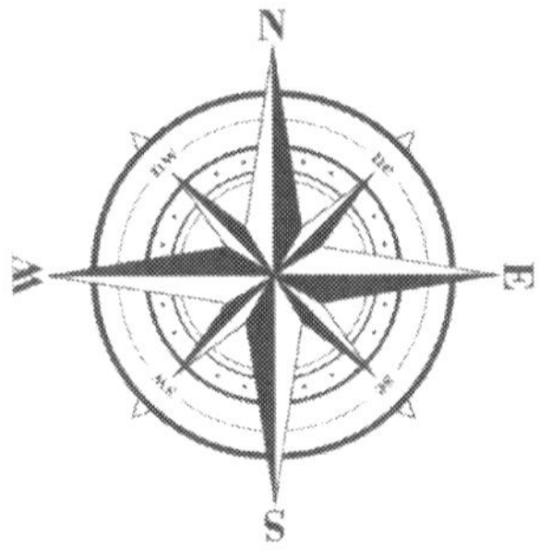

Autonomous Municipality of Sipicciano

AD 1239

"I think you're taking advantage of me."

The stable owner chuckled. "No, my friend, it is you who is taking advantage of me. This is a long-distance horse. He'll take you three times as far in a day as the one you traded me."

Sir Ricardo smiled as he counted out several coins, placing them in the man's palm. "I suppose then it is a fair trade."

"It is. Come back at the top of the hour and I'll have everything ready for you."

Ricardo thanked the man and left. Three days of hard riding had exhausted him and his horse, and no matter how well fed or watered, the overnight hours were simply not enough for the poor creature to fully recover and meet his needs. A fresh horse was necessary. Not to mention the fact he required supplies.

In his mind, he had broken the journey up into three-day stages. Anything longer would require more supplies, which would weigh down his horse. If he were using Templar resources, he would be doing much the same. Unfortunately, he wasn't, despite his desperate desire to sleep with a roof over his head rather than a tent. The nights were cold, which taxed him and his horse, yet he had no choice. In the days since he had left Rome, he had seen scores of Templar messengers racing past in groups, far more activity than there normally should be.

And he was now convinced it must have something to do with him.

Yet there was still a possibility it didn't concern him at all. He had planned on traveling the entire route incommunicado with his brothers due to the nature of the mission, though he had never thought his journey would be consumed by concerns that his order might not have his best interests at heart. His orders had been given to him by the Templar Master's sergeant and had been labeled *non contramand.* It meant only the Templar Master, in person, could override his orders.

What concerned him was that Rome was aware of this, and also aware that any orders they might be sending out in an attempt to call him back were meaningless, the entire thing a useless endeavor. Because the Order wasn't known for wasting its time, he had to assume the messages weren't meant for him, they were meant for his brothers, and those instructions would be to stop him. And if that were the case, what had changed?

He pressed his hand against his chest, feeling the document concealed underneath his cloak. If only he knew what it was he carried, it might help him decide what to do. Could his order have discovered what the document was and decided it shouldn't be delivered? Or could they have discovered his destination, the emperor's court, and made the decision that they didn't want to get involved in the feud between the papacy and the Holy Roman Emperor? Yet no matter the reason, due to his orders labeled non contramand, there was nothing that could be done.

Yet he had to know. And he did have an option. He could return to Rome, meet with Sir Enrico, and find out for himself. Yet it would mean a six day delay in his mission at a minimum, and if it were indeed urgent that this document reach the court on schedule, he would have failed in his mission. Non contramand orders were only issued when there was no doubt of the urgency and necessity of the mission, and when there was concern someone might attempt to interfere. Any order that these messengers might be carrying could be just that—an attempt to interfere. They might not have even come from the Templar Master.

The monk he had met with had been terrified. Something important was going on here. Something big. If it involved the Church and the Holy Roman Emperor, there could be nothing bigger. No, he had to follow his orders. He had to continue on mission. There was no room for any doubt.

He continued to walk the streets of the town when he rounded a corner, the flag of the local Templar commandery fluttering in the cold breeze. Several of his brothers were out front closely watching those passing by, and if the goings on weren't merely a figment of his imagination but were indeed genuine, they were no doubt seeking him. Though they would have no idea what he looked like.

He glanced down at his garments. Nothing he wore, at first glance, would identify him as a Templar. He frowned. That wasn't correct. His boots were Templar issue. An experienced knight might notice that.

Another messenger galloped up, coming to a halt in front of the commandery, one of the knights stepping out and taking the reins as the messenger leaped off the back of his steed and raced inside.

And Ricardo made a decision.

Perhaps not a smart one.

He strode across the street and down an alley, then cut up toward the rear of the commandery. He headed quickly toward the fenced-in rear where the stables were located, his eyes scanning the area. He spotted no one, so quietly opened the gate, slipping inside before closing it behind him. Several stable hands were tending horses, but nobody paid him any mind which wasn't surprising. After all, this wasn't the Holy Land, overrun by Saracens.

He walked toward the rear of the building and positioned himself near a window, partially open, voices carrying.

"When was this dispatched?"

"Last night from the Templar Master."

The distinctive snap of a wax seal breaking had Ricardo leaning in closer, holding a hand up to his ear. A paper crinkled then there was a curse. "You're dismissed but hold for a return reply. And get me my sergeant."

"Yes, sir."

Footfalls followed, replaced moments later by heavier ones. "You wanted to see me, Sir Martino?"

"Close the door."

The door shut and Ricardo shifted his position slightly, desperate not to miss a word. The paper crinkled once again as if Sir Martino was shaking it. "An urgent dispatch from Sir Enrico Teutonico himself."

"Am I permitted to know what it is about?"

"Yes. Everyone is to be informed. We are to be on the lookout for one of our own. Sir Ricardo Gabillone needs to be stopped at all costs."

"Do we know why?"

"Who goes there?"

Ricardo spun to find a squire approaching. He backed away from the window, raising his hands to show he wasn't armed.

"Sir Martino, someone listens at your window!"

Ricardo cursed and continued to retreat as several others took notice and stopped what they were doing. The window swung open and a man Ricardo assumed was Sir Martino due to his white tunic peered out.

"What's going on here?"

Ricardo continued to retreat, the gate only paces away, his hands still up. "I was merely looking for a warm meal."

"Sir, I saw him listening near your window."

"I'm sorry. I heard voices and was going to ask for your assistance but didn't want to interrupt."

Martino regarded him, doubt filling his eyes. "If you're hungry, why come through the back? You could have asked one of the brothers at the front."

Ricardo's back pressed against the gate and he lowered his head. "I'm merely a weary traveler and certainly not worthy of being among honored men such as yourself. I didn't want to disgrace this place with my presence. I was merely going to ask for some provisions and then continue on my way."

Martino pursed his lips. A man of his experience would definitely not believe the story outright. He was likely weighing whether he should be concerned. If the story were true, there would be no risk to the Order. But if he were indeed eavesdropping, the part of the conversation overheard would be of no importance to anyone but the man they were seeking.

Ricardo unlatched the gate. "I'm sorry for intruding. I'll be on my way." He pushed the gate open when Martino held up a hand.

"Wait."

Ricardo froze. He didn't want any trouble, not with his own brothers.

Martino pointed at the squire who had issued the initial challenge. "Provide him with a day's rations. Is there anything else you require?"

"No, sir. A day is enough to get me home where I have family that can tend to me."

"Very well." Martino flicked a wrist at the squire who ran inside. Martino wagged a finger at Ricardo. "And sir, in the future, don't be listening at someone's window. And remember, those in need are always welcome at the front door of any Templar facility."

Ricardo bowed deeply, his heart filled with warmth at the truth in the words spoken. "You have my word and my thanks."

Martino disappeared from the window, closing it behind him. The squire appeared a moment later with a canvas bag and handed it to Ricardo.

"I gave you two days' rations. You look hungry."

Ricardo smiled as he took the bag. "Thank you, Squire. May God bless you for your generosity."

The squire held open the gate and Ricardo stepped off Templar property. The gate swung closed when the squire stopped, his eyes narrowing. He pointed at Ricardo's feet. "Those are fine boots."

Ricardo cursed to himself as he looked down at his footwear. "They are that. Yesterday, I met a man, one of your order, who offered a trade. Who was I to say no? His boots were far finer than mine."

The squire smiled. "He must have sensed your need."

"He must have. Mine were leaking and water-logged and I was in true misery. He must have sensed that when he came upon me. I suppose, since he was riding a horse, he felt his need wasn't as critical as it would be for someone on foot. It was why when I arrived in town and saw the flag, I thought perhaps his generosity would be repeated." He held up the bag. "And it has been, exceedingly so."

The squire bowed. "It was our pleasure to serve."

Ricardo returned the gesture. "I've wasted enough of your time. May God bless you and your brothers."

"And may God watch over you as you journey home to your family."

The gate closed, the latch locked, and Ricardo hurried back to the stable, his heart heavy from lying to his brothers. But he had no choice. He didn't know what the orders that had arrived said, but they involved him. And with his orders issued as non contramand, he had to assume something nefarious was afoot.

From now on, just as the monk had predicted, he could no longer trust his own brothers.

They could very well kill him where he stood.

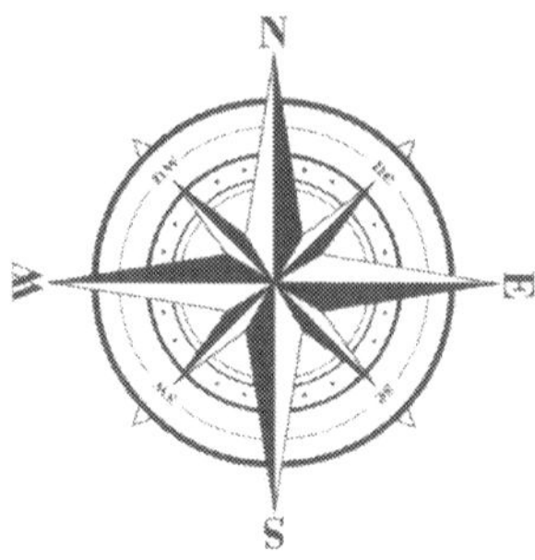

Giovan Battista Pastine International Airport

Present Day

Alexie Tankov stepped off the private charter and took a moment to enjoy the early afternoon Italian sun baking down on his skin. Much better than Belarus. Belarus was temporary. He had no intention of spending the rest of his days there, but it served his purposes. It was aligned with his former homeland of Russia, it wasn't an ally of any of the countries that might demand he be arrested on sight, and the right bribes had anyone he needed looking away. Also, it was fairly centrally located since most of the items his clients were after were not located in the Americas.

He headed for the charter terminal. They were a team of eight, all in civilian attire, packed light for a few days of fun in the sun. Clean identities and passports should mean they wouldn't have a problem gaining entry.

Arseny Utkin came up beside him, holding up his phone. "They're live casting the dig. I just reviewed the footage. It looks like they found the document, but they haven't confirmed it yet. They're not going to attempt to open it until they get it in a lab."

"Good. We don't want it destroyed before we can deliver it to our winning bidder."

"Speaking of, you're going to like this."

Utkin tapped on his phone several times then held it up, showing a monster-high eight-digit number. "That's the latest bid."

Tankov whistled as they entered the terminal. "Post that the scientists have confirmed there is a document inside the folio. That should juice that up into the nine figures."

Utkin's thumbs went to work. "I wonder what they plan to do with it."

"Is it one of our Religion of Peace buyers?"

"Yep."

"Well, I have no doubt they'll claim they want it so they can destroy it, but I know these people. I've watched them drink, do drugs, and sleep with prostitutes. They're only Muslim when it suits them. There's no way in hell they're going to destroy something they paid a hundred million euros for."

Utkin agreed.

Tankov handed over his passport, ending the conversation. Within minutes, they were outside, two large SUVs waiting for them with local contacts behind the wheels. Tankov climbed in the passenger seat of the lead vehicle. "Leo, good to see you again." Handshakes were exchanged.

"And you, my friend. Ready for a little fun in the sun?"

Tankov chuckled. "Absolutely. I assume you got everything I asked for."

"Of course. Body armor, weapons, it's all in the back. Everything on your list."

"Perfect. I'm looking forward to working on my tan."

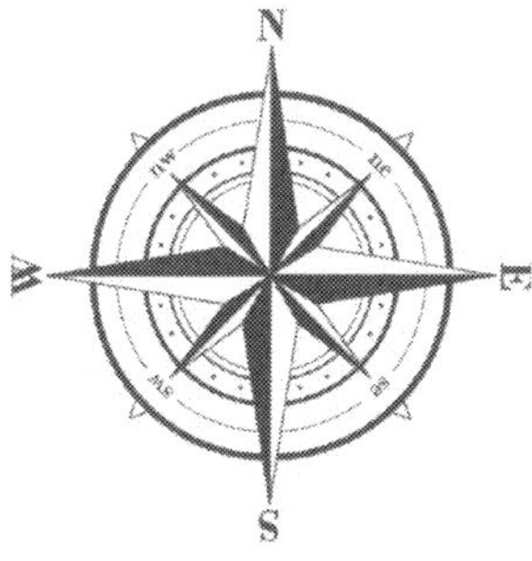

Rest Stop off Highway A1

North of Sipicciano, Italy

Lorenzo Bruno parked at the far end of the rest stop and took a moment to assess the scene. "I count two police cars."

"So do I." Salvatore Greco pointed toward the tree line. "Sightseers, gawkers. They heard about it on the news, so they come by to see what's going on, discover it's as boring as watching paint dry, and leave. They won't be a problem."

"Unfortunately, there'll probably be a constant stream of them. Remember, we're not expecting trouble, so we're just going to hang back and observe. The first sign the Treatise isn't being taken to the Vatican, we act."

Alessio Conti held up his phone from the back seat. "I just watched a recording of them confirming there's something inside this leather case that they found on the body. They said they're not opening it until they get it back to a proper lab."

Bruno chewed his cheek for a moment. "We need to find out where that lab is. If it's at the Vatican, then good. But if it's at some other institution, we may be forced to act. We can't risk it falling into the wrong hands. I get the sense nobody here is treating this as the threat it is."

Conti bit his lip. "How far are we willing to go with this? Are we really going to kill?"

"I doubt that'll be necessary. We're dealing with a bunch of academics. Unless we see a threat to the document here, we just follow it. If they take it to the Vatican, then we trust that His Holiness will do what's necessary. If it goes somewhere else, it'll be some academic institution. All we'll need to do is walk in, flash our guns, they'll pass out, piss their pants, whatever, and we'll walk out with the document and put it in the Vault ourselves. No matter what, this is all done before midnight tonight and not a single drop of blood will be shed."

"Let's hope you're right," said Greco. "But unfortunately, I'm not sure you are."

Bruno stared at his friend. "Why not?"

Greco pointed ahead and Bruno cursed at the sight of half a dozen cars emptying, filled with what were clearly Muslim agitators, their Palestinian kaffiyehs on full display, most with thick beards, too often the sign of radicals.

"Something tells me they're here for the Treatise as well."

Bruno frowned. "We better call for reinforcements."

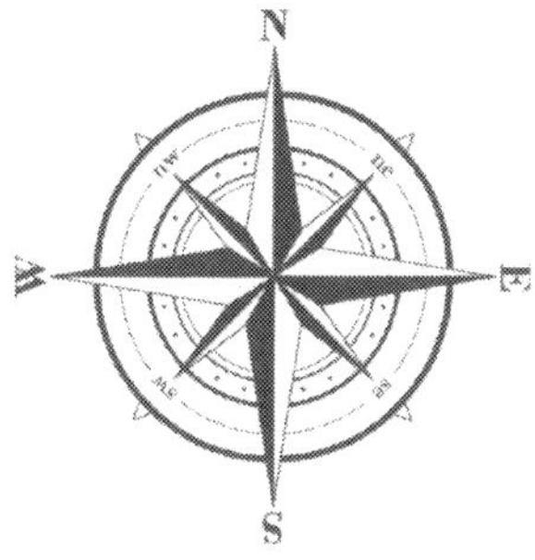

Discovery Site

North of Sipicciano, Italy

Acton climbed from the hole then helped Tommy and Mai out, Father Esposito gracious enough to grant them a few minutes alone so they could see the site before the body was removed.

"That was unbelievable!" exclaimed Tommy. "Who knew archaeology could be so exciting without all the bullets and bombs?"

Acton chuckled. "A lot of the archaeology you've been exposed to isn't really archaeology, it's interrupted archaeology."

"So, who do you think he was, Professor?" asked Mai.

Acton spotted Esposito being interviewed by a reporter nearby, her cameraman recording the proceedings. "Well, who do you think he was?"

Mai shrugged. "I don't know. I didn't spot any markings, and his garments appeared to be those of a commoner. But there's no way the pope would have entrusted something like this to just anybody. It had to be some sort of trusted courier, or perhaps not a courier but a trusted confidant or lieutenant, somebody he could not only trust with the secrecy of what was being carried, but also had the ability to deliver it. If we assume the message originated at the Vatican and the destination was Padua, that's three or four hundred miles on horseback. That's quite the journey. And if others might want to get their hands on it, the pope would probably want somebody who could handle himself in a fight."

"Those guys in the silly outfits?" suggested Tommy.

"You mean the Swiss Guard? No, they didn't exist for a few hundred more years. But there's another possibility."

Tommy's eyebrows shot up. "Who?"

"Who do we know existed back then that was loyal to the Church and good in a fight?"

Mai smiled. "Templars."

"Exactly. I'm betting our friend down there is a Templar, but unfortunately, whoever he was, was traveling incognito, so we may never know. Hopefully, when we're able to examine him properly and we've excavated the entire site for other artifacts that might be buried around him, we'll be able to figure that out."

"Too bad they didn't carry ID back then like we do now," laughed Tommy.

Acton chuckled then frowned when he heard something coming from the trees. "What the hell is that?" He beckoned their driver over, as he could hear a chant repeated by an approaching group.

"Yes, Professor?"

"Can you understand what they're saying?"

Lombardi cocked an eyebrow, apparently hearing it for the first time. "It's not good, sir. I think they're saying, 'Burn it now.'"

Acton cursed as the first of the group emerged from the trees, an angry mob of what appeared to be Muslim youths wearing Palestinian paraphernalia rushing up to the police line, rage in their eyes that only religious fervor could create.

"This is about to turn into a shitshow."

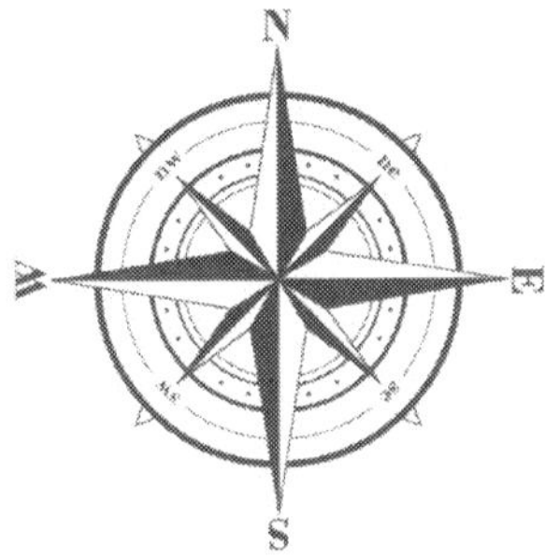

En Route to Padua

AD 1239

Templar Master Sir Enrico Teutonico raised a hand, bringing the small procession to a halt. He was traveling with two knights, three sergeants and half a dozen squires. It was the smallest entourage he could risk, for the Templars did have enemies. If he were to stumble upon a hostile foe alone, they might find it too irresistible to not attempt to take him down. But a force this size would never be harassed. It slowed him down slightly, but not enough for it to matter in the end. But now, as a Templar messenger raced toward them, a hand raised in the air, he wondered if perhaps good news was about to be delivered, and that Sir Ricardo had been found and stopped without incident.

He didn't want anything to happen to the man despite the Vatican's insistence that he be stopped from delivering his message. If half a dozen knights had intercepted the man, he would surrender. Of that, he had no doubt. He would listen to what their orders were and certainly resist the urge to fight overwhelming odds in which he might die, and so might some of his brothers.

The messenger came to a halt, indicating the flag carried by one of the squires. "Do I have the honor of addressing Sir Enrico Teutonico?"

Enrico nodded. "You do. Do you have a message for me?"

"Yes, sir. From the Templar outpost in Sipicciano." A folded paper was produced. Enrico snapped the wax seal and opened the page to find a letter from Sir Martino da Canelli. His eyebrows rose as he read the incident of a man claiming to be a traveler, caught eavesdropping while wearing Templar-issue boots.

"Interesting." He handed it to his second-in-command. "What do you make of it?"

The experienced knight pursed his lips. "Either the eavesdropper was Sir Ricardo himself, or Sir Ricardo is traveling with wet boots."

"And which do you think is more likely?"

The man grunted, handing back the message. "I have little doubt Sir Ricardo was the eavesdropper. A hungry man would have approached either the front door or the squires tending the animals in the back. He would not have listened at a window waiting for an opportunity to ask for help from voices belonging to those he could not see."

Enrico agreed. "I believe you are correct. And unfortunately, if you are, this new information is concerning."

"Why is that, sir?"

"First, it confirms that he's traveling incognito—he's not wearing any of his Templar-issued gear, except for the boots. But more importantly, he lied to his brothers. It means he has already come to the conclusion that he cannot trust us. And that means we might not be able to stop him without killing him."

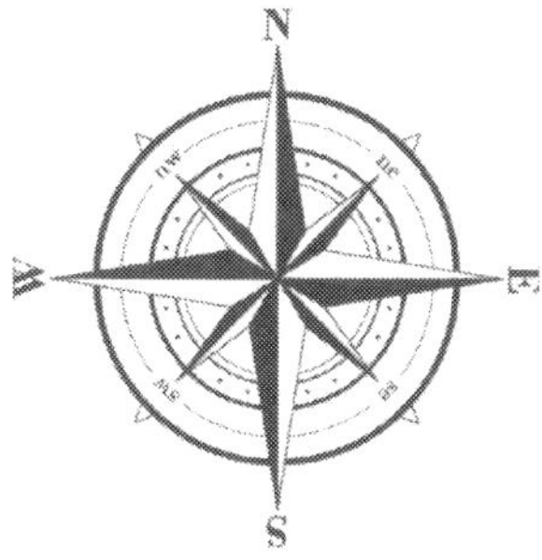

Ostia, Italy

Present Day

Sergeant Will "Spock" Lightman cocked an eyebrow at the sight before them and Command Sergeant Major Burt "Big Dog" Dawson smacked his forehead. "You two do know you're in public, right?"

Sergeant Carl "Niner" Sung grinned. "I think that's the point."

Sergeant Leon "Atlas" James stood in stunned silence, his head shaking. "How in the hell did you arrange this?"

Niner placed a dainty hand on his chest. "What makes you think *I* had anything to do with it?"

"Because there's no way in hell that not only would I pack a Speedo, but you'd be here with one that matched."

Niner raised his hands over his head and did a dainty hip twist. "I think it's rather fetching, don't you?"

Spock snorted. "It looks like you're packing a Vienna sausage and Atlas has a whole roll of kielbasa tucked away."

Niner took an exaggerated look. "How does that thing even fit in there?"

The impossibly-muscled Atlas glanced down then grinned. "Well, let me tell you, it's a complicated process involving twists and turns."

Niner spun, addressing the bar beside the beach they were at. "Ladies, please don't excite my friend. You could get him arrested for indecent exposure."

Snickers and laughter erupted and Atlas appeared slightly uncomfortable. He took a seat on a bar stool between Spock and Dawson. "I still want to know how he arranged this."

Niner dropped between Atlas' man-spread legs, twisting around and striking a pose as he took a selfie. Atlas shoved him away and Niner expertly rolled, his Delta Force training kicking in. He checked out the photo. "I think that turned out rather nicely." He tapped on his screen and a moment later all their phones beeped. Dawson pulled up the message and couldn't help but laugh.

Spock held out the phone so others who had gathered could see. "I'm not sure what's bigger, your head or Atlas Jr."

"Definitely Junior," rumbled Atlas in his impossibly deep voice.

"Just a second." Niner tapped away. "I promised Vanessa and Angela I'd send them the result of their handiwork."

Atlas tossed his head back and groaned. "How did I know those two were involved?"

"That's what you get for letting your girlfriend pack your bag when you're being deployed."

"I did *not* let her pack my bag. She added the Speedo to the bag after I had put it by the door. How was I supposed to know we were gonna get a couple of days' leave?"

Dawson eyed his comrade. "You should expect the unexpected. That's the job."

"An unexpected beach vacation?"

Dawson shrugged. "Hey, you could have gone to the quartermaster and asked for some standard-issue shorts."

"Yeah, but then I'd be out here in camo."

Spock eyed the big man. "Me thinks the lady doth protest too much."

Atlas eyed Spock. "Huh?"

"I think Kong really wanted to display Kong Jr."

"That's ridiculous."

"Yeah, sure it is, brother."

Niner, facing the three of them, jerked his chin toward the bar behind them. "Is that the Doc?"

They all turned to see a news report playing on the TV, the footage on a loop, something in Italian written below. Dawson squinted, watching as what appeared to be Palestinian protesters caused more trouble somewhere, though this looked different. Usually, the protests were in the streets, but this appeared to be a forest.

"Now they're pissing off Mother Nature?" commented Spock.

The camera flipped to a different angle showing four policemen forming a human barrier between the mob and what appeared to be a counter-mob. The numbers weren't large but something was going down.

Niner pointed as the angle changed again. "There!"

Dawson cursed. Acton and his wife Laura were clearly visible along with Tommy Granger and Mai Trinh. "Where is this?" he asked, flagging the bartender.

The bartender glanced at the screen. "It's a rest stop a few hours north of here."

A buxom blonde leaned in. "I'll tell you what they're saying if you give me five minutes alone with him." She winked at Atlas.

Atlas held up his hands. "Sorry, sweetheart. I'm taken."

"I don't care about you. The question is, is *he* taken?"

Niner chuckled. "Sorry, darling, but unfortunately his girl back home has a lock on that thing." He gestured toward the TV. "But those are our friends. Can you please let us know what's going on?"

The mischievous smile on the girl's face disappeared. "They're your friends?"

"Yes."

"Oh, I'm sorry. I didn't realize." She listened to the TV, the bartender having turned it up. "It looks like they're at a truck stop a few hours north of here. Oh, yeah. This was on the news last night. I remember seeing it. Apparently, some boy fell into a hole and broke his ankle. They found a body inside that was there, they think, for hundreds of years, so a team from the Vatican was sent in to investigate. I guess they found a letter from some pope on the body. They're saying they believe there's some ancient document that's been found. Sorry, I don't know how to translate that into English."

"Treatise of the Three Impostors," filled in the bartender.

Dawson quickly googled it as the woman continued to translate.

"I guess these Muslim youth have shown up and are demanding it be burned because they consider it blasphemous."

Dawson frowned. "Wonderful. And the response?"

She shrugged as the newscast changed to the weather. "I don't know, sorry."

Dawson turned to the bartender. "You said it's a few hours north of here?"

"Yeah, on the A1 Highway."

Dawson rose, as did the others. "Where's the nearest car rental place?"

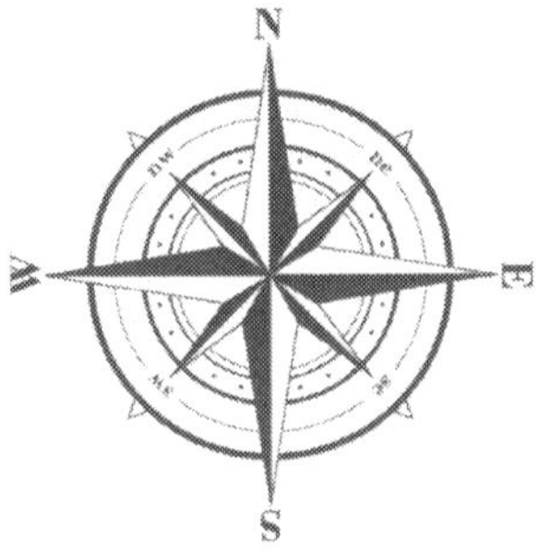

En Route to Padua

AD 1239

Brother Alberto continued north at a steady pace, the long-distance horses they were riding rapidly closing the gap Sir Ricardo's head start had provided him. A brother embedded within the Templar Order had informed them that Ricardo had been spotted this morning in Sipicciano, a town less than two hours ahead. After Father Francis had informed him of what was in the folio he had given Ricardo, Alberto had met with Keepers leadership, and it had been decided it was simply too dangerous for this document to exist.

While there was the possibility it could weaken the emperor, there was doubt as to what that might mean. There was a distinct possibility weakening the emperor's position might cause a war, and wars were unpredictable. With the emperor having a power base in Sicily to the south, and a significant number of allies in the north, the Papal States could find themselves squeezed. And if Rome were sacked once again, as it had been before in history, Christianity could find the emperor sitting in the Chair of Saint Peter rather than the pope.

He pulled his cloak tighter against the stiffening breeze. The sun was up, though provided little warmth today, the cloud cover thick. But at least it wasn't raining, as it had for most of their journey. He was cold, damp, and miserable, as were the others with him, yet no one complained, for this was an important mission in service of God. Perhaps at no point in history had the Church ever been so threatened, and it was the Keepers' job to preserve it, not just from those on the outside who would do it harm, but those on the inside who would do the same, though perhaps unintentionally.

This was a plan set into motion by people other than him, and when briefed on the treatise and its contents, he immediately knew that anything involving it could come to no good. He had no desire to kill Sir Ricardo, yet the man had to be stopped. Though perhaps the damage had already been done. A messenger had reached them this morning from Padua, indicating the court there was in chaos, the pope's letter, sent ahead of the actual treatise, apparently having its desired effect. Should the actual text arrive, war might be inevitable, and the emperor, like a cornered animal, might lash out at his greatest foe.

The Church in Rome.

Ricardo had to be stopped, and unfortunately, with his orders being issued as non contramand, he feared the man's life was already forfeit.

Though only if they could find him.

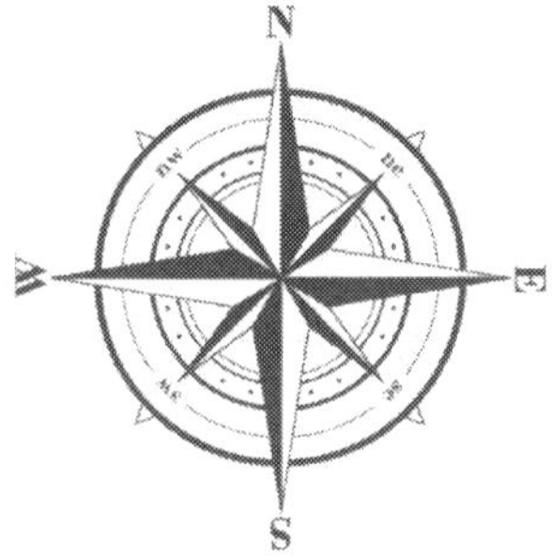

Discovery Site

North of Sipicciano, Italy

Present Day

Acton took in the rapidly escalating situation. Four police officers could only hold back this crowd if they were willing to use their weapons, and there was no way they would, not unless their lives were threatened. He had already seen one of them on their radio, so reinforcements would be arriving eventually, but how long they would take to get here he had no idea. The only way to defuse the situation would be to get the hell out of here.

He turned to their driver Lombardi then pointed at the terrified Tommy and Mai. "Take the two of them back to our car as discreetly as possible. Call Mario Giasson, let him know what's going on."

"Yes, sir."

Acton turned to Tommy and Mai. "You two go with Lombardi. Get in the vehicle. We'll be along shortly. If things get out of control, you leave. Understood?"

They both nodded and Mai rushed into Laura's arms, hugging her. "Why don't you come with us before it's too late?"

"We need to get the artifact out of here, otherwise, this mob will destroy it. Don't worry, we're not going to risk our lives, but we just want you two safe."

Mai sniffed hard, wiping her eyes, and Lombardi beckoned them. "Let's go before they surround us."

Acton noticed more were coming through the trees and he turned to Father Esposito, who walked up to them, concerned.

"My understanding is you two have been in more situations like this than I have. What's your recommendation?"

"Abandon everything. If they destroy your equipment, it doesn't matter. It can be replaced. All we need to do is take the case with the folio."

"What about the body?"

Laura dismissed the concern. "They don't care about that. All they care about is the document. They might destroy it since that's what mobs do, but let's be honest, it's the document that's important, not the messenger."

Esposito's head slowly bobbed in agreement. "All right. I'll go get the case."

Acton heard the hesitation in the man's voice. He was scared, and rightfully so. "I'll get it. Here's what we'll do. I'm gonna get the case, and when I come out of the tent, I want all of your people, including yourself, to join the counter-protesters as Laura and I head to our vehicle. Count to thirty, then leave. Get to your cars then we'll head back to the Vatican. Agreed?"

"Agreed."

"Okay. Tell your people. We're doing this now."

Esposito gathered his team as Acton and Laura headed for the tent. The case was sitting on the table as it had been left. Unfortunately, it was large and conspicuous, and it wouldn't take a genius to figure out what was inside.

"This might not be such a good plan after all."

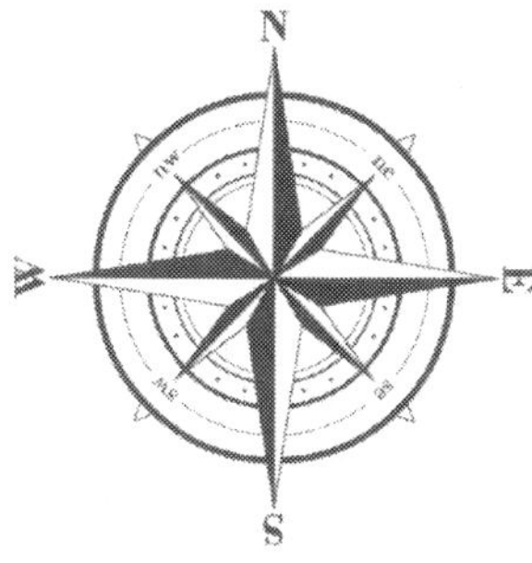

St. Thomas' Hospital

London, England

Reading pressed the button to elevate the head of the bed a little more as his doctor entered the room. Spencer stood, both of them desperate to hear the results of the test taken hours before. "What's the good news, Doc?"

The doctor frowned as he worked his tablet. "Unfortunately, it's too early to tell right now. There's a marker we look for and it is showing an elevated result. Now, your heart was under a lot of stress during the episode so this isn't uncharacteristic. What we need to do is wait for eight hours after the initial attack ended and test again. If we're lucky, the number's gone down, indicating no damage. But if it stays elevated, then things could be more serious."

"Do we need to be concerned?" asked Spencer. "I mean, what are we talking about here? What's typical?"

"Typically, the number goes down. It's just that at the moment, it's a little higher than we like to see after one of these episodes. How long was it before the paramedics arrived?"

Reading shrugged. "I'm not sure. Certainly under thirty minutes from when I woke up, but I don't know how long it was happening while I was asleep. It could have been five minutes, it could have been five hours."

The doctor waved the tablet. "Based on these results, I'm guessing it wasn't five minutes. In the future, if you have another attack, it's essential you call emergency immediately. Minutes can count."

"I understand. So, now what?"

The doctor tapped his watch. "We wait eight hours from the point you were given the injections."

Reading groaned. "Eight hours?"

The doctor flashed him a grin. "Look at the bright side. It's already been more than half that."

"Yeah, Doc, not to throw cold water on that, but how many hours will we be waiting to see the next set of results?"

The doctor shrugged. "Unfortunately, we're understaffed and our hospitals are overwhelmed. We're doing the best we can."

"We know you are, and it's appreciated," said Spencer. "Is he allowed to get up and stretch his legs?"

"Yes. Just watch your IV and don't be a hero."

Reading smirked. "Then you obviously don't know me."

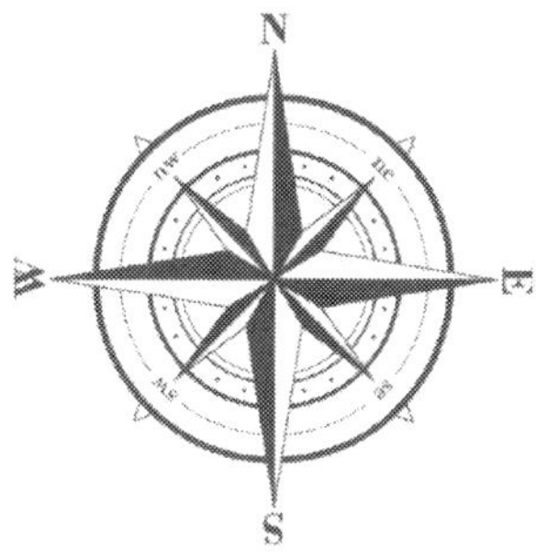

En route to Discovery Site

Italy

Dawson ended the call with his commanding officer, Colonel Thomas Clancy, as Spock pulled their rental SUV out onto the road.

"You got a location for me?"

Niner leaned between the seats and programmed the destination into the GPS. And cursed. "Three and a half hours. Too bad we couldn't borrow a Black Hawk."

Dawson cocked an eyebrow à la Spock. "We might not be able to get a Black Hawk, but I wonder if we can rent a helicopter."

"That's a crazy enough idea, it might just work." Niner sat back and worked his phone. "Let me make some calls."

"Where am I heading?" asked Spock.

Dawson gestured ahead. "Just keep heading toward the trouble, just in case there's no way to rent one."

Atlas leaned forward. "What did the colonel say?"

"He said stay off the news and don't make what we do on our vacation his business."

Atlas chuckled. "That sounds like the colonel."

Spock gunned them through a traffic light just as it was about to turn red. "I've got a question."

Dawson regarded the man. "What's that?"

"How the hell are any of us gonna afford to rent a chopper?"

Dawson frowned. "Hadn't thought of that. Normally I'd call the professors in a situation like this."

"Why don't you?" said Niner. "They'll probably just put you in touch with that fancy travel agent slash spy they've got working for them."

Dawson looked up from his phone. "Good idea. She could probably get us a chopper in a heartbeat." He brought up Acton's phone number. "Let's hope he's answering."

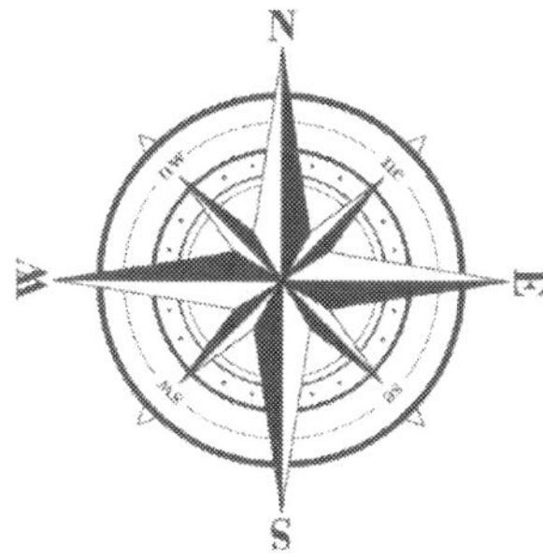

Discovery Site

North of Sipicciano, Italy

Acton gripped the case tightly as he stepped out of the tent and into the sunlight. He gave Esposito a nod and the priest/scientist joined the crowd of counter-protesters with his staff, thickening the blind for their escape. Acton headed in the opposite direction with the case held in front of him. Laura kept behind him and slightly to his left, blocking the mob's view of what he was holding as best she could without it looking too obvious.

Her phone pinged and she checked it as they stepped into the trees. "Tommy and Mai are in the vehicle."

"Tell them we're on the way." Acton's phone rang and he cursed as it echoed through the trees. He was forced to lower the case—it was too heavy to hold in front of his chest with one hand. He reached into his pocket and fished out his phone with the intention of turning it off when he noticed the call display said 'BD.' He handed the phone to Laura. "You better take it."

Somebody shouted behind them and Acton turned to see several of the mob pointing toward them, and he cursed.

"Time to run!"

Davide's heart raced as his fist pumped in the air, screaming the counter chant of "foreigners go home" adopted by the crowd in response to the "burn it now" demand from the Palestinian mob. So far, only insults had been thrown, but one of the pieces of shit had tried to snatch his yamaka.

"They're getting away!" shouted one of the Palestinians, pointing toward the trees behind Davide and his friends. He turned and saw the man and woman leaving the area, the man gripping a large case that had to contain the document they were all here about. The mob surged forward and one of the police officers cursed as he drew his baton, the other three following suit, but it didn't deter the hate-filled group.

They stormed forward, shoving the police to the ground, some of them kicking the officers as they were down, and it enraged Davide. He pushed through the crowd of counter-protesters and charged at one of the mob kicking the police officer he had spoken to earlier. He knocked the attacker to the ground then began kicking him.

"How do you like it, you piece of shit? How do you like it?" He continued to kick when from out of nowhere a fist connected with his face. He hit the ground hard, his ears ringing, his world spinning.

"Davide!" cried Salamone from nearby as somebody kicked him in the side and he cried out. Something dark swung across his field of vision and his attacker screamed in agony, dropping beside him as the officer rolled to his knees then pushed to his feet, hauling Davide up beside him.

The man swung his baton again, catching one of the mob in the head, slicing open his cheek. Davide reached down and grabbed a tree branch dropped by one of the attackers and began swinging as Salamone and Zaccaria joined him, wielding their own makeshift weapons. They set upon those attacking the other officers and created a circle, their backs to each other, holding off the mob when a gunshot rang out.

And everything changed.

Acton cursed at the gunfire. It was far enough away that they shouldn't be in danger, but the mob was after them and there was no way to know if any of them were armed as well. He could hear them racing through the trees behind them as Laura spoke to Dawson on the phone.

"Yes, I'll have her contact you…I've gotta go…running for our lives…yeah, I know…what else is new…good luck to you too." She ended the call and worked her phone between glances up to make sure she wasn't about to run into a tree. He didn't bother asking what was going on. It was more important she focused on whatever she was doing.

Something hit him in the back and he stumbled, cursing as he lost his footing and tripped over a tree root. Laura reached back and hauled him to his feet. "Let's go! Let's go!"

He pushed forward, his back aching from what must have been a fairly hefty rock. He glanced over his shoulder and grimaced at the sight. At least ten were just behind them, two of them within paces. They were going to be overtaken. These were teenagers and young men in their early twenties, and his legs had seen better days. Hauling this huge case wasn't helping—it was just too much to keep ahead of them.

Laura stuffed her phone back in her pocket, signaling an end to whatever she and Dawson had been discussing.

"What's going on?"

"BD and a few of the others are in Italy on leave. They're heading our way. I just sent a message to Mary to reach out to them to see if she can arrange transport for them."

"When will they get here?"

She did a shoulder check. "Not soon enough."

"That's what I figured." He could hear the breathing of those behind him. He had seconds at best. He cursed. He swung the case gripped in his right hand across his chest, then back, flinging it to his right as a flurry of gunfire erupted behind them.

Davide lay on the ground, curled up in a bundle as three of the officers opened fire on the mob while one of their comrades bled out not three paces from where he screamed in terror. Gunfire replied, the mob armed, at least some of them, but most were scrambling to get out of the way of the police response.

"Where the hell's that backup?" shouted the officer from earlier into his radio.

Davide couldn't make out the response but when the radio was discarded on the ground beside him, it was clear the officer wasn't happy. Salamone and Zaccaria scrambled away on their hands and knees as Davide pushed up and crawled over to the wounded officer. He pressed his hand on the neck wound just above the body armor. He was certain it was a lucky shot, but that was all a matter of perspective. It was certainly unlucky for the officer.

More gunfire rang out from the crowd. The counter-protesters had scattered with the first shots but he couldn't leave. This was now his fight too. These people had to be stopped. They were a scourge on Italian society. There was no loyalty here. These weren't his countrymen. These were people with their own agenda, their own hatred, and they had no place in civil society.

He retrieved the officer's weapon from its holster, determined to take action.

"No, don't!" gasped the officer.

Davide stared down at him, tears in his eyes, his entire body shaking with fear. "If I don't, we're going to die."

The officer stared into his eyes then acquiesced. "Don't forget the safety."

Davide stared at the weapon. He had never held one before and it was a lot heavier than he had expected. He spotted the safety on the side and pushed it, the small switch sliding as the gunfire continued around him. He turned, keeping the weapon out of sight, and peered into the mob, searching for whoever was firing at them.

One of the officers dropped beside him and he glanced over. "Are you all right?"

The man gripped his chest. "Looks like my vest caught it."

"Can you see the shooter?"

"No, but I think he's to our right in the trees."

Davide swung around, peering through the mob and spotted an opening they had left, an opening that led straight to a shooter hiding behind a tree. He took aim, lining the bastard up like countless video games had taught him, then he said a silent prayer, begging for forgiveness for what he was about to do.

And squeezed the trigger.

Acton burst onto the pavement, gripping Laura's hand. A horn sounded repeatedly and he glanced over to see their SUV with Lombardi behind the wheel rapidly approaching. It shuddered to a halt and they both jumped in. "Let's get the hell out of here!"

"You don't have to tell me twice." Lombardi hammered on the gas as the mob erupted from the trees, several of them reaching the SUV, pounding on the windows as they gained speed, soon leaving them behind.

"Don't let up. There was gunfire."

"You got it."

Laura twisted around, reaching out for Tommy and Mai. "Are you two all right?" Tommy's eyes were wide, his cheeks pale, and Mai was shaking, her face stained with tears.

"I think so," managed the poor girl.

"What about you two?" Tommy gasped and pointed at Acton's back. "You've been shot!"

Acton's eyebrows rose and he twisted his head around, struggling to see his back. An impossible task. Laura grabbed him by the shoulders and spun him around, tearing open his shirt then sighing with relief.

"It's just a cut. It's not a bullet hole."

Acton gave Tommy a look. "What are you trying to do? Scare the shit out of me?"

Tommy's jaw dropped, aghast. "I'm sorry!"

Acton laughed and reached back, smacking the kid on the leg. "I'm just joking. We all have to calm down. We're safe now." He pointed at the road, Lombardi now merged with the highway traffic. "Any sign of pursuit?"

"Nothing yet, but small problem."

"What's that?"

"We're heading in the wrong direction."

"Where are the others?"

Lombardi glanced in his sideview mirror. "They're behind us. It looks like everybody got away."

"Get on the phone and confirm that. Make sure we didn't leave anybody behind."

"What's your recommendation? Keep heading north and get to a police station, or turn around and head south to the Vatican?" Lombardi pointed ahead. "There's a butterfly ramp just ahead. I need to know in thirty seconds what you want me to do."

Acton glanced at Laura. "What do you think?"

"The Vatican's south. BD and the others are south."

"South it is."

Lombardi cut their speed dramatically and took the off-ramp. "I hope this was all worth it."

Laura reached under her jacket and pulled out the leather folio, Tommy and Mai gasping from the back seat. "Oh, it was worth it all right."

Jihad roared in frustration as he hurled the empty case against a nearby tree. "They tricked us! It's not in here!" He pointed to the parking lot. "After them! They can't be allowed to get away!" The crowd charged toward their cars as the gunfire behind them dwindled then stopped. He hoped it meant the police opposing them were dead, but it didn't matter. So far, he had failed. The infidels had tricked him and the blasphemous document was no longer here. The man and the woman had played him for a fool, played them all for fools.

He emerged from the trees and shouted to the crowd. "Does anybody know where they went?"

Somebody replied to his left. "The only way they can go is north!"

He leaped into his car, his friends piling in with him. He fired up the engine and gunned it toward the highway, determined to catch them. Unfortunately, he had no clue what kind of car they were driving. He punched the steering wheel repeatedly, the frustration overwhelming. "Keep your eyes open. Look for anything suspicious. We need to find those bastards."

Haasim pointed across his field of vision and Jihad batted the idiot's hand away. "Are you trying to get us killed? Do you realize how fast I'm going?"

Haasim held up his hands. "Gee, sorry, but I just thought you might like to see the three SUVs with Vatican emblems going by on the other side."

Jihad took his foot off the gas and twisted around, struggling to catch a glimpse of them, but they were out of sight. He spotted an exit ahead and cranked his wheel, crossing two lanes of traffic, horns blaring in protest as he took the exit ramp at the last second. He glanced back to see at least half a dozen other vehicles following him. They weren't alone. They would catch the bastards and punish them for what they were doing.

And destroy the blasphemous insult to Islam once and for all.

"You can let go, son."

Davide flinched at the voice behind him. It was the officer from earlier.

"And you can lower that gun."

His weapon still pointed at the tree where he had emptied the magazine toward the shooter, the man's body lying out in plain sight now, a large pool of blood staining his clothes and the ground.

"Just put the gun down on the ground. You're safe now."

Davide's entire body trembled violently. He released his grip on the weapon and it fell to the ground. One of the other officers stepped over and picked it up.

"That's one hell of a shot, kid. You ever thought of joining the force?"

Davide's eyes bulged and he shook his head, then flinched again when someone patted his hand behind him. He spun around to see the officer with a grim expression.

"You can let go, son."

Davide's eyes narrowed, confused. He had already let go of the gun and was about to say so when he gasped, realizing what he meant. He stared down at the wounded officer, at his hand still gripping the man's neck in a desperate attempt to stop the bleeding, but the officer's eyes were closed now, his face sickly pale, the blood no longer pumping through Davide's fingers.

"He's gone, son. You tried your best but he was beyond saving."

Davide jerked his hand away, soaked in blood, then twisted around and vomited, the horror finally registering. He stared out at the carnage, his hands and knees pressed into the blood-soaked dirt. Bodies crumpled where they had been shot, others writhed in agony, some felled by the police, some by their own shooters as they fired through the crowd, like most of these people, unconcerned with innocent lives, instead focused only on killing.

Shouts erupted from the woods and the officer cursed, drawing his weapon and aiming it into the trees. Davide squeezed his eyes shut, terror once again gripping him at what was to come when cries of relief surrounded him and he forced his eyes open to see the long-awaited reinforcements emerging from the forest, the shock on their faces at the carnage making him realize just how out of control things had become.

For these were the professionals, and if they were horrified, he had no idea how he would ever recover from what had happened on what was to be a fun day that had instead drawn him into the hate that filled too much of the world.

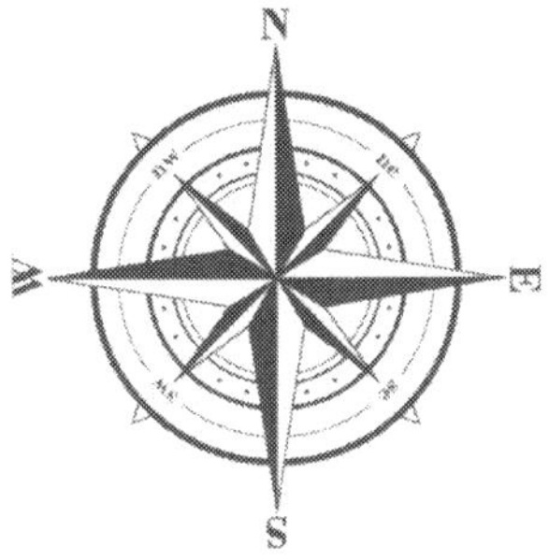

En Route to Padua

AD 1239

Ricardo patted the long neck of the mighty beast he rode. These endurance horses were bred for covering long distances, three times the normal length of ride that the average horse could manage, and it could do so for several days before it would need a proper rest. He had planned on a journey of almost two weeks to reach Padua, as he had set out on a normal horse, not having expected a long journey. The stable at which he had supplied himself in Rome had no endurance horses available. He had made do, though he had to assume those who might be pursuing him didn't suffer such an affliction. They would have left Rome upon the proper steeds.

Now that he had the proper ride, he should hopefully keep ahead of anyone. Yet he couldn't help but continue to ask why, what had gone wrong, what had changed? If he only knew what the document he carried contained, perhaps he could make a decision himself. Yet he had sworn not to look at it, and his orders were to obey to the letter the instructions given him by the man he met. No matter how much he wanted to, he couldn't look at it, nor should it make a difference.

A thought occurred to him that provided some comfort. Messengers had been passing him day in and day out in both directions. Certainly, the Order would have sent a message to Padua, where the head of the Electoral College was currently located. If the message shouldn't be delivered, this man would know by now, and since he was a man of honor, he would surely take the proper action when presented with the document. He nodded to himself, satisfied with this possible scenario. It had to be so.

He frowned. There was another possibility. It could be that it had been decided the man he was to deliver it to couldn't be trusted with it or shouldn't see it.

He growled in frustration. There was simply no way to know, and there was still the possibility that this was the very intrigue that had led to all the secrecy in the first place. The Vatican hadn't sent the document themselves. They had reached out to the Templar Order, and the Order hadn't used the normal messenger network. It had instead assigned him covertly, with non contramand orders. The Vatican must have realized that someone would attempt to stop the delivery of this document, and that could be what was happening here, that someone was issuing false orders to interfere with his original mission.

He squared his jaw. He had his orders. They were issued as non contramand, and he had taken an oath to deliver this message to Padua.

And he had never not followed an order nor had he ever broken his oath.

He forged ahead, bracing against the growing wind, his leg protesting once again, signaling a change in the weather. He rubbed at the pain just above his knee, damning the Saracen responsible for the umpteenth time.

He rounded a bend in the road and frowned at the sight ahead. Four men blocked his way, all on horseback. There were a few people ahead of him, some behind, the road containing a fairly steady flow of traffic throughout the day. Those not traveling alone, along with those on foot or with carts or carriages, were waved through unchallenged. They were clearly searching for a lone rider. If he turned around, it would look suspicious and they would likely pursue him. And there was nowhere to turn off.

It could be something innocent, unrelated to him, but he doubted it. It was simply too coincidental. He would have to bluff his way through, for he wasn't the only traveler alone on horseback, and it wasn't like he had posed for an artist to create a portrait they might hold up to identify him as the man they were seeking.

Yet who were these men? They wore no colors that identified them. In fact, from where he stood, they appeared to be monks. It made no sense. They certainly weren't from his order, nor were they from the Church or from any army controlled by the emperor. Yet these monks in their long, dark brown cloaks, made no attempt to hide the fact they were armed, their swords clearly visible. Were they warrior monks like himself, or mere brigands, highway robbers?

He gripped his sword, pulling it out slightly, making certain it hadn't become stuck in the damp weather. He drew his dagger and tucked it in his saddle where he could easily reach it with his left hand. He didn't want to kill, but anyone who interfered with a Templar's orders immediately forfeited their life.

He approached the four men with as pleasant an expression as a weary traveler could muster. The cart ahead of him was waved through, and as soon as it cleared, the gap was closed, one of the men holding up a hand.

"Identify yourself."

"By what authority?"

The man appeared taken aback, apparently unaccustomed to being challenged. It was perhaps not the wisest of moves on his part, but he was frustrated. If he could identify these men, perhaps he could identify his adversary working to prevent him from successfully completing his mission.

"That's none of your concern," the man finally replied.

"I think it is my concern. In fact"—Ricardo turned in his saddle, waving a hand at those behind him—"I think it's all our concern. What gives you the right to interfere with our free passage? What gives you the right to delay us in our travels?"

"We…we have our orders," stammered the man. "Now, identify yourself!"

"Who gave you these orders?"

All four men exchanged looks.

"If you can't tell me who issued your orders, then I have to assume you're highway robbers and are up to no good. Perhaps I'll just turn around and report you to the nearest Templar outpost. They can send a contingent to deal with you."

The man held up his hand. "That won't be necessary. We work on behalf of the Church in Padua. We have an important message for a traveler named Sir Ricardo. Are you him?"

"I am not. I'm merely a traveler heading north on family business."

Another spoke. "You match his description." He gestured at Ricardo's footwear. "And those, if I'm not mistaken, are Templar issue."

Ricardo rolled his eyes and stroked his beard. "Three of you match my description, and the footwear were a gift from a Templar I encountered on the way two days ago."

"And why would he give you his footwear?"

"He was a good Christian and saw that I was in need. He told me it wasn't a bother as he would merely get a new pair at the next outpost. He was inconvenienced for a couple of hours while his good deed would be appreciated for months, if not years. Now, are you going to let me pass?"

More looks were exchanged before they finally made a hole.

"Thank you, gentlemen." Ricardo urged his horse forward with his legs and winced as a sharp pain jolted him. An involuntary gasp escaped and one of the monks drew a sword.

"It *is* you."

Ricardo's head snapped toward him. "What makes you say such a thing?"

The man pointed at Ricardo's right knee. "We were told Sir Ricardo has a leg wound from his battles in the Holy Land. Show us your leg."

Ricardo frowned. "And if I don't?"

"Then die."

"I don't think I like those options. How about I introduce a third?"

The man stared at him, puzzled. Ricardo pulled the dagger from under the saddle, his hand whipping out, the blade sailing through the air and embedding itself in the man's chest. Ricardo drew his sword, urging his horse forward as he swung, slicing open the nearest man's chest, revealing a large tattoo of Saint Peter's Cross. He let the sword continue to swing over the animal, whinnying in fear, the steed not battle-trained like a Templar one, instead a creature that had likely never heard a blade near its ears.

He parried a thrust from one of the two remaining monks, throwing the man off balance. He swung his sword back, catching the man on the arm, his enemy's weapon clattering to the ground as he surged through the roadblock. The fourth dropped his sword and curled up into a ball in his saddle, reciting the Lord's prayer in Latin.

Ricardo came to a stop and pushed the tip of his blade against the man's shoulder. "Who are you?"

The man whimpered but said nothing.

"Look at me!"

The man twisted his head and Ricardo cursed. It was a boy, his face covered in pimples, his beard mere tufts of what was yet to come.

"Why did they send a boy to do a man's job?"

"We were all that was available. The Keepers are few in this area."

Ricardo's eyebrows narrowed. "Keepers? What are you talking about?"

The boy vehemently shook his head. "I've said too much already."

Ricardo pressed the tip of his sword harder against the boy's shoulder and he winced. "Tell me."

The boy sniffed. "The Keepers of the One Truth were established by Saint Peter before he died, to protect the Church from those who would do it evil from both inside and out."

It was a rehearsed line. "Who do you report to? Who is your master?"

"I don't know. I'm not a real member. Not yet."

"Tell him nothing," gasped the man whose chest was opened by Ricardo's initial swing of the sword.

Ricardo turned his attention to the man, using his sword to open the man's tunic so he could get a better look at the tattoo. "And who are you to him?"

"He is my son, and he knows not of what he speaks."

"Oh, this was a little too specific. I think he knows exactly of what he speaks. And your tattoo of Saint Peter's Cross seems to back up his story. Who issues your orders?"

"You'll get nothing out of me or any of us. You'll have to kill us."

"I have no desire to kill anyone. I merely want to know why you're trying to stop me from accomplishing my mission."

The man collapsed back down on the ground, but maintained eye contact, his pain evident. "That I cannot say. However, our orders were to stop you from delivering that which you have been tasked. It was hoped you would listen to reason, but our orders were to kill you if you refused."

Ricardo sighed, sheathing his sword. "Tell your master that you all fought bravely, but that I took you by surprise. Also, tell your master not to interfere again for I will not be stopped. I have no desire to make the Keepers of the One Truth my enemy, whoever you might be."

"We are on the same side, Templar, of that I can assure you."

"Then stay out of my way. I have no desire to kill those who serve God." Ricardo urged his steed forward, leaving the scene of battle behind, finally with some answers that unfortunately merely left him with more questions. Who were the Keepers of the One Truth and why did they want to stop him in his mission? And more critically, how did they know about his wound? Only those within the Order could possibly know. It meant one of his brothers had betrayed him, or the Order had been infiltrated by these Keepers.

When this mission was over, these questions needed to be answered.

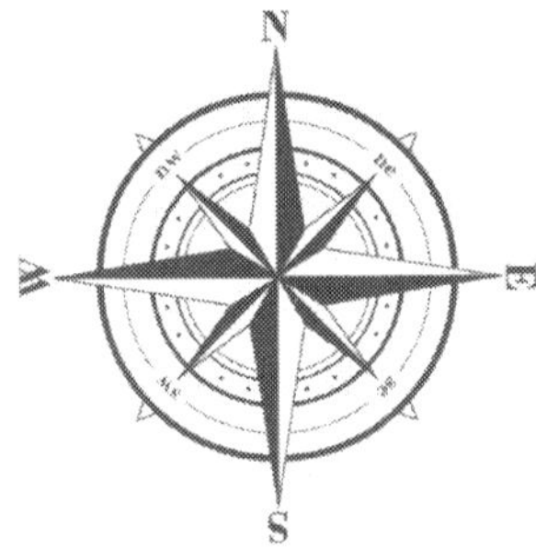

Heading South on Highway A1

Italy

Present Day

"Does this thing have lights and sirens?"

Lombardi shook his head. "No, it's not technically a diplomatic vehicle. It's just property of the Vatican and licensed in the Vatican."

Acton looked back to see the stream of cars racing out of the rest stop on the opposite side of the road, hands pointing in their direction extended out windows. "They've spotted us."

"They're going to have to make the same loop we did."

"Which means we have less than a five-minute head start, so I suggest you floor it. Use whatever lights you do have and try to clear a path. Otherwise, that mob will catch us, and at these speeds, somebody's gonna die."

Lombardi guided them to the far left of the highway, hammering on the gas. He reached over and activated his flashers.

"Do you have a weapon?"

"Glove compartment."

Acton leaned between the seats and popped open the glove compartment, removing a SIG Sauer P226 MK25.

"There should be three spare mags in there."

Acton grabbed them and Lombardi glanced over at him as he honked on the horn in an attempt to clear a path ahead of them.

"Do you know how to use that thing?"

Acton smirked at Laura. "I've been known to fire at a few targets."

"That's right, I forgot you're American."

Acton chuckled. "We're not all gun crazies."

"You're not?"

"Not all of us. I am. You should see the arsenal we have at home, but with the things that have happened to us, we'd be fools not to be armed."

"I always wanted to visit America, but now I'm not so sure."

Acton inspected the weapon as Lombardi took the shoulder, forcing his way up along the guardrail, cars ahead of them honking horns and swerving out of the way. "Are our friends with us?"

Tommy twisted around. "Yes. It looks like they figured out what we're doing."

"Good."

Lombardi swerved around a car ahead. "Should I try to keep us all together, or if I see an opportunity to get ahead, take it?"

"Take it. We're the ones with what they're looking for. If they catch up to the others, they can stop and let them search their vehicle. We have to keep ahead of them for as long as we can."

Lombardi frowned. "You're talking three and a half hours."

"How are we for petrol?" asked Laura.

"Full tank. I filled up at the rest stop."

"Good thinking. Do you know if the others did the same?"

"No, the others didn't have drivers, but don't worry. I filled up all the vehicles." Lombardi shrugged. "I was bored."

"Thank God."

Acton agreed. "If we're lucky, a lot of those chasing us didn't think to do the same, not to mention the fact they almost all appeared to be teenagers. I know at that age I was always riding on fumes." He sat back, tightening his seatbelt. "Oh, and don't worry about visiting the States. As long as you stay away from schools, you should be fine. It's almost never as violent as this day has been here in Italy."

Lombardi grunted. "Point taken."

"Tell you what," said Laura. "You get us out of this alive, and we're paying for your vacation."

Lombardi glanced in his mirror with a grin. "Deal!"

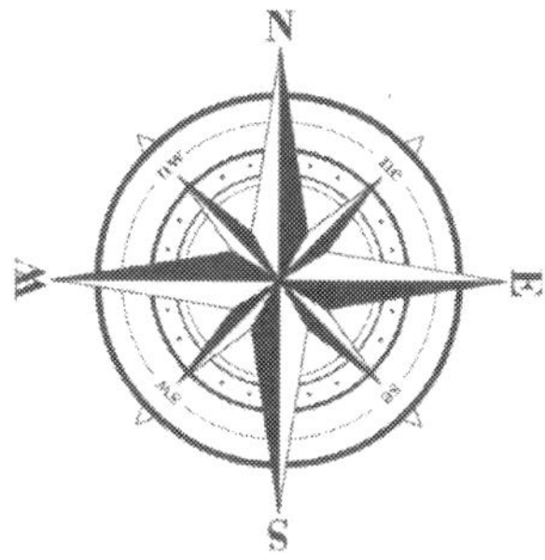

Giasson's Office

The Vatican

Giasson sat behind his desk, running a hand over his bare scalp, wishing he had hair to pull. He had shaved it years ago to support Marie-Claude when she was battling cancer. The fight was long won, the cancer a thing of the past, but he had liked the look, and so had she. The fact his family on both sides suffered from male pattern baldness made it just a matter of time regardless. He was fortunate to be one of those who had no surprises hidden under his hair.

He sighed heavily. Once again, the troublesome academics were causing him a headache, though in their defense, this wasn't their fault. They just seemed to be magnets for trouble, though when they found it, they didn't shy away. Too many pieces of history had been lost by inaction, and the professors had had enough, determined to fight back whenever they could.

Like today, apparently.

There was a tap at his door and his second-in-command, Martino Rizzo, leaned in. "We might have trouble brewing. Looks like we've got some Palestinian protesters gathering at the front gate."

Giasson cursed, flashing back to the mob that had stormed the Vatican when an ancient piece of the Koran was found on the body of a Templar Knight. Far too many had died that day, and he wasn't taking any chances this time, not with another document that could have the Religion of Peace calling for blood, heading their way. "Seal us off. Shut down everything. Get anybody who's not a resident out while we can. Put His Holiness' helicopter on standby and clear his evac path. Call back all security personnel and open the armory. I want everyone licensed to carry, armed. And remind everyone of the new protocols. We will not lose the Vatican a second time under my watch."

"No, sir, we won't."

Giasson flicked his hand, dismissing Rizzo. "See to things. I have some calls to make."

"Yes, sir." Rizzo headed back into the main security office, closing the door behind him as Giasson picked up his phone and dialed his counterpart with the Rome police. Hopefully, they would stop this before it even got started.

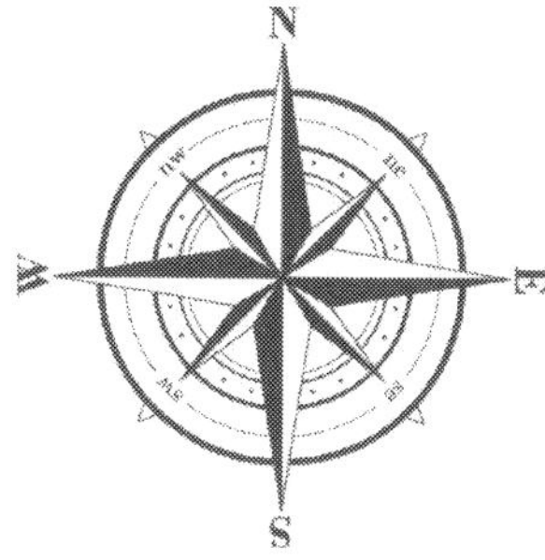

Jetex Rome Ciampino Airport

Rome, Italy

"Are you sure you know how to fly this?"

Dawson began flipping switches, turning knobs, and checking indicators as he sat in the pilot's seat of the large Sikorsky S-92 medium-lift twin-engine helicopter.

"My friend can fly anything," said Niner, reassuring the helicopter tour company operator. A hefty premium had apparently been paid by Mary, the professor's travel agent, to rent a helicopter big enough to carry the four of them plus evac the professors and their young friends.

Without a pilot.

Dawson strapped in then looked down at the man. "Don't worry. My uncle taught me how to fly."

"Your uncle?"

"Yeah. Uncle Sam." Dawson reached out and grabbed the door, yanking it shut as Niner climbed into the copilot's seat, Atlas and Spock sitting in the rear. "Everyone on comms?"

A trio of replies filled his ears as he pulled up on the cyclic and the beast of a machine strained then lifted off the ground, the owner of the tour company scrambling out of the way, the terror on the man's face likely worry over what would happen if the authorities discovered he had let someone other than one of his own pilots take out a chopper.

Atlas' voice rumbled in his ear. "BD, we've got a problem."

"What's that?"

"I just checked and they forgot to mount the fifty cal."

Dawson laughed. "I'll be sure to mention it in my comment card."

Niner glanced over at him. "So, just what the hell is the plan?"

"Intercept the professors, load everybody on board, get out of Dodge."

Niner shrugged. "Sounds simple enough. What could possibly go wrong?"

Spock groaned over the comms. "You had to say it, didn't you? You just jinxed the mission."

Atlas stepped forward and leaned between the seats. "I just found one weapon we can use, BD. A bomb. Not exactly a smart bomb, but it'll be partially guided because I'll be the one tossing his narrow little ass out the window."

Niner flipped Atlas the bird. "If we really need to do some damage here, you should be the one we're dropping." He jerked a thumb toward the rear. "Now sit your magnificent ass down. All that muscle is destabilizing the airframe."

Atlas shoved Niner's head with a meaty palm then disappeared into the back. Niner grinned at Dawson. "He loves me."

"Clearly. If you two are done flirting, contact the professors and see if we can get a fresh set of GPS coordinates on them. Then try to find an LZ where we can rendezvous. I wanna be in and out nice and smooth. No complications."

"Exactly the way I like it."

Dawson gave his friend a look. "I really hope you're talking about Angela."

Niner grinned.

But didn't reply.

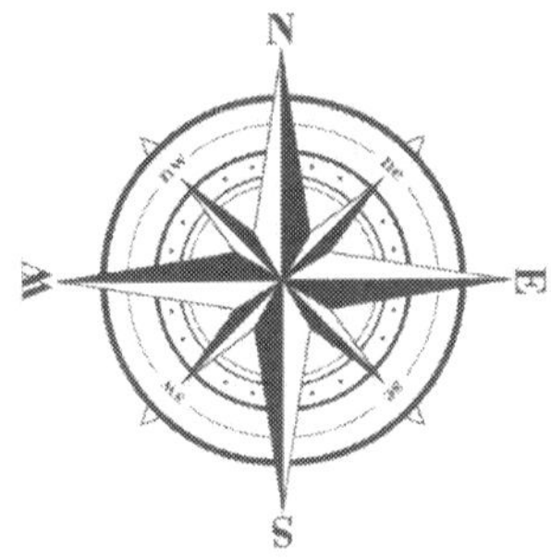

Heading North on Highway A1

Italy

Tankov inspected his weapons as did the others while they headed north on the A1 toward the professor's last known location. He didn't expect to fire any shots today, in fact, he was counting on it. A heavy engagement could lead to airport lockdowns, and his intention was to retrieve the item and be out of the country before the sun set.

He pulled out his phone and dialed Utkin in the second vehicle. "Deploy the drone. I want eyes on the highway ahead."

"The chances of us spotting them like that are pretty slim."

"I know. I just don't want to run into any surprises."

"Gotcha. We'll pull over and deploy now."

Tankov ended the call and his local contact glanced at him. "Expecting trouble?"

"When Professor Acton and the lovely Professor Palmer are involved, I always expect trouble. They have friends in very high and very low places. It's always best to be as prepared as possible when it comes to them."

"Professors? You mean like schoolteachers."

"These aren't your ordinary schoolteachers. Trust me."

"Interesting. I think I'd like to meet them. Just how lovely is this Professor Palmer."

Tankov leaned back and smiled. "She's the kind of woman you change your life for."

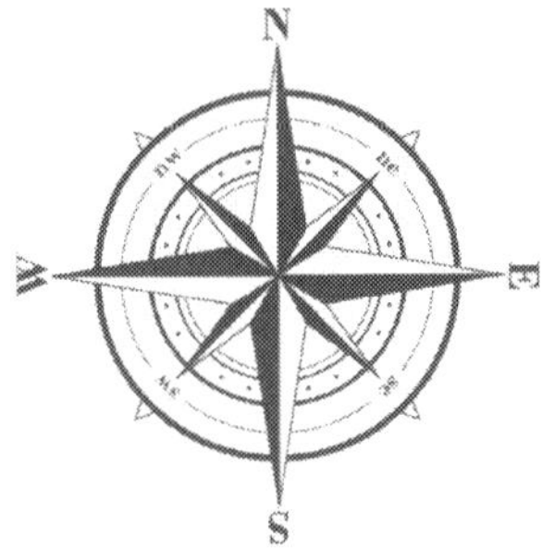

Heading South on Highway A1

Italy

"I don't think we have a choice. You saw what happened when you tossed the case. They were on it like bridesmaids after the bouquet. Push comes to shove, we're going to have to sacrifice the document to save ourselves. You saw the hate in their eyes. They're out for blood."

Acton pursed his lips at Laura's words. She was right, though normally he was the one to suggest something unorthodox. "You're right, of course. Let's do it, but do it as safely as we possibly can."

Lombardi glanced in the rearview mirror. "I can't promise to keep us steady, professors."

Acton dismissed the man's concerns. "You do what you need to keep them behind us and don't worry about what we're doing. Just keep your eye on the road and keep as much distance as you can between us and that mob. I'm taking full responsibility for what we're about to do, understood?"

"You got it, boss."

Laura removed the folio from her satchel and laid it on the seat between the two of them. Tommy and Mai both held up their phones, recording the event as Laura carefully opened the cover then widened the opening inside with her fingers.

Acton leaned over and peered in. "Definitely at least several pages, folded in half by the looks of it." He took a deep breath. "Everybody ready?"

Nods all around.

He reached in with his thumb and forefinger and gently pulled just a fraction, looking for any give. They didn't budge.

"Well?" asked Laura.

"It seems to be stuck. I'm gonna try to gently break any bond between the paper and the leather." He gently pulled up on the top of the folio then reached inside, probing with his fingertips, gently pressing down on the pages, separating the top page from the leather case. He could sense it giving way and he just prayed he wasn't shredding the page. He reached deeper inside and continued to feel the ancient paper separate.

"How's it going?"

"The paper feels intact as I pass over it. So far so good, I think. There's no way to know yet if there was writing on the top of the page that we're losing, but even if we are losing the ink, if we do get it back to the lab, the computer scan should be able to pick it up." He reached the end, his fingertips touching the bottom of the folio. "That's one side down."

"How do you want to do this? From the bottom or do you want to flip it?"

"Let's flip it. It worked the first time, let's see if we get twice lucky."

"Hang on!" shouted Lombardi, and Acton jerked his hand away from the folio as Laura pressed down on it protectively. Lombardi hammered on the brakes, sending everyone tumbling forward, his hand on the horn, pulsing at the drivers they were sharing the road with. He pressed on the gas, shouting an exaggerated thank you at whoever had finally gotten out of his way. "Sorry about that."

"No worries. Like I said, do what you gotta do. Saving our asses is more important than this."

"Agreed."

Acton drew a deep breath, returning his attention to the task at hand. "Shall we?"

Laura nodded. She flipped the folio case completely back and he pulled up on the top again, repeating the process, and a couple of minutes later the page was free. He removed his hand and took a deep breath again, his heart hammering.

"This is it, history being made. If we're right, we could be the first people in almost eight hundred years to see the Treatise of the Three Imposters, a document long thought to have been a hoax, to have never existed. Here goes nothing."

He reached in and gently squeezed on the bundle of pages, then gave it a slight tug. It slid smoothly. He flashed a smile at Laura then continued to pull, the pages slowly revealed, and a collective sigh escaped as he freed them from the folio that had secured them for almost a millennium. He held it up reverently as Tommy and Mai angled their phones for better shots as Laura took photos.

He placed it down on the seat. “Now to see what we’ve really got here.”

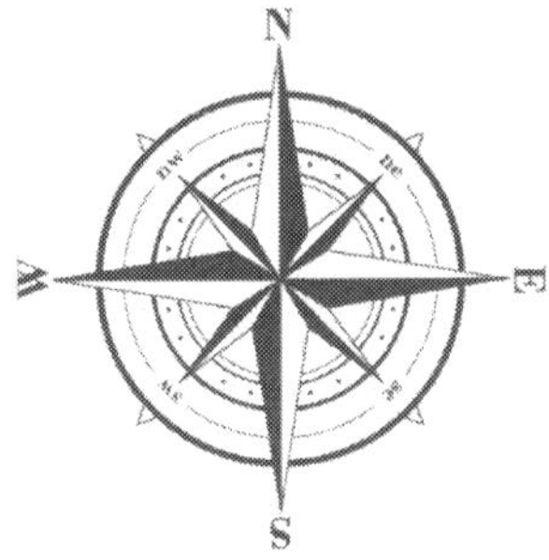

The Vatican

Rome, The Papal States

AD 1239

Father Francis rose from his desk as Cardinal Simon entered, holding up a sheaf of papers. "I must see him at once."

"Yes, sir." Francis opened the doors to the pope's office and stepped inside, closing them behind him. "Your Holiness, Cardinal Simon is here to see you, apparently on urgent business. It looks like he has a message."

His Holiness pushed aside the document he had been reading and closed his eyes, pinching the bridge of his nose. The man appeared exhausted. They all were. The past several days had been the most stressful of his life, especially considering it was his error that had compounded their misery. "Show him in, but only if he has good news."

Francis headed for the door then stopped. "Your Holiness?"

The pontiff waved a hand at him. "A bad attempt at humor. Let's see what the man has to say."

"Yes, Your Holiness." Francis opened the doors and beckoned Cardinal Simon inside, the man and his entourage wasting no time, the news he had to impart evidently important. He was about to close the doors and return to his desk when His Holiness held up a finger.

"Remain with us, Father Francis."

Francis bowed then closed the doors, delighted to be included, for he was desperate to know what was going on.

Cardinal Simon handed over the message he gripped. "It's from the head of the Electoral College, confirming what we suspected would happen. The emperor has been accused of being a heretic." He smiled. "One of the Electoral College members read your letter in open court."

Francis tensed as his heart raced. The fact one of the princes had publicly read the accusation in open court meant at the very least, some of the Electoral College hadn't entirely dismissed His Holiness' letter despite the lack of proof offered with it.

"And the emperor's reaction?" asked His Holiness.

"Outrage and indignation. His exact quote is in the letter. Apparently, he said, 'The three impostors theory has not passed my lips.'"

Francis cocked an eyebrow at the choice of words, and His Holiness caught his reaction.

"What is it, Father?"

Francis' cheeks flushed and he cleared his throat. "I'm sorry, Your Holiness. I just found his choice of words interesting."

"In what way?"

"Well, he used the word 'lips.' He didn't deny writing it, he denied saying it."

His Holiness' eyebrows rose as he leaned back. "A very interesting distinction, don't you think?"

Simon agreed. "It is, and it's a distinction, I'm ashamed to say, I missed. By using those words, if he did indeed pen the treatise as we suspect, then he technically didn't lie to the court."

His Holiness continued reading the letter, several pages long, then smiled. "I assume your people have read this?" Simon confirmed it with a nod. His Holiness picked up the pages and held them out to Francis. "Read this so you're properly informed."

Francis stepped forward, taking the pages with trembling hands. He retreated to the back of the room, quickly reading the message from the head of the Electoral College responsible for choosing who the next emperor would be.

"It would appear the emperor's court is divided, as is the Electoral College," observed His Holiness.

Simon agreed. "It does appear so. Sending the letter ahead with the accusation, but no proof, has led to the speculation we anticipated. All talk of taking away the power of the College of Cardinals to choose the next pope has been forgotten. All anyone is talking about is your accusation, and the fact that proof is on its way."

Francis finished reading the letter, detailing much of what was being discussed. It appeared His Holiness' plan of lobbing an accusation without proof had had its desired effect. Holy Roman Emperor Frederick II stood accused of being a heretic by the pope, and those within the court and the Electoral College who supported His Holiness over the Holy Roman Emperor, were making hay with the unfounded claim. The longer it took for the actual treatise to arrive, the better, for it would allow doubt to foment further.

"When do we expect the messenger to arrive?" asked Simon.

His Holiness turned to Francis who stepped forward. "We can't be exactly sure, as he's using private resources and not Templar. We have no idea where he exactly is right now. Depending on the type of horse he's riding, it could be as little as five days from the time he left to as many as fourteen."

Simon's head bobbed. "Let's hope it's closer to fourteen. If two weeks should pass with the court in turmoil, the emperor's power grab will certainly fail."

"Agreed," said His Holiness as Francis returned the message.

"Then I think, perhaps, when this current crisis is dealt with, it might be time to put an end to this problem once and for all."

His Holiness regarded the cardinal. "Just what are you suggesting?"

Simon stepped closer to His Holiness' desk, lowering his voice slightly. "The Holy Roman Emperors have been thorns in our side for over a century. The current emperor, particularly so. The man has already been excommunicated. His questioning of our faith, even before the discovery of the treatise, is well known. If there has ever been more of a skeptic on the throne, I can't think of one. For this man to have any sway over the matters of the Church is untenable."

"Again, while I agree with everything you said, what is it you're suggesting?"

"We should make our move against him now while he's been weakened by this accusation. Excommunicate him again. Demand the

Princes of Christendom swear fealty to you and the papacy, and reduce him to nothing more than a figurehead with no power. Destroy his family name, and when he dies, we're not dealing with an heir who holds a grudge and perhaps views that match his father's. I fear that entire family has been touched by evil."

His Holiness' head slowly bobbed and Francis gulped at the implications of what was being proposed. Simon was suggesting a war of words between the Vatican and the Holy Roman Emperor, and wars of words had the nasty habit of turning into all-out conflict.

If this went too far, they could be at war.

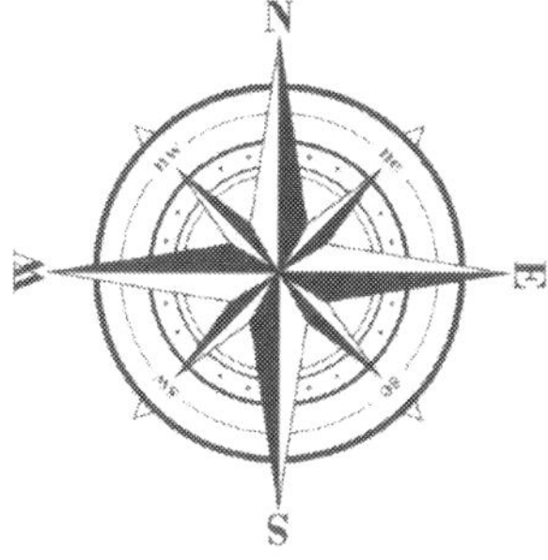

Heading South on Highway A1

Italy

Present Day

Jihad gripped the steering wheel as he shoved the gas pedal to the floor. His pulse pounded in his ears as his heart raced, rage consuming him as the traffic continued to get in his way. He could see the infidels ahead, but every time he thought he was about to close the gap, some fool would block his path.

If only he had a gun.

When the man had thrown the case, he had thought they were victorious. But when he discovered it was empty and he had been played for the fool, he had seen red. Never in his life had he been so angry, and for the first time he had a true thirst for blood. He wanted to kill them, kill them all. Not just the man and woman who had tricked them, not just the team from the Vatican. He wanted them all dead.

All the infidels.

All the Christians.

All the Jews.

Everyone who didn't embrace Islam or bow down before it. This was his day and no one was stopping him. Today, he would die a martyr, but not before he got his hands on the blasphemous document and destroyed it, condemning its insults to Islam to oblivion.

"Go! Go! Go!" shouted Haasim as he pointed to a gap in the traffic. Jihad hammered on the gas, swinging them to the right as he punched through the opening. They surged past half a dozen cars then he jerked the wheel to the left, putting them back in the fast lane with the shoulder giving him a little bit of room but not enough, as too many cars intentionally blocked them.

They were all in on it.

Every one of them.

All in his so-called home were anti-Muslim. They must be seeing the keffiyehs around their necks, the proudly displayed Palestinian colors causing the racist Italians to get in his way. But Allah was on his side and he would catch the infidels. He would punish them for tricking him.

Then he would kill them for attempting to spread more lies about his faith.

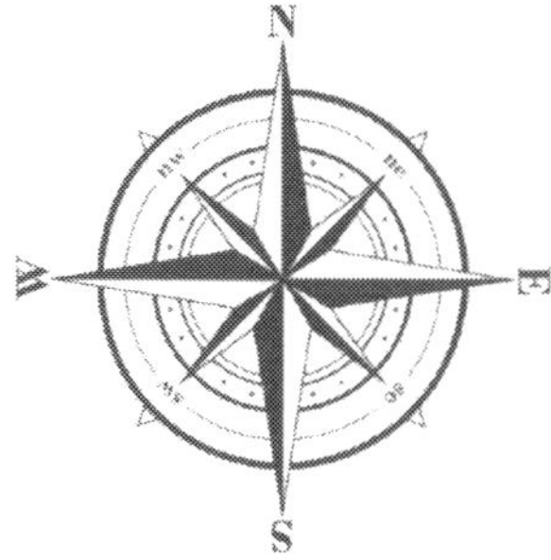

Giasson's Office

The Vatican

Giasson watched the security monitors through the glass that separated his office from his team. He had just got off the phone with Father Esposito who sounded terrified, as did the passengers in the vehicle with him. So far, the small convoy was managing to keep ahead of their pursuers but the gap was closing and they were still hours from Rome. Local authorities appeared to be in disarray and details were sketchy. At the moment, all police resources in the area were responding to what sounded like a massacre at the dig site. Esposito didn't know what had happened. All he knew was that a mob had descended on the site, and as they were making their escape, heavy gunfire crackled behind them.

Acton had coordinated their escape and everyone had made it out unscathed, but it meant getting the Italian police to respond to what was happening on the highway was next to impossible. At the moment, anything phoned in by drivers witnessing the pursuit would be interpreted as hooligans out street-racing. He had just finished informing his counterpart in the Rome police about what was actually happening, and she had promised she would do what she could to coordinate a response, but he feared it would come far too late.

Rizzo knocked on his closed door and Giasson waved him in. His second-in-command entered, a frown creasing his face as he held up a tablet. "We've been monitoring social media. Posts are going out on the usual sites calling for people to rally at the Vatican in support of the Palestinian cause."

"Any mention of the Treatise?"

"Not yet. Whoever's behind this, I think, is just trying to get a lot of the useful idiots out."

Giasson's head bobbed. Useful idiots were the worst type of protester. They had no idea about any of the facts surrounding what they were protesting. They were just out there because it was a protest. Today, it might be to support Palestinians. Tomorrow, it could be animal cruelty. The day after, a cancellation of their favorite TV show. He didn't worry about them. They were meant to make an event's cause seem more supported than it actually was. Get fifty people who truly believed in something out there protesting and it wouldn't even make the news. Get fifty people plus 500 morons and the press would get all riled up, claiming a cause was clearly supported by the masses when it actually wasn't.

But this wasn't a protest to support the Palestinians. If he wasn't mistaken, this was an attempt to clog the streets around the Vatican, and if they succeeded, Esposito's team, even if it reached Rome, would never get within the walls of the city.

"Sir, what are your orders?"

Giasson sighed and regarded Rizzo. "Crowd estimates?"

"A couple hundred outside the front gate. A few dozen at each of the others, but more pouring in every minute."

There was a tap at the door, Francesco Russo, one of their newer recruits, poking his head in. "Sir, there's something you're going to want to see."

"What is it?"

Russo jerked his chin toward the TV in Giasson's office. "Channel twenty-four. They've got a reporter out front."

Giasson picked up the remote and switched the channel then cursed. Now that the news was covering it, things could only get worse. "What's our status?"

Rizzo's frown was even deeper now. "We just got the last of the tourists out a few minutes ago. All gates are closed. Anybody who works or lives here who isn't in an essential position has been encouraged to leave."

"His Holiness?"

"The chopper's ready, the route's cleared, but he's indicated he's not leaving."

Giasson leaned back in his chair and groaned. "That man will be the death of me."

Rizzo chuckled. "I can see his point of view. Right now, there's not much going on. A few hundred protesters outside our gate isn't exactly unusual, and the circumstances are different than last time."

Giasson cocked an eyebrow. "Are they?"

"Well, yes. The relic was found here."

"Yes. And in this case the relic's being brought here. If it arrives, what will these people do?"

Rizzo pinched his chin. "Last time it was terrorists who had organized things. This time there's no indication that's what's happening."

"True. But, unfortunately, a mob doesn't always need a leader to cause havoc. Fanatics of any stripe who feel hard done by can quickly get out of control. When mob mentality takes over, normally good people can turn bad with the slightest provocation." He sighed. "I don't know what this world is coming to, but I fear where we're heading can bring only chaos."

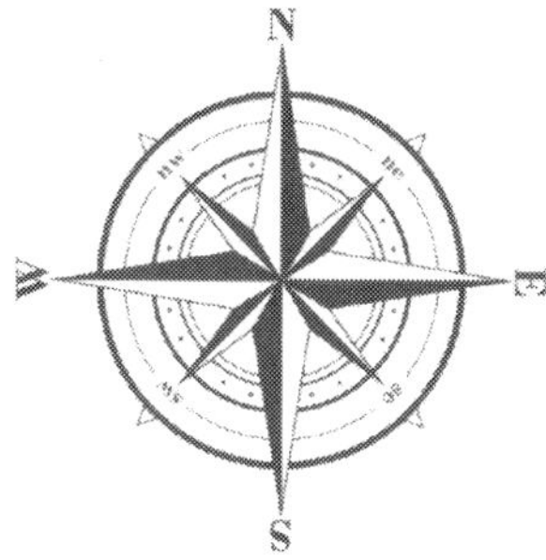

Heading South on Highway A1

Italy

Acton kneeled on the floor, his legs angled in such a way as to lock him in place as Lombardi continued to swerve in and out of traffic, expertly keeping them ahead of their pursuers. Laura sat wedged in the corner, bent over, one leg curled up under her, her other foot extended, pressing against the bottom of the driver's seat.

"Are you sure we should do this?" asked Mai as she and Tommy were jockeyed around the rear row.

Acton regarded her. "Of course we shouldn't be doing this, but we don't have a choice. If they get their hands on this, it'll be destroyed regardless. We'll never know what it said. This might be our only chance to ever read the text of the Treatise and fill in this gap in history."

"And you're willing to die for that?" asked Tommy incredulously.

Acton looked up at him. "Who said anything about dying? They're coming after us whether we do this or not."

"We could always throw it out the window."

Laura dismissed the young man's suggestion. "First of all, they probably wouldn't realize what we had thrown out the window, and second of all, James is right. This is a piece of history and we're stuck with it for now. If they catch us, we'll surrender it and hopefully that'll be the end of it. But if we have a chance to discover its secrets before that, then we should. Now, if you feel strongly about this, however, we'll stop."

Tommy stared at them both, his eyes darting between his two mentors then finally to Mai. "What do you think?"

"I want to know."

Acton grinned. "That's my girl."

"Fine. Do it. I guess I'm curious too why someone would want to kill us over some pieces of paper."

Lombardi glanced in his rearview mirror. "Don't forget how many they slaughtered just because of some cartoons. This thing sounds far worse."

Acton agreed. "Then I suggest we find out why they want to kill us over something they've never seen or probably heard of before today. No point in everybody being ignorant." He returned his attention to the pages, zooming in with his phone and taking some photos. "It appears to be six pages folded in half. They appear to be in remarkably good condition. I'm gonna see if I can remove the innermost page."

The pages were now slightly fanned out, which boded well for successfully extricating each page. If they were stuck together due to excess moisture, his efforts would likely shred them, but the leather folio and the relatively controlled conditions of what Acton assumed was at some point a root cellar, appeared to have left things in reasonably good condition. He just wished he had his satchel and the tools it contained. Unfortunately, it had been left behind in the rush to escape.

He reached in, pinched the edge of the innermost page, and took a deep breath, holding it before gently pulling. The page slid out and he sensed no resistance. He continued to pull in one continuous motion, focusing on the sensation in his fingertips, ready to stop at the slightest hint of resistance. But none came, and the page was soon free. He looked at the others excitedly and no one said a word, all eyes glued on the exposed page.

"Somebody tell me what's going on. If I'm going to die for this, I want to know why."

Acton exhaled and a nervous laugh escaped at Lombardi's outburst. "I've got the innermost page out," he reported. "If we assume the pages are folded the way you normally would today, then hopefully it is the first two pages of the Treatise, since it appears there's writing on the back side. We don't know about the inside yet." He gestured at Tommy. "Take a good photo of what's exposed now and run it through your app. Make sure it gets uploaded into the cloud. If something happens to us, I want there to be a record."

"Yes, sir." Tommy leaned over the seat and positioned his phone, taking a series of photos before climbing back.

"Now I'm gonna try to flip the page." Acton gently picked up the piece of paper around the curled crease in the center and flipped it over, wincing as a sliver broke off in his fingers. "That's what I feared."

"Don't worry about it," said Laura. "We knew this could happen. We don't have a choice, like you said."

Acton leaned back. "Okay, Tommy. We're ready for you."

Tommy leaned back in, taking photos of the newly exposed portion of the document then returned to the rear row as Acton looked up at Laura. "The only way we're seeing the inside is if I force it open. It doesn't seem too brittle but it was brittle enough for this little piece to break off." He held up the fingertip-sized piece of parchment. "What do you think?"

She glanced out the window. "I think they're getting closer."

Acton inhaled again. "Then here goes nothing." He gripped either side of the page between his thumbs and forefingers then slowly spread them apart. His heart pounded as the page continued to spread, the text inside revealed, and he stopped. "Tommy, can you get in there? Maybe you can get a good shot without me having to open it all the way."

Tommy leaned over, performing an acrobatic act that had Mai holding his legs and Laura gripping his belt. He took several shots. "Pull me up." Mai and Laura hauled him up, pushing him back into the rear row, and he examined his handiwork. "I think I got it. I should be able to manipulate this to turn it into a flatter image."

Acton smiled, gently closing the page back up, giving Laura a chagrined look. "I guess I should have thought of that sooner."

She reached out and squeezed his forearm. "None of us are exactly thinking straight right now. I know I didn't think of it either."

"Holy shit!"

Acton pushed his hips forward and groaned at his aching back as he rose to see an excited Tommy holding out his phone. "I ran it through the app. The top of the inner page translates to Treatise of the Three Impostors!"

A wave of gooseflesh washed over Acton as the moment of discovery, of confirmation, overwhelmed him, their dire situation momentarily forgotten. Laura reached out for him and he grabbed her, hugging her hard as Tommy and Mai did the same.

"So, is it worth dying for?" asked Lombardi from the front seat, bringing reality back to the situation.

Acton chuckled as he let go of Laura. "Definitely not. But at least if we do die, it won't be in ignorance."

"Bah! I don't care about ignorance. I've already found my positive way of looking at my impending death."

Acton hesitated to ask. "What's that?"

"I won't have to pay for my damned ex-wife's car repairs."

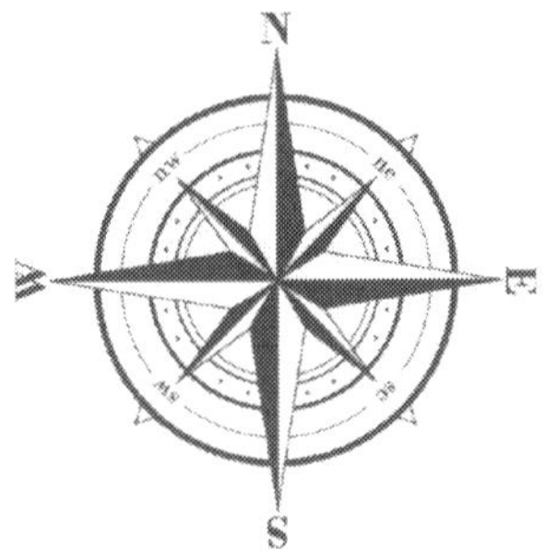

Discovery Site

North of Sipicciano, Italy

Davide spun and cried out at the sight of his mother and father rushing toward him. He collapsed into her outstretched arms and wept, unable to control his emotions any longer. His father wrapped his arms around them both and the three of them stood there, a family reunited, as the horrors of what had taken place a short while ago replayed on the back of his eyelids, a preview of what he had in store for perhaps the rest of his life.

His mother gently pushed him away and stared down at him, gripping him by his face, her thumbs wiping the tears from his cheeks. "Are you all right? Are you hurt?"

"I'll be fine."

His father regarded him. "That's not a yes or no. Did they hurt you?"

Davide looked away, ashamed. "I was kicked a couple of times and someone punched me."

His mother gasped. "Oh no! We need to get you to a hospital, get you checked out."

Davide dismissed the idea vigorously. "I just want to go home. The paramedics already looked at me." He stared at them. "How did you know to come?"

"Zaccaria's mother saw it on the news, so I called your father at work. He came and picked me up and then we came straight here."

Davide stared at his feet. "I'm sorry you had to leave work, Dad."

His father reached out and gripped his shoulder, giving it a squeeze and a shake. "You're my son. You'll always come first."

Davide's eyes burned and he squeezed them shut, battling the tears that threatened to flow. "I'm so sorry!" His shoulders shook and his father embraced him as he cried like he hadn't in years, his entire body convulsing as he relived the horror. He sniffed hard, his head pressed against his father's chest, the scent of his cologne filling Davide's nostrils, and for the first time since it had all started, he felt safe. "I killed a man."

"What?"

"I'm so sorry. I didn't mean to. I mean, I did mean to, but I had to. I didn't want to. I swear to God, I didn't want to, but I had no choice! He was killing us!"

"Oh, my poor boy!" wailed his mother, her voice a shriek.

"Mr. and Mrs. Levi!"

Davide jerked away from his father, sniffing hard and rapidly wiping the tears away as Salamone and Zaccaria rushed toward them. But when he spotted the tears streaking his friends' faces, his shame was washed away. His mother extended her arms and embraced his friends, then pushed them back quickly, grabbing each and spinning them around, checking for wounds.

"Are you two all right?"

They both nodded, but it was clear they were damaged as he was. His ribs hurt, he was bruised, but the physical scars of today would fade. It was the mental ones that terrified him, and his were worse than his friends. They hadn't struggled and failed to hold the life force inside a man's body. They hadn't opened fire in desperate defense and killed a man attempting to kill him. Only he had gone through that.

"Are you Davide's parents?"

Davide flinched and spun toward the voice as the officer whose name he had learned after the fight was Brambilla, approached. Davide's parents turned, his father acknowledging the man.

"Yes, we are."

Brambilla extended a hand. "I'm Constable Brambilla. I thought you should know, your son is a hero. In fact, if it weren't for all three of these boys, a lot more people could have died here today."

Salamone and Zaccaria smiled broadly, Salamone slapping Davide on the back. "All we did was follow Davide, but when the gunfire started, he's the one who stayed. He's the one who fought. We just ran away."

Davide reached out and gently pushed his friend. "Hey, you were the smart ones. I was just too stupid to leave."

Brambilla squeezed Davide's shoulder. "Your son should receive a medal. Me and the other officers had been overwhelmed and were being assaulted on the ground. Your son and his friends came in and helped beat back the mob, allowing us to get back on our feet and defend ourselves properly. When gunfire broke out, your son's friends and most of the crowd sought safety, but your son stayed behind and placed his hand on the neck wound of one of our officers in an attempt to save his life. When the fire intensified, your son took the downed officer's service weapon, identified the shooter, and neutralized him, saving countless lives. If it weren't for him, I can confidently say me and my fellow officers would be dead, as would probably countless more civilians."

His mother sniffed. "And your officer, the one my boy tried to save?"

Brambilla frowned, his eyes closing for a moment as he bowed his head. "I'm afraid he didn't make it."

"I'm so sorry." His father cast a hand over the scene. "What was this all about? What did so many die for?"

Brambilla frowned. "An eight-hundred-year-old document that a group of radicals felt was blasphemous to their religion."

His mother closed her eyes, tears flowing. "Religion is supposed to bring comfort and joy. Why is it that so many use it to spread so much hate?"

Brambilla grunted. "Ma'am, if you figure that out, you let me know, because this is far from over."

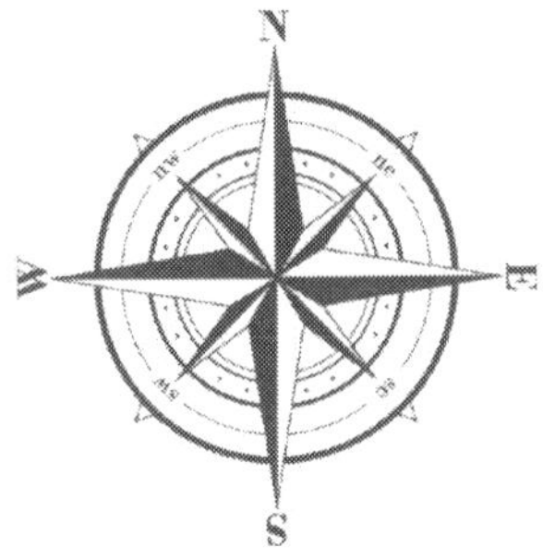

Heading North on Highway A1

Italy

Tankov held a tablet computer in his lap, watching a live feed from the drone as it raced down the highway they were on. The radio was tuned to a news station covering a mass shooting event involving police and Palestinian protesters that, from the sounds of it, had happened at their destination.

"We need to confirm the story," he said, his phone paired to the car's Bluetooth, Utkin on the other end of the line.

"I'm trying. The details are really sketchy right now, and I don't read Italian."

"Then pull over and switch out your driver. Sergey, you drive."

"You got it boss," replied Sergey.

"Do you want me to pull over?" asked Tankov's driver, Leo.

"Yeah, you better. We could be heading straight into a massive police presence, and if they search us, we'll be going to prison for a long time."

Leo pulled them over to the side of the road and Tankov turned in his seat. "Vlad, you drive."

"Yes, sir."

Seats were switched and they were soon underway again, Leo working his phone. As a local, he would know the news sites, he could read the language of the social media posts, and he could confirm far quicker what was going on than they could.

"I've got it, and you were right. They've got live footage from a camera crew that was interviewing the scientist in charge of the dig site we're headed for, when a bunch of Palestinian protesters showed up demanding the document they had found be burned because it was blasphemous to Islam."

Tankov cursed. "Do we know if they succeeded?"

"No, but apparently, some of them were armed and a gunfight broke out. At least half a dozen dead including a police officer, a couple of dozen wounded. A major police operation is underway, but there are not a lot of details on that yet. But I can guarantee you we don't want to be showing up anywhere near that rest stop. They're going to have roadblocks and probably vehicle searches because of the weapons that were involved."

Tankov punched the dash in frustration, his easy payday slipping away. "Keep searching. We need to find out what happened to the scientists and to our two professors. I guarantee you that if there was any way to save that document, they found a way. Find them, find our payday."

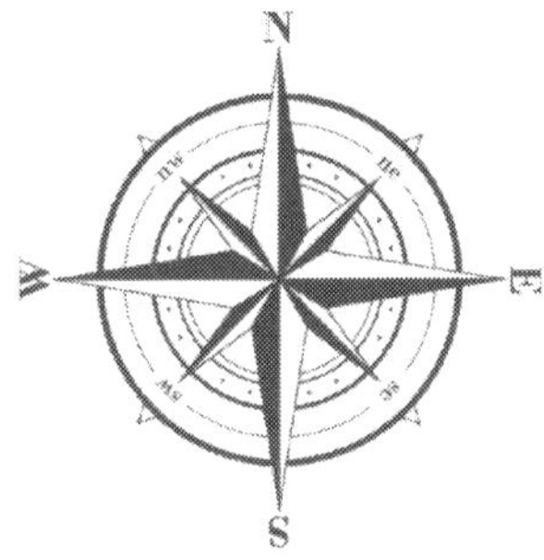

Heading South on Highway A1

Italy

Jihad smashed his open palm against the steering wheel repeatedly, frustrated that he couldn't gain on the SUVs with their large engines, his budget Fiat unable to compete. Traffic was slowly thinning out, about half what it was. The pursuit was now simply flat-out racing with little dodging in and out of traffic.

"Look!" Haasim pointed at a bridge ahead, flashing police lights visible. "They're blocking the on-ramps!"

Jihad gripped the steering wheel even tighter. "Good. The fewer cars that get on, the fewer we have in our way."

"Why don't they just block the road?" asked Ziad from the back seat.

"They'd just create a traffic jam then we could get them on foot. They want the traffic to keep moving until there's not enough of it to matter."

"What are we going to do when we catch them?"

"We kill them. This has already gone too far. I have no intention of spending the rest of my life in an Italian prison. I intend to slaughter those who would bring harm to Islam, those who would allow the prophet, peace be upon him, to be insulted. And then I intend to attack any police who try to arrest me so that they're forced to kill me and I become a martyr." He inhaled sharply, filling his lungs with bravado. "Today, we fulfill our dream. Are you with me, brothers?"

"Allahu Akbar!" shouted Ziad, the others joining in, fists pumping the air as a tingling sensation rushed through Jihad's body, a religious fervor overwhelming him in an ecstasy-laden burst of hormones, a sign from Allah that He was pleased with what His vassal was doing.

A Mercedes GLC SUV whipped past them, a Palestinian flag flying out the passenger window, and Jihad cheered. "Go get them, brothers!" The Mercedes raced up behind the trailing SUV and rear-ended him. Both vehicles fishtailed wildly, the Mercedes driver applying his brakes, killing his speed as the driver and onboard computers struggled to maintain control.

But Jihad didn't care about them.

If they lost control and got themselves killed, they would die martyrs, for they would have sacrificed their lives for the cause. All he cared about was the Vatican SUV that continued to lose control.

"There he goes!" cried a jubilant Haasim.

Jihad smiled as the SUV teetered over onto its side, skidding along the highway, sparks spraying across the pavement in front of them, and he found himself silently praying it erupted into flames and engulfed those inside, delivering the most painful death he could imagine. He steered clear of the wreckage and blasted past it.

Haasim stared at him. "Aren't we going to stop?"

Jihad pointed at the other two Vatican vehicles. "No. If what we seek is inside, then our brothers will find it and destroy it. But if it isn't, we can't let these two get away. Don't worry, brothers. Our time will come."

Father Esposito groaned, and it took him a moment to reorient himself. His seatbelt was holding him in place for the most part, but his limbs were all hanging to his right. Somebody whimpered behind him and he took a sharp breath, forcing open his eyes he hadn't realized were still squeezed shut from the terrifying accident. He pushed the airbag out of his way and turned to see Father Emanuel in the passenger seat pressed against the shattered window, the scarred pavement visible underneath.

He reached out and shook Emanuel's shoulder. "Father, are you all right?"

The man groaned and Esposito breathed a sigh of relief that his friend was still alive.

"Is everybody all right back there?"

He received four uncertain replies, everyone still shaken. He reached down and loosened his seatbelt, twisting around and pressing his right foot against the passenger headrest. He unclipped his seatbelt then balanced himself, finally taking a proper look at his companions in the rear. Everyone was clearly shaken up, and he had no doubt they all suffered bruises and scrapes, but everyone was alive, a minor miracle considering how fast they had been going when they had been rammed from behind.

His pulse raced as he remembered exactly what had caused this. The pursuit. It was then that he noticed the sounds of tires screeching, of engines revving, and of people shouting, anger in their voices, not concern. These weren't good citizens coming to help. This was the mob hell-bent on killing them simply over words written almost a thousand years ago.

He closed his eyes for a moment, asking God to forgive them, for unlike Christianity, the religion these people practiced had never evolved and was still trapped in the Dark Ages where Christianity once was just as wicked.

Somebody hammered on the roof, slightly disorienting him since the sounds were to his side and not above. More fists hammered all around them, shouts, mostly in Arabic, sending terror through his heart when two words were heard over all the others, two words that brought horror to those they didn't embolden.

"Allahu Akbar!"

Something hit the windshield and it splintered.

"We've got to get out of here!" cried one of the students, the youngest on the team, still a layman. He reached for the door handle and Esposito swatted his hand away.

"No, we can't leave." He cursed. "Make sure the doors are locked. I think when there's a crash they automatically unlock." He twisted around and pressed the central locking button just as someone leaped onto the driver's side of the vehicle overhead. He could hear them trying the door to no avail, then the heel of a shoe slammed into the glass. It held, though it wouldn't for long.

Father Emanuel looked up at him from his twisted position in the passenger seat. "What do we do, Father Esposito?"

"There's nothing we can do but pray." Esposito crouched down and extended a hand to Emanuel and his other to those in the back seat, and together they created a makeshift prayer circle, Esposito closing his eyes along with the others as those outside continued their efforts to break in.

"Our Father, who art in Heaven, hallowed be thy name."

Something was shouted outside and suddenly the hammering stopped.

"Thy kingdom come, thy will be done, on Earth as it is in Heaven."

Hope filled his heart as, for whatever reason, those determined to reach them backed off. Perhaps their prayers were being answered.

"Give us this day our daily bread, and forgive us our trespasses."

Gunfire erupted, revealing why the assault had been stopped. He gripped his companions' hands tighter and continued.

"As we forgive those who trespass against us."

Sirens sounded in the distance, rapidly approaching as the first of the bullets made it through the roof. Esposito dropped, falling atop Emanuel, and covered his friend's body.

"And lead us not into temptation, but deliver us from evil."

His entire body shook as the sirens grew louder, the gunfire shredding the roof, holes torn through the cloth liner allowing sunlight to shine through like heavenly beams.

"For thine is the kingdom, the power and the glory, for ever and ever."

Something hit him in the shoulder and he cried out in agony then gritted through it, determined to finish what he had started. "Amen!"

The others echoed him, their voices providing him with comfort in their final moments, when tires screeched outside, the machine guns drowned out by police sirens. Shouts in his familiar Italian could be heard, and the direction of the gunfire changed, the loud pinging sounds of bullets hitting the metal of the car suddenly falling silent. More guns entered the fray and he squeezed his eyes shut harder, praying silently for God to save his brothers and the other innocents, begging He take his life rather than the blameless.

The guns fell silent but no one moved, uncertain as to what was happening. He heard shouts from outside, all in Italian. It was the police. He was certain of it. Somebody smacked on the roof.

"Is anybody alive in there?"

Esposito gasped out a relieved cry. "Yes, yes, we're alive!"

"Any wounded?"

"I don't think so. Is anybody hurt?" he asked the others, and a series of 'no's' was the reply.

Emanuel tapped him on the arm. "Father, you're bleeding."

Esposito twisted around to see blood soaking his shoulder, and the sight of it had him dizzy, leaving Emanuel to reply for him.

"We've got one wounded in here. Looks like he was shot in the shoulder. There's a lot of blood."

"All right, hang tight. The paramedics are coming up now. We'll get you out of there in a minute."

"It's all right, Father. You're going to be all right."

Esposito inhaled, his world coming back into focus. He thanked God for saving them, then he gave Emanuel a chagrined look. "I'm sorry I'm so heavy."

Emanuel chuckled. "Perhaps now you'll lay off the cannolis."

Esposito laughed then winced. "It would appear to be God's will."

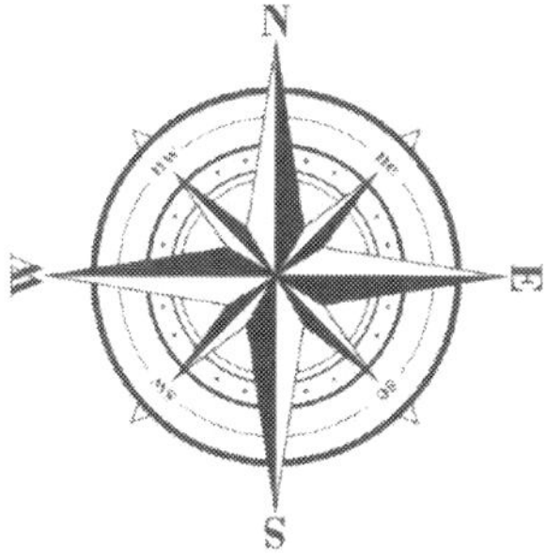

En Route to Padua

AD 1239

Sir Ricardo continued toward Padua, less than two days ride with his current steed, yet that was if he took a direct route. He couldn't risk another encounter like he just had with the so-called Keepers of the One Truth. He had no idea who they were, nor if they were even real, though the tattoo shown by the boy's father was large, intricate, and a commitment. The Keepers had to be real, and if that was the best they had to offer, at least in this region, they shouldn't prove to be much of a problem.

But his Templar brothers wouldn't be dealt with so easily, nor would he dispatch them so willingly. They were his brothers, his family. Yet his orders. He growled in frustration. As he continued with other travelers, some on foot, some on horseback, he continued the search for a solution. Why had he been stopped? Because he was a man who matched the description they had been given, was wearing Templar-issue boots, and more critically, was traveling alone on a horse.

He pursed his lips. Could it be so simple? Merely give up his horse? Travel on foot? He dismissed the idea. It would mean turning two days into weeks, many weeks. It would mean he failed in his mission. But perhaps while traveling on foot wasn't the answer, ridding himself of the horse might be.

He spotted a man ahead with a limp and pulled up beside him. "How much farther do you have to travel, sir?"

The man looked up at him, the weathered face revealing a life hard lived. "Three days, if my leg holds out."

"Then may I propose a trade?"

The man eyed him. "I'm afraid I have nothing of any value."

Ricardo gestured at the man's feet. "How about your shoes?"

The man stared down at the well-worn pair, his eyes widening. He pointed at Ricardo's boots. "What need have you of my shoes when the boots you wear are so fine?"

"I find they're a little too tight for me. Perhaps they'll fit you better."

The man smiled, revealing several rotten teeth and little else. "Sir, if you're willing to make such a trade, I'd be a fool to refuse."

"Then it's a deal." Ricardo dismounted and they both sat on a log beside the road, removing their footwear before making the exchange. Ricardo cringed at the smell, but it was for a good cause. They both stood, the man ecstatic over his new boots.

"Never have I ever had such fine boots. I again ask, sir, why? Why would you make such an uneven trade?"

Ricardo patted the man on the back. "I have my reasons and they're nothing to concern yourself with." He regarded the man. "Do you know how to ride a horse?"

"I do, sir. However, it's been a few years."

Ricardo removed enough rations for several days' travel along with his bedroll, then handed the reins to the man. "Treat him well, and he'll do the same."

The man's eyes shot wide. "I couldn't."

"You must. It's God's will."

"Are you an angel?"

Ricardo laughed. "No, I am a mere mortal, but I serve God and I sense you're in more need than I am."

"If it's God's will, then who am I to refuse?"

"Indeed." Ricardo helped the man on the back of the horse. He smacked the hindquarters of the beast and she whinnied, surging forward. "Have a safe journey!" he called after the man who gave an unsteady wave as he held on to the creature for dear life, leaving Ricardo with the distinct impression it had been far more than a few years since the man had ridden. But as he disappeared in the distance, two problems had been solved. One, he no longer had his Templar boots that had already betrayed him, and two, he was no longer a man traveling alone on horseback.

But he now had a third problem. He was a man with no means of transport.

A horse nickered behind him, the grind of wooden wheels on the hard road approaching. He turned to see a man with a cart laden with goods. He pulled several coins from his purse and hailed the man. The man pulled on the reins, coming to a halt beside Ricardo, his eyes glued to the coins. Ricardo held them up higher. "My good sir, do you have room for a weary traveler?"

The man eyed the coins, greed in his eyes. "I do."

Ricardo smiled and climbed on, sitting beside the man. A hand was held out and Ricardo deposited the coins in the filthy palm. "How far can you take me?"

"I have two days' travel north. I'll take you as far as I'm going tonight. We can discuss my fee in the morning for tomorrow's journey."

Ricardo chuckled. "Indeed, we shall."

The man flicked the reins and they were soon underway, Ricardo having solved his third problem. He was no longer a man traveling alone on a horse. He was a man with a companion on a cart.

With the vilest pair of shoes one could imagine.

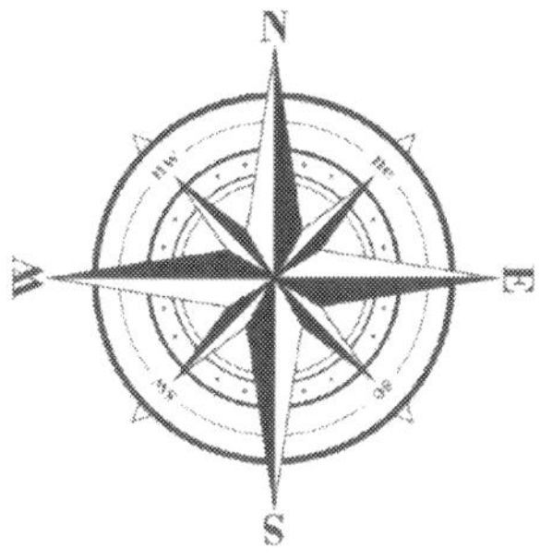

Giasson's Office

The Vatican

Present Day

Giasson pinched the bridge of his nose hard, his eyes squeezed shut as he listened to the update from his Italian counterpart. "And you're sure Father Esposito is going to be all right?"

"Yes. The bullet just grazed him. It sliced open his shoulder a bit so there was quite a bit of blood, but it didn't go deep. The paramedics are treating him at the scene, then he'll be taken to a local hospital where he'll receive proper stitches. Everyone else just has bumps and bruises, but they're all going to be checked out."

"And the perpetrators?"

"Two had automatic weapons. They're dead as are three others that were attacking the vehicle. There are a few wounded, but let's just say no innocents beyond Father Esposito were hurt."

"Thank God for that."

"Indeed. From the photos I've seen, it's a miracle that anybody survived. There are so many bullet holes in that roof, I can't believe they weren't all killed."

Giasson's eyes darted upward. "Perhaps God's will was at play."

"Perhaps."

"What about my other people?"

"They're still being pursued. We've shut down all access to the highway south of them, which is thinning out the traffic. Once it's light enough, we're planning to intervene, but right now, anything we do could cause a traffic jam that would leave your people vulnerable."

"I understand. And the help we requested?"

"Already on its way. You should start to see them arriving in a few minutes."

"Good. We'll talk to you soon." Giasson ended the call, his shoulders slumping in exhaustion. He hadn't been this stressed in years.

"So?" asked Rizzo, waiting in the doorway.

Giasson threw his hands up in frustration. "Father Esposito and the others with him are confirmed fine, but the others are still being pursued. They're saying the traffic is still too heavy to risk a roadblock. At the speeds they're apparently driving, all it would take is somebody to do something unexpected ahead of them and they could get into an accident. There's just so many things that could go wrong." He leaned back. "They did say reinforcements are arriving any minute now to help manage our protesters. What's the updated crowd estimate?"

"About a thousand from what we can tell, but there's also a good number of counter-protesters. At least a few hundred. More of both groups are pouring in. I do have an idea, however."

"What's that?"

"Well, we've been looking at the social media accounts that are encouraging the protests, and we've been able to link some of them to people who were at the shooting. If we were to somehow make it obvious that these terrorists are actually behind this protest, I'm willing to bet a lot of people would change their minds about coming. They wouldn't want to be associated with the murder of a police officer."

"How would we go about doing that?"

"We could use our own social media accounts."

Giasson immediately dismissed the idea with a flick of his wrist. "No, we can't be seen to be behind this." He leaned forward and tapped his desk. "I've been at meetings in this very building with imams and other religious leaders claiming to want nothing but peace. In the next breath, I see them on TV at protests. They're the usual organizers of these things. Let's reach out to every one of them that we know and present them with the evidence of what their people are supporting. They can spread the word to their flocks to stay home. Otherwise, it'll damage their cause."

Rizzo flashed a smile. "Good idea. I guess that's why they pay you the big bucks."

Giasson snorted. "If only. If I really wanted money, I would have gone into politics. It's amazing how they go in poor but come out rich."

He pointed at the door. "Now get the word out. Let's see if we can head this off before someone gets killed."

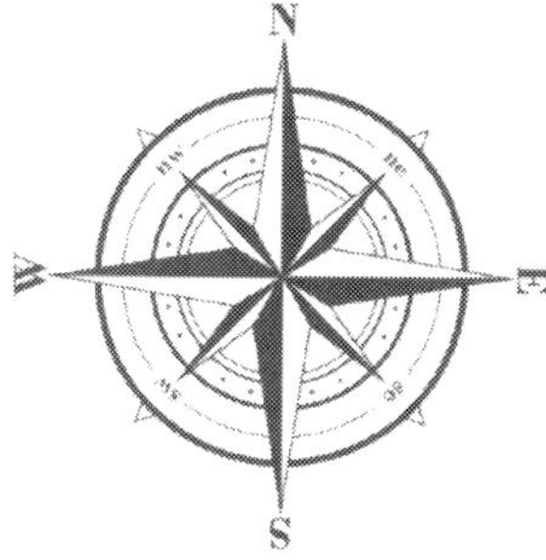

Heading South on Highway A1

Italy

With the entire Treatise photographed and translated, Acton and the others were now all strapped in properly as Lombardi continued to earn his free vacation. The traffic had thinned dramatically, but it was still too heavy, and the going theory that the police weren't intervening with the roadblock because of the traffic jam it would cause had been confirmed moments ago by a brief call with Giasson checking on their status. Acton wasn't able to pump him for more information because a call came in from his Italian counterpart, but Giasson had promised a call back. For now, everyone except Lombardi was reading the Treatise of the Three Imposters, Tommy's app doing a bang-up job.

"It's remarkable how analytical it is," commented Laura. "There's no emotion here. No hyperbole. There are also no facts."

Tommy leaned forward. "I suppose you could say there are facts surrounding his argument against the virgin birth."

Acton agreed. "True, we know the virgin birth is impossible scientifically, but that's where faith comes in. What he's arguing is that since there's no proof there's a God, then faith can't be used to explain something that science says is impossible. He claims we only have Moses' word about things like the burning bush or the Ten Commandments being delivered by God, that since the virgin birth is impossible, Jesus was just a man who spoke eloquently, but wasn't the son of God, and Muhammad was just an illiterate who made up the story so that he could subjugate his people. If God were real, he would have simply given Muhammad the ability to read and write, rather than force him to memorize the text over years." He wagged his phone. "It really is quite well written. Whoever did this was well educated, well informed on the subject."

"And clearly a skeptic," added Laura.

"Definitely."

"You can see why this thing has been called the Atheist's Bible," said Tommy.

"I prefer the Heretics Bible. Everything is about these three so-called imposters, these heretics who made up everything, lied about everything, and invented religion as billions know it today, all for their own purposes. Since it argues that these faiths are invalid, then we all are the heretics. It's really quite a fascinating theory."

Mai looked up from her phone. "I just don't understand why he would do this. Why would the emperor write this? He would have to know putting these types of thoughts on paper could be dangerous."

"That's the $64,000 question, isn't it?"

Mai eyed him, confused.

Acton smiled. "Old game show."

"Oh."

"But that's why the document has always been dismissed. Frederick II was always thought to be a very intelligent man, very well educated. Yes, he was a skeptic, so attributing a document like this to him was within the realm of possibility, but for him to actually write it down was always thought to be incredibly stupid."

"Arrogance," suggested Laura. "He had a massive ego, and as the Holy Roman Emperor, probably felt he had the divine right to say whatever he wanted."

"Even if he didn't believe in that divinity?"

Laura flashed him a grin. "I didn't say it was a well-thought-out theory."

"It's as good a theory as any and a definite possibility. People with egos who think they're untouchable do and say incredibly stupid things without thinking of the consequences all the time. He could have written this treatise simply to prove to himself how brilliant he was, and perhaps to decide what side of the argument he was actually on."

"Do you think it's real?" asked Tommy. "Or is this a fake?"

"Well, there are two parts to that question, aren't there? It's definitely real. What we have here is definitely the Treatise of the Three Imposters from 1239 that was referred to by Pope Gregory IX. So, what this proves is that the pope was referring to an actual document when he leveled the accusation against Frederick. That fills in a major gap in our known history. The second part of the question, though, is if this real document is actually a fake from the thirteenth century? Did Frederick write this, or did someone else write it and make it look like he did?"

"Is there any way to know?"

"I doubt it. We'll be able to do tests and confirm that the paper came from the right era, the ink, the folio, even the bones of the messenger. Handwriting analysis will probably confirm the pope's handwriting and the emperor's match other samples that we've confirmed are genuine. But, just like today, back then there were forgers. It's likely that we'll never be able to prove one way or the other whether he actually wrote it. All we can do is theorize that this is indeed what Pope Gregory was referring to, and if he believed it was genuine, it explains his actions and also explains why it led to the downfall of the emperor and his family."

Tommy glanced nervously behind them at their pursuers. "So, these people want to kill over a document that might not even be real?"

"It would appear so."

"I just don't understand those people. How can they all be filled with so much hate?"

Acton raised his hand. "Now, by those people, if you mean all Muslims, then no. Let me stop you right there. These people are fanatics, brainwashed into hating anything different than them, anything that disagrees with them, and they exist in all religions, including Christianity."

"But why is it always them that you hear about on the news?"

"Oh, there's no doubt there's far more radicals in Islam than any other religion. But you have to look at where most followers of Islam are from. They're from poor countries, so they're easily swayed by charismatic speakers who convince them, just like the good Christians of Nazi Germany, that someone else is to blame for their problems. You have to dive deeper than the headlines to truly understand what's going on. And make sure you don't get that deeper dive from social media when radicals in our own country label anything that the mainstream media says as a lie, just because it disagrees with their opinion. Are they any more radical than a young Muslim man who says something is blasphemous because it disagrees with what he was taught?"

Tommy grunted. "Never thought of it that way."

"Me neither," chimed Lombardi from the front.

Acton turned his attention to their driver. "How are we doing?"

"The traffic's thinning out quite a bit."

"Isn't he a little close?" asked a nervous Tommy, checking the rear again. "I mean, how fast are we going?"

Lombardi glanced at his dash. "A little over one-sixty."

"Holy shit!" exclaimed Tommy and Lombardi laughed.

"Kilometers per hour, about one hundred miles per hour. Still fast. Father Christoph is driving the second SUV. He's drafting me. It allows us to split the drag between the two of us, so we're actually going a little bit faster together than we could apart."

Tommy's eyes widened. "You mean like in NASCAR?"

"Exactly, though they go quite a bit faster than we are."

Laura, an expert driver, checked the second vehicle for herself. "Is he a good enough driver for this?"

"Don't worry about him. He races cars as a hobby."

Mai's jaw dropped. "Priests race cars?"

Lombardi laughed. "Priests do all kinds of things. They're normal people like you and me. It's just their day job is different."

"And there's no shagging," added Acton.

"James!"

Acton gave his wife a look. "As if you weren't thinking it." His phone rang and he glanced at the call display. "Father Esposito!" He took the call and put it on speaker. "Father Esposito, are you all right?"

"We're all fine. By the grace of God we made it out of there alive."

"Perhaps someone was on your side."

Esposito chuckled. "If you saw how many bullet holes were in our car, you wouldn't be saying 'perhaps.'"

"Are you secure?"

"Yes, there are dozens of police around us now and all the troublemakers here are either dead or arrested. My concern is for you. What's your status?"

"We're still on the A1 heading south to Rome. So far, both vehicles have managed to keep ahead of the pursuers." He glanced back. "But if there are a hundred meters between us, I'd be surprised. It won't take much for them to overtake us."

"My understanding is the police are trying to put together a response. Hopefully, you'll see something soon if what I just overheard was correct."

"What did you overhear?"

"I'm not sure I should say, just in case they're monitoring the call somehow."

Acton frowned but had to agree. "You're right, Father."

"Now tell me, were you able to see the Treatise? Is it real?"

"We managed to extract all the pages and translate them. We've uploaded them to our own servers just in case something happens to us."

"Is it what we thought?"

Laura leaned in. "It *is* the Treatise of the Three Imposters and it reads as a dry analysis of how Moses, Jesus, and Muhammad lied about their encounters with God and how there's no proof any of it happened. Therefore, anything they said is not the word of God but merely the word of men, guided or misguided. Tommy Granger's translation app has done an excellent job. We'll send you the text now if you want."

"Yes, please. I suppose there's no real way to know if Frederick II actually wrote it."

"No," said Acton. "Unfortunately, unless we find some other document that corroborates this, I doubt it. But it does, though, answer the question of whether a document existed that Gregory IX referred to. Listen, with what's happening and the speeds we're traveling at, there's a very good chance the document could get destroyed. We've got the photos. We've got the translations. What do you want us to do?"

There was a pause. "What do you think we should do?"

Acton checked with Laura who gave a slight nod. "My inclination would be to release this publicly now so that there's no chance it's lost forever due to ignorance."

"That would be my inclination as well," agreed Esposito.

"So, we have your permission?"

"Do it. Let's make sure ignorance doesn't win the day."

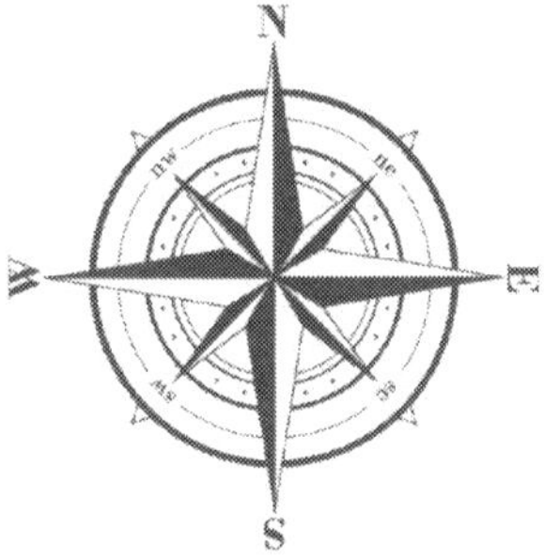

Heading North on Highway A1

Italy

Tankov pointed at the tablet he was staring at. "What the hell was that?"

Utkin, still on speakerphone, replied. "I'm not sure."

Tankov backed up the footage then replayed it, zooming in on the opposite side of the road. "It looks like the police are shutting down all the on-ramps to the southbound highway."

"Now why the hell would they do that?"

"I don't know." It was too much of a coincidence not to be related to the shooting. "Keep the drone heading north, but make sure it doesn't miss a square centimeter of the southbound lanes. Something's got to be going on there, and if I know our professors, it has something to do with them."

"Roger that."

Tankov leaned forward, peering out the windshield at the other side of the highway. "Is it my imagination or is the traffic a lot lighter over there?"

Leo glanced over. "Oh yeah, that's way lighter than it should be for this time of day. They must have on-ramps shut down quite a ways north. Definitely a big operation. If I had to hazard a guess, I would say they're funneling someone somewhere. If there was a terrorist shooting, they could have made their escape on the highway and the police could be pursuing them."

"Why not just set up a roadblock?"

"With that kind of traffic? If they are after terrorists with automatic weapons like we heard in that newscast and they get stopped in a traffic jam, they could kill dozens if not hundreds." Leo shook his head. "No, I'd do exactly what the police are doing. Thin down the possible victims."

"Check your live footage, then back up about thirty seconds," said Utkin over the Bluetooth.

Tankov glanced down at his tablet, dragging his finger to the left. He watched as the drone sped over the southbound traffic. Something flashed by and he pressed his finger against the screen again, slowly backing it up. "What the hell was that?"

"Looks like two SUVs drafting each other, being pursued by eight to ten other vehicles, and then a few miles back of that, a shitload of police."

"So then, what are we looking at here? Who's who in this scenario?" asked Leo.

Tankov slowly drew his finger over the tablet, replaying the short segment he was concerned about. "We know who the police are, obviously. They're in the rear, pursuing somebody, most likely terrorist suspects. The hodgepodge of cars between them and the SUVs are likely the terrorists, but it makes no sense. There are too many of them, too uncoordinated, so they're definitely after the SUVs, not trying to escape." He wagged a finger at the screen. "A hundred euros says our professors are in one of those SUVs with the artifact we're after, and that these are the fanatics who stormed the dig site chasing them, and the police are trying to figure out how the hell to stop this mob on wheels without getting the people in the SUVs killed."

"What do you want us to do?" asked Utkin.

"This is definitely them. It has to be. It's the only explanation that makes sense. Turn the drone around. I want live coverage of them."

"You got it, boss."

Tankov turned to Leo. "Do you have some local contacts in this area?"

"Of course."

"Good. Start making some calls. We might need a little more muscle."

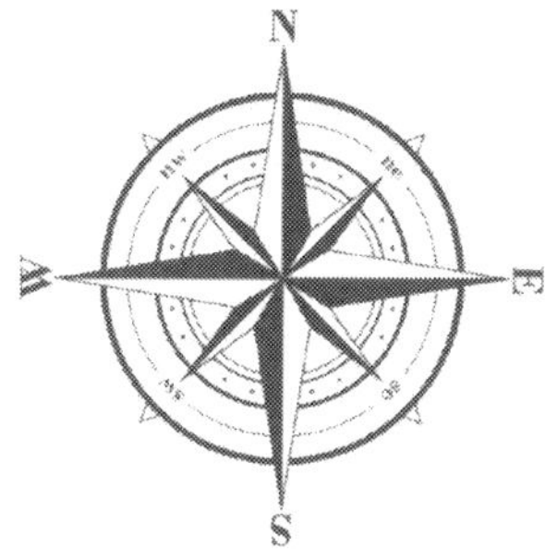

En Route to Padua

AD 1239

Sir Ricardo's companion grunted, jerking his chin at the road ahead. "There's another bloody roadblock. I wonder who they're after."

Ricardo shrugged. "Must be somebody important. This is the third one in two days."

"And hopefully the last." Another jerk of the chin. "My home is just ahead, after that bend." His companion, whom he had learned was named Marco, craned his neck, looking toward the sun now low on the horizon. "The hour grows late. You're welcome to stay with my family tonight."

Ricardo regarded him. "For a price?"

Marco tossed his head back and laughed. "No, I think you've paid enough. Providing you with transport was a service, but inviting you into my home as a guest is the Christian thing to do."

Ricardo smiled. "I would be honored."

"Then it's settled. We don't have much to offer, but my wife is a good woman and a good cook. She'll feed you well tonight, then send you on your way tomorrow morning on a full belly."

They approached the checkpoint, this one manned by four Templars. Ricardo tensed as he mimicked Marco's mannerisms. As a knight, every encounter was entered into with confidence and the knowledge he was nobility, and a Templar, a soldier of God. But a display like that in this situation would merely draw undue attention. Marco's shoulders were rounded inward, his chin pressed against his chest, everything about him suggesting a meek man who was no threat. Ricardo did the same and eyed his sword lying at his feet where he prayed it would remain.

His new travel arrangements had allowed them to pass through two different checkpoints, including one manned by Templars yesterday evening, everyone simply waving them through. Hopefully, this would be no different. But should he be challenged, he was torn as to what to do. He didn't want to kill his brothers. He didn't even want to wound them, and because there were four of them, it would certainly be a fight to the death should he not surrender. These men would be merely following orders. He had absolutely no doubt they were not involved in any conspiracy to stop him from fulfilling his mission.

Yet he still had his mission and it was his duty to complete it. He growled in frustration.

"Are you trying to get us killed?" hissed Marco. "Be quiet!"

Ricardo said nothing, instead, clenching his jaw shut. He kept his head down and peered up as the carriage in front of them was waved through. They were next. Marco flicked the reins and the horse snorted, the cart jerking forward.

"Move along, move along," said one of the knights, and Ricardo fought the urge to cringe for he recognized the voice. It was Sir Bartholomew, a man he had served with in the Holy Land for almost a decade. If Bartholomew saw his face, there was no way he wouldn't recognize him. If he turned away, it could look suspicious, though if there was anyone he could trust in the Order, anyone who would listen to what he had to say, it was Bartholomew. Yet he didn't know the others and he didn't know what they had been told about him. He couldn't take the chance. All he could do was trust in God to get him through this latest challenge.

The cart continued forward, and in the corner of his eye he could see Bartholomew and another knight to his right carrying on a quiet conversation.

"Halt!" ordered Bartholomew, and Ricardo's shoulders slumped as Marco yanked back on the reins, bringing them to a halt, their horse protesting with an angry sniff.

"Sir Ricardo, did you not think I would recognize you?"

Ricardo sat upright as there was no point in attempting to hide anymore. He faced his old friend. "Sir Bartholomew, it's been a long time."

"Indeed. Several years since we last served together in the Holy Land. You're aware that half of Christendom is looking for you?"

"I am."

"Can you tell me why?"

"They haven't told you?"

"No, and I never believed you could be involved in something until now."

Ricardo regarded the old warrior. "And what makes you now think I'm guilty?"

"You're in disguise, obviously attempting to hide. An innocent man wouldn't."

"He would if he were being pursued by those who would prevent him from completing his mission."

Bartholomew dismounted, as did the others. "Search the cart."

Ricardo waved them off. "There's no need." He reached down and retrieved his sword, passing it over.

Bartholomew took it and frowned. "I never thought I'd see the day that you of all people would surrender your sword, and I certainly never would've thought it would be to one of your brothers."

"Certainly wasn't how I thought things would end," agreed Ricardo. "But if it is to end this way, I'm pleased that I am surrendering my blade to a friend."

"I'm pleased you still see me as such, despite the circumstances. Now, why don't you explain to me what's happening?"

"I have orders from Sir Enrico Teutonico himself. They were issued as non contramand."

Bartholomew cocked an eyebrow at the unusual qualifier. "What can you tell me of these orders?"

"Nothing. I swore an oath. However, it was made very clear to me that should people discover I was on this mission, there would be those who would attempt to stop me."

Bartholomew chewed his cheek for a moment. "As we now stop you?"

"Exactly."

"I'm conflicted, brother."

"As am I."

"Will you come peacefully to the commandery?"

Ricardo shrugged. "I have no desire to injure or kill my brothers, despite being confident I could best all four of you."

Bartholomew smirked. "You were always a confident warrior. Overconfident on occasion."

"I'll come with you, but I ask only one thing."

"And what is that, my friend?"

"That I am not questioned, nor am I searched, until I see Sir Enrico himself, the only man who can countermand my orders."

Bartholomew's head slowly bobbed. "Perfectly reasonable. Agreed, brothers?" he asked, addressing the others. All agreed but one who was squinting as he peered down the road.

"Someone approaches."

Everyone turned to see a group of men on horseback, ten strong, all in monk's cloaks.

Ricardo cursed.

"Do you know who they are?" asked Bartholomew as he and the others mounted their horses.

"I can't be certain, but I suspect they're members of The Keepers of the One Truth. They've already made one attempt to intercept me, and it was clear their intent was to kill me if I didn't surrender to them."

Bartholomew tossed him his sword. "Then what you have said must be true. Someone is attempting to interfere with your mission."

Ricardo turned to his travel companion. "Go, now. Don't look back. Don't slow down. But if they do stop you, tell them the truth. I was a stranger you picked up yesterday and gave a ride in exchange for some coins. You didn't discover there was anything untoward going on until just now."

Marco stared at him, his eyes wide, his entire body shaking. "And what of you?"

Ricardo smiled at the man's concern. "My fate is sealed and my duty is to protect the innocent, and the best way to do that is for you to leave now." He stepped forward and smacked the horse on the ass. Hard. It protested then pulled the cart forward, leaving the scene of what might be an unavoidable battle.

"Get behind us," ordered Bartholomew and Ricardo complied, his sword at the ready, wishing he was in his armor as his brothers were.

The approaching riders slowed, coming to a halt barely ten paces from the line of Templars blocking the road.

"Identify yourselves!" barked Bartholomew.

A rider advanced. "I am Brother Alberto, and we are on urgent business. Move aside, Templar."

"Brother, that's him!"

Ricardo cursed as the boy from yesterday pointed at him.

"He's the one who killed my father!"

Swords all around were drawn as Alberto, the man Ricardo now recognized as the one who had given him the folio in the alleyway, stared at him in shock. "In the name of Saint Peter, we demand you surrender Sir Ricardo to us!"

"Over my dead body," replied Bartholomew.

Alberto shook his head, genuine disappointment on his face. "I regret that this is your response. You will find we are much better trained than those Sir Ricardo encountered yesterday. You will not survive."

Bartholomew smirked. "Today is as good a day to die as any."

"So be it." Alberto turned to his companions. "Kill them all!" The Keepers charged and Bartholomew glanced back at Ricardo as the other Templars advanced to engage.

"Get out of here now! We'll hold them as long as we can!"

Ricardo refused. "I stand with my brothers!"

"No, if they're as skilled as they claim, we won't survive. And if they aren't, we'll find you after we dispatch them. But you must continue on your mission, for it's clear to me those who would do evil wish you to fail."

Ricardo wanted to say something profound. Something to thank his brothers, to thank his friend, yet he wasn't given the chance.

"Run, my friend! And should God will it, we'll find you soon. And should He not, I'll be waiting for you with our fallen brothers."

Swords clashed, grunts and screams filling the air. Ricardo ran from the melee, guilt wracking him. He had never run from battle before, and it left a sickening feeling. His brothers were fighting and possibly dying so he could fulfill a mission they had been told must be stopped. But he was all the more convinced, as they now were, that his mission must proceed, these Keepers, whoever they were, far too determined to stop him.

Ironically, this was the danger the monk Alberto had spoken of.

A horse rapidly approached and he spun to see one of the Keepers had broken through. He raised his sword, ready to defend himself, though he stood little chance, the rider in armor revealed underneath the brown cloak billowing in the wind, and he, wearing the clothes of a simple traveler. He prepared to parry the blow. Their blades clashed, sparks flew, and his enemy's weapon, heavier than his own, combined with the momentum behind it, inexorably slid up his blade.

He grunted as he stood his ground, pushing into the blow as hard as he could, then ducked as his opponent's steel cleared the tip of his own. He winced as his shoulder was sliced open and his sword fell to the ground. The rider turned and Ricardo reached down, gripping his blade in his left hand as blood poured from the gaping wound. With the last of his strength, he rushed forward and plunged his sword into the side of his enemy. He pulled the man from his saddle as he writhed in agony, then hauled himself atop the snorting beast.

He glanced over his shoulder to see only Bartholomew now stood, surrounded by the enemy, several more turning to leave the battle and pursue him. There was nothing he could do to help his friend. He urged the horse forward, guiding it with his knees as he gripped his bleeding shoulder. It was too deep.

Unless he could find help, he wouldn't survive the night.

He rounded a bend in the road, briefly out of sight of his pursuers. His eyes scanned the area for any means of escape, and he spotted something to his right. He released his grip on his shoulder and grabbed the reins, slowing and guiding his horse hard. The beast burst through some underbrush and they emerged onto a forgotten laneway, perhaps once belonging to a farm now abandoned. He urged the creature forward, grabbing on to his shoulder once again in a futile attempt to stem the bleeding, and prayed his pursuers would be too hasty in their pursuit to notice where he had left the road.

He charged forward through the thick trees, the laneway almost reclaimed by nature, wherever it led evidently abandoned decades ago. He rounded a bend, the beast following their path on instinct, when it whinnied and came to a rapid halt just before a downed tree, sending him sailing head over heels. He hit the ground hard, gasping in pain. He took a moment to recover then pushed to his knees before rising to one leg. He reached out for the reins, dangling over the horse's neck, but it backed away.

"Come here, you fool."

A snort was the response.

"Come here!" he snapped. He struggled to his feet, his body weak, and stared into the creature's eyes. Even if he could manage to wrangle it, there was no way he was mounting it. He was too drained. His shoulders collapsed. He took in his surroundings and spotted something through the trees when shouts echoed from the road.

His deception had been discovered.

He stepped over to the horse, making no attempt to grab the reins, then smacked it on the ass. It reared up on its hind legs then charged forward, leaping over the log that had caused it to stop, and continued to gallop down the laneway, leaving fresh hoof prints obvious to even the most inexperienced tracker.

Ricardo stepped into the trees surrounding the laneway, putting as much distance as he could between him and the forgotten path, as the pounding of horses' hooves approached. He hid behind a thick growth of bushes and watched as his pursuers passed him, and breathed a sigh of relief as they showed no signs of slowing.

He pushed to his feet in search of a place where he could die in peace, and where that which he carried, for what so many had died, would never be found.

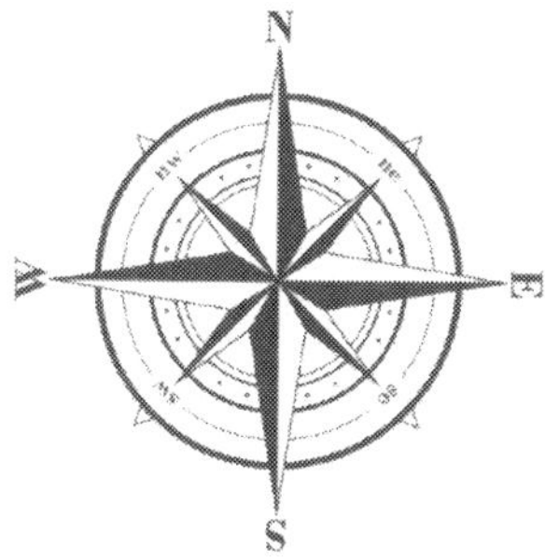

Heading South on Highway A1

Italy

Present Day

"Roll up your windows and turn off your air conditioning."

Jihad stared at the phone, half a dozen of his brothers now on a conference call as they continued to pursue the infidels. "What the hell good is that going to do?"

"Closing your windows will reduce your drag."

Jihad reached for the controls and put the windows up. "And why am I turning off the air conditioning? We're going to roast in here."

"It'll give you a little bit more power. Not much, but we don't need a lot to catch these bastards. We just need a lucky break, and Allah willing, we'll have it soon."

Jihad killed the air conditioning and the effect was immediately felt. In speed and heat.

Haasim tugged at his shirt. "We're going to die like this."

Jihad shot daggers at his friend. "You complain about the heat while we fight for the prophet, peace be upon him?"

Haasim shifted uncomfortably, turning his head away. "Sorry, it's just that it's hot. You know I can't stand the heat."

Jihad could already feel the difference in temperature, but they were once again gaining on their enemy. "It's working!" he cried, shaking Haasim. "Allah is on our side!"

Haasim smiled, tugging again at his shirt. "Was there ever any doubt?"

Jihad spotted something ahead on the side of the road, and his eyes bulged as he realized what it was. "Brothers, look to the right. There's a police officer there. I think he's going to deploy a spike strip. Someone take him out."

"I've got him!"

Jihad checked his rearview mirror to see one of his brothers swinging to the right. The officer's foot came back as he prepared to kick out the strip. The car barreled toward him and Jihad giggled in glee at the terror on the man's face as they blasted past him. He adjusted his rearview mirror then cringed before screaming "Allahu Akbar!" at the top of his lungs when their brother's car made contact, the blood spatter so large he was sure the infidel had been cut in half.

He redirected his attention to the road, pressing his accelerator to the floor once again as he grinned at the others. "I don't think we'll be worrying about spike strips again."

Tommy and Mai both cried out in horror at the sight behind them, Acton squeezing his eyes shut for a brief moment, saying a silent prayer for the officer they had just seen killed.

"This is too much! This isn't right!"

Acton reached back and squeezed Mai's hand. "No, it's not. It's not right at all."

"We have to do something," sobbed Mai. "We have to do something before someone else is killed."

Acton sighed. "I'm open to suggestions."

"What if we just stop and give them the document?" asked Tommy.

Laura dismissed the idea. "It's too late for that. You heard what happened at the dig, what happened with Father Esposito's SUV, and now what just happened with that poor officer. They're out for blood. They want martyrdom. They're going to do whatever it takes to get themselves killed by the police. They're not going to surrender. If we stop, they're just going to kill us all."

"Then if I'm going to die, I want the world to know why." Tommy wiped his cheeks clear then activated his phone's camera. "It's time to tell the world."

Utkin sat in the back of the SUV, monitoring the drone footage as Sergey guided them off the northbound highway. "They're coming up fast."

"Copy that," said Sergey as he turned onto the bridge crossing the highway.

Utkin pointed ahead. "Right up there."

"Got it."

Utkin addressed Tankov over the Bluetooth connection. "We're in position, boss. ETA less than two minutes."

"Acknowledged. Are your people in place?"

"Yes," replied Leo from Tankov's end. "They're already closing in on their position. They'll be ready."

"Good. Let's not screw this up, people. We've got one chance at it."

Sergey pulled over to the side of the road, throwing on their flashers, then popped the hood. He climbed out and pushed it up so if anyone were to look, they would assume the vehicle had broken down. But Utkin didn't pay any mind to what was happening around him. He continued to stare at the footage and the distance indicator between the drone and themselves that rapidly counted down. He stared out the window at the highway below and spotted their targets.

"Here they come!"

The two passenger side doors opened and the team climbed out, their assault rifles ready. Sergey was tossed a weapon and the five of them leaned over the guardrail, aiming at the traffic below. "Here they come. Watch your arcs."

"Yes, sir," echoed the men.

Utkin trained his sight on the lead SUV as the driver inside spotted them and pointed. "Fire!"

"We've got shooters!" shouted Lombardi, pointing at the bridge ahead.

"Everybody down!" ordered Acton as he lunged forward and draped his body over Laura, Tommy doing the same with Mai as he continued to broadcast live to his hundreds of thousands of followers. Gunfire erupted ahead of them and Acton squeezed Laura tight underneath him, preparing to either be torn to shreds or for Lombardi to lose control. At the speeds they were going, there was no way he could see them surviving, and if they did crash, it would just give the shooters a stationary target to finish the job.

As the gunfire rattled overhead, it had him wondering who it was and how the hell they were missing. These weren't AKs, they were HKs, if his ear wasn't lying to him.

"They're not shooting at us!" shouted Lombardi, the relief in his voice palpable.

Acton pushed up, peering ahead, just in time to see the bridge with the shooters flash by.

"Is it the police?" asked Laura.

Lombardi shook his head as he stared back, his foot obviously lifting off the accelerator as they slowed rapidly. "I don't think so. It looks like they're shooting all the cars behind us."

Acton rose and stared out the back window, the second SUV having backed off, giving him a good view as at least a dozen cars spun out of control, some smoking from their engine compartments having been torn apart by whoever it was on the bridge.

Laura sat up beside him. "Are they shooting just the bad guys?"

"It looks like they're shooting everybody," said Mai, now pressed against the back window.

Acton agreed with her assessment. "That's definitely not police, but it's obviously not the terrorists, otherwise, they would have shot at us."

Tommy squirmed around and held up his phone, recording what was happening behind them. "They definitely are targeting some of the guys who were chasing us." He pointed. "I recognize that red car. It's been after us the whole freaking time."

Acton spotted the car careening into the guardrail as the traffic behind them came to a rapid stop, the traffic jam the police had been fearing now a reality. But they were ahead of it. Whoever was on the bridge had created the perfect scenario. They were clear of their pursuers with a nearly open road ahead.

The question was, who the hell were they?

Utkin tossed his weapon over the bridge, as did the others, a panel van pulling up beside them. The door slid open and everyone climbed inside as police at the roadblock at the far end of the bridge sprinted toward them, their weapons drawn. The door slid shut as the van surged forward, leaving the police in its dust, Leo's contacts having come through.

"Everybody hang on!" warned the driver as he took a hard right. "Two minutes to the next switch."

"Understood," replied Utkin as he dialed Tankov.

"Report."

Utkin grabbed the seat in front of him as the driver took another wild turn. "Mission accomplished. It was like shooting fish in a barrel."

Jihad gripped the steering wheel, his heart hammering at the close call. He glanced over at Haasim. "Are you all right?"

His friend pried his fingernails out of the vinyl dash then opened his eyes slightly, the scream wailing from his mouth during the entire event finally stopping. "What the hell was that?"

"There were people shooting from the bridge. It had to be the police."

"They're trying to kill us!" exclaimed Ziad from the back seat. "I can't believe they tried to kill us!"

"Of course they tried to kill us. They're infidels, and we're Muslim." Jihad checked his rearview mirror then put the car in reverse, backing up slightly and twisting the wheel to get around the wrecked car in front of him.

"What does that mean?" asked Haasim, his voice still quavering.

"It means that today we will die at the hands of Allah's enemies in defense of His word and that of the prophet, peace be upon him. Tonight, we are martyrs who will dine in Jannah together!" He hammered on the accelerator, clearing the crash, and checked his rearview mirror to see several of his brothers following. This would soon be over now that there was almost no traffic in their way. They would kill the infidels, destroy this blasphemous document, then in a final showdown with the police, join those who had gone before.

What a glorious day.

"Allahu Akbar!"

"You need to see this." Haasim shoved his phone in front of Jihad's face and he angrily battered it away.

"What did I say about doing stupid shit like that? Are you trying to get us killed? You don't get in Jannah for getting in a car accident!"

"Sorry, but you need to see this."

"What is it?"

"Somebody on our Telegram group posted it. It's a live feed. Somebody in one of those SUVs is broadcasting."

Jihad stole a quick glance then thought better of it. He had to keep his eyes on the road. "What are they saying?"

Haasim cursed, punching the dash. "They did exactly what you said they would! They published pictures of that treatise thing as well as translations!"

"Translations? How the hell are they doing that?"

"I don't know, but I'm just reading the comments here, and apparently it's been published in English, French, German, Italian, Spanish, Arabic, and they're promising more to come."

Jihad growled, the pit of rage already burning in his stomach reaching a new temperature. This was what they had always intended to do, to embarrass Islam, to insult it. He gripped the steering wheel tighter, his knuckles turning white. "I'm going to disembowel them!"

"They're saying here that there's no way to confirm that the document is genuine."

"What does that mean?" asked Ziad.

Haasim continued to read. "It looks like they're saying they believe the document is real, but they don't know if this emperor guy actually wrote it."

Jihad wiped the sweat off his forehead, the car an oven. "It doesn't matter who wrote it. The words were written, they exist, and now these kafirs have put them out there for the world to see. They're claiming our religion, everything we believe in, is a lie, that the prophet, peace be upon him, was a liar. It doesn't matter who wrote it. All that matters is we punish those who spread the lies." He turned his head slightly toward the Bluetooth speaker. "My brothers, did you hear what we just discovered?"

At least half a dozen voices confirmed it.

"This has to end now. Haasim, can you tell which one they're in?"

"Yes. The camera is showing that there's an SUV behind them, so they're in the lead vehicle."

"Good. Brothers, if someone has a gun or if someone is willing, take out the second vehicle. That will slow down the first one. They won't be able to draft."

"I'll take care of it," said someone.

Jihad pulled slightly to the right, opening up a gap. He glanced in his rearview mirror to see one of his brothers leaning out, an AK-47 gripped in his hands, muzzle flashes erupting. The trailing SUV swerved as it attempted to avoid the shots slamming into its rear windshield, but the speeds were too high for those types of maneuvers. The driver struggled to maintain control, his brake lights flaring, allowing them to rapidly close the gap.

And seconds later, they were passing him, their brother with the assault rifle opening up on the rear tire, shredding it, bringing the infidels to a screeching halt.

"Two down. One to go."

"We've got trouble!"

Acton turned toward Lombardi who jerked his chin ahead at a smoking car.

"Oh no, they're ahead of us!" cried Mai.

"What do I do?"

Acton leaned forward to get a better look. "Just keep going. We don't have a choice."

There was a car of some sort parked on the side of the road ahead, thick black smoke billowing out of it. He didn't think it was one of the mob since the car sat alone. They rapidly closed the distance and Acton breathed a sigh of relief, sitting back as they whipped past the vehicle, its owner sitting on a guardrail pulling at his hair as his notorious British sports car burned.

Acton grinned at Laura. "You know what they say, just another grand until another repair."

Her giggle was cut short by gunfire behind them and they all turned, gasping in shock as the SUV behind them was taken out and quickly overwhelmed by the pursuing mob.

There was no way they would survive.

Tankov unhooked from the rope he had rappelled down with, three of his team plus several locals dropping beside him as the last surviving SUV, confirmed through drone footage to be from the Vatican, raced toward them, followed by half a dozen cars.

"Take out their engine. I don't want anybody inside killed." He opened fire with the others, and moments later steam and light gray smoke burst from the engine compartment, bringing the SUV to a rapid, unceremonious halt. The cars in pursuit locked up their brakes, the mob they had heard about on the news pouring out, some of them with guns.

And he smiled. "Take them out!"

Jihad dove to his left, rolling on the ground as heavy gunfire ripped down the highway toward them. He hadn't even noticed the gunmen in the road. All he had seen was the infidels he was chasing coming to a stop. It had to be the police. They had already killed so many of his brothers today, he was quite certain they intended to kill them all to eliminate any witnesses, to silence all dissent.

Haasim cried out behind him and he spun to see his best friend on the ground, blood pouring from a head wound. This was it. This was where he earned his martyrdom. This was where they would all die to meet again in Jannah for an eternity of bliss.

He pushed to his feet and grabbed a crowbar from the hand of a fallen brother, then using the SUV as cover, he raced forward. He reached the rear window and whacked at the glass. It splintered but held. He continued to swing over and over, screaming in rage. He could already taste the blood of the infidels on his tongue when he finally made a hole in the glass. He dropped the crowbar and it clattered on the pavement as he reached in and grabbed the shattered glass with his bare hands, yanking the entire frame out. He tossed it aside then retrieved the crowbar as he climbed up on the bumper, raising his hand, preparing to strike the man and woman in the rear seat, barely older than him, yet responsible for so much hatred.

"Now you die!"

A man popped up from the middle row, a pistol gripped in his hand, and he pointed it directly at Jihad's forehead. "You first."

The trigger squeezed, and for the last brief moment of his existence, Jihad celebrated.

I did it!

Tommy screamed and Mai wailed as the body of their assailant collapsed on the ground behind them with a thud. Acton withdrew the weapon and placed a hand on Tommy's shoulder as Laura embraced Mai.

"It's over. You're going to be all right."

Tommy nodded, though Acton was quite certain the young man thought he was full of shit. Gunfire continued, suggesting no one was safe, but he didn't have time for this. He turned back toward Lombardi.

"Are we dead in the water?"

"Yeah, we're not going anywhere."

"Who are these people?"

"They're not police, and they're not part of the mob. I don't know who they are."

Acton climbed forward, bracing himself on the dash as he peered through the windshield and cursed. "It's Tankov!"

Laura leaned forward to get her own look. "That's good, isn't it? It means they're not here to kill us. They just want the document."

Acton turned around. "Okay, everybody stay down and we might just survive this."

The gunfire continued to rapidly dwindle to nothing, and Lombardi raised his hands. "Here they come."

Tankov strode forward, keeping a wary eye out for survivors, his gun aimed at the driver who had his hands up. This was turning out to be far more public and far more fun than he had expected. It was always a good day to kill fundamentalist scum, though it would mean a more difficult escape.

But that was the next part of the plan. Right now, he had to concern himself with completing the current phase of the mission.

He stopped in front of the SUV. "Professor Acton, all we want is the document. Hand it over and nobody gets hurt."

There was no reply, and he rolled his eyes.

"Professor Acton, don't make me ask twice."

The rear passenger door pushed open and a hand appeared holding up a leather case. "Don't shoot! It's yours!"

He recognized Acton's voice and smiled. "So good to see you, Professor."

"I wish I could say the same."

"What? No 'thank you' after we just saved your lives?"

"Fine, thank you."

"That didn't sound sincere. Is your wife there with you?"

"Why does that matter?"

"I just wanted to say hi."

Acton stepped out, holding up the folio. "Do you want this or not?"

"I do."

"Then let's cut the bullshit. Am I bringing it to you, or are you getting it?"

"That doesn't look like paper to me. Show me what's inside."

Acton flipped open the folio then reached in, partially pulling out several pages folded together.

"That'll do."

Acton stuffed them back in and Tankov motioned to Vlad to retrieve it, when one of the locals issued a warning.

"We've got company."

Bruno wove through the traffic jam they had become stuck in. The moment they had seen the Vatican scientists leave the rest stop, he and the others had followed. They had been forced to allow the fundamentalists to get ahead of them—they were simply too dangerous and showed no regard for the safety of others. But that disregard had left an opening in their wake, and he and the others had followed them as if tailing an ambulance through city streets.

Though whatever had happened here to create this traffic jam, they hadn't been witness to, only the aftermath. The road was completely blocked, there was no way through, and the police were directly behind them. They couldn't be caught here, so the decision had been made to move forward on foot.

"I don't see them," said Greco.

Bruno scanned the cars ahead as they reached the front of what turned out to be an accident scene. "Neither do I." He jumped up on the hood of a car, its owner protesting, but he ignored them. "It looks like they both got away." He hopped down and continued forward.

Several of the extremists were clustered around their wrecked cars, uncertain as to what to do. He was tempted to kill them all, but that wasn't his job. Justice would be delivered by the police arriving any moment now. His job was to make sure that document was delivered to the pope, and with the two Vatican vehicles nowhere to be seen, he needed transportation.

He spotted a bright red pickup truck on the side of the road, not exactly a common sight in these parts, but it was perfect for their needs. He pointed then jogged toward the truck, the others following. The owner was standing by the open driver's side door, on his phone, with his back to them. Bruno tapped him on the shoulder and the man turned around, dropping his phone and shoving his hands into the air at the sight of the gun pointed at his chest.

"Keys?"

They were handed over and Bruno gently pushed the man out of the way. "Thank you for cooperating."

Bruno jumped behind the wheel as everyone else piled into the extended cab or the exposed bed. He fired up the engine, put it in gear, and pressed on the accelerator, leaving the carnage behind, though only for a minute. Greco pointed up ahead and to the left at several cars clustered around one of the Vatican SUVs. Someone was reloading an assault rifle as half a dozen kicked at the windows and yanked on the doors.

He took his foot off the accelerator. "Take them out!"

Windows rolled down on the driver's side, and those in the back positioned themselves to engage.

"Try not to hit the SUV. Those are friendlies inside. Single shot only."

Weapons settings were changed as he coasted up unnoticed. Someone in the rear seat opened fire, the rest joining in, the one holding the AK-47 taken out first, the rest felled moments later. Bruno leaned out the driver's side window and honked his horn. "Are you all right?"

The passenger window rolled down and a man poked his head out. "We're fine. Thank you for helping."

Bruno smiled at the man then hammered on the gas. There was no time to waste.

"What the hell's going on up there?" asked Greco, again pointing ahead.

Bruno leaned forward, peering through the windshield and cursed at the sight of the third SUV stopped, its engine smoking, half a dozen men spread across the roadway with assault rifles, and Professor Acton standing beside the vehicle with the leather folio held up in the air. "Take out the gunmen!" he ordered as he hauled his weapon off his lap and shoved it through his window, resting the muzzle on his side-view mirror.

He squeezed the trigger, uncertain as to whom it was he was now fighting.

Tankov dove to the right and rolled, coming to a stop and aiming his rifle toward the red pickup truck that had just rushed up to the scene, looking so out of place in Italy. He opened fire as the rest of his team scattered. Acton disappeared back inside the SUV, slamming his door shut as Tankov attempted to get a bead on the engine of the approaching truck, carrying at least five guns, four of them lined up in the bed.

"Who the hell are these people?"

Vlad opened fire. "I've got no damn idea, but I don't think they like us."

"No shit!"

Acton covered Laura once again with his body, reaching out and pushing Tommy and Mai down as gunfire raged from two directions. Mai's screams had turned into whimpers, the poor girl going into shock. This was too much for anyone to handle.

"Do we know who they are?" asked Laura, and Acton shook his head.

"I just got a glimpse of them. Looks just like a bunch of civilians in a pickup truck. Like something out of Dukes of Hazzard."

"Dukes of what?"

"When we get home, we're working on your American culture education, and I'm getting you a pair of Daisy Dukes."

"What are those?"

"Don't you mind. It's more for me than you."

"I don't think they're shooting at us!" cried Tommy

Acton had to agree. So far, not a single shot had been heard impacting their vehicle, which meant the new arrivals weren't the ones chasing them. His brief glimpse hadn't revealed any keffiyehs or out-of-control beards, just clean-shaven, casually dressed men. But why were they here, and who were they?

"Could it be another group of art thieves? Competitors of Tankov?" suggested Laura.

"That's as good an idea as any."

"How the hell do you know all these people?" asked Lombardi, sprawled across the front seats as he attempted to use the dash as a shield.

"We haven't exactly lived a quiet life." Acton turned to Laura. "If they are a rival group, we can't count on them being as friendly as Tankov's people."

She cocked an eyebrow at him. "Friendly isn't exactly the way I'd describe them."

"No, but in our past few dealings with them, they haven't killed us."

"That wasn't always their choice."

Acton's phone pinged with a message and he fished it out of his pocket, his eyes narrowing at the text.

"Who's it from?"

"BD."

"What's it say?"

"Head into the dust."

"What the hell's that supposed to mean?" asked Tommy from the rear row, his voice filled with uncontrolled panic when Lombardi pointed.

"Look!"

Dawson expertly controlled the massive Sikorsky helicopter, lowering them rapidly toward the highway, his nose up, relying on instinct and training not to slam into the ground. "Eat this, assholes!"

Dust billowed all around them as the massive rotors worked their magic, delivering a textbook dusting to everyone below. They had followed the A1 north and it didn't take too long to spot the final showdown from above. He had no idea who was fighting it out. All he knew was he couldn't risk letting either side win because then they could focus on the professors.

He glanced over at Niner, peering out his side window, helping gauge their distance. "Do you see them?"

Niner shook his head. "No! Let's just hope they got that message!"

Acton pushed his door open as the wind and dust howled around them, the thunder of helicopter rotors overwhelming. He took Laura by the hand then helped Tommy and Mai out, pointing toward the mayhem ahead of them. "Just head into the dust! Keep moving forward! Everybody grab the next person's wrist!" He turned to Lombardi who had crawled out the passenger side. "You take up the rear! Make sure nobody gets left behind! Let's try to get over to the guardrail and use it as a guide!"

Acton led the way, leaning into the wind, shielding his eyes with his hand as he struggled to breathe. He got them around the front of the SUV then kept heading left until he bumped into the guardrail. He changed his direction, following the metal divider as the blades continued to thunder, his grip like iron on Laura's wrist. He pressed onward, struggling for breath, his mouth filled with dirt and grit, his eyes watering as the dust continued to pound them. He couldn't make out anything. He couldn't see his hand in front of his face. But the roar of the helicopter continued to grow louder, and he wasn't certain, but it appeared the gunfire had stopped.

He kept going, kept pressing forward, and just prayed he didn't bump into Tankov or one of his men.

Or worse, a helicopter blade.

Tankov hunched over, his back to the helicopter. He covered his eyes and mouth as best he could, but it didn't help. He couldn't see anything, and he could barely breathe. Whatever helicopter was doing the dusting was not only piloted by an expert, but it was big, the power of the rotors incredible, the dust overwhelming. They weren't equipped for this. None of them even had goggles.

This fight was lost.

And with the connections the professors had, those responsible were liable to be Delta, and he had no desire to die today.

"Abort! Abort! Abort!" he shouted as loud as he could. He broke to his right, heading for the divider running down the center of the highway. His shins hit the guardrail and he cursed then climbed over the divide. He peered to his right, struggling to see the oncoming traffic through the dust, but couldn't see anything. Vlad made it over, and they huddled together until the rest of the team joined them.

Tankov pointed north. "Let's go until we can see, then we'll get across when it's safe!"

Everyone nodded and Tankov rose, sprinting along the side of the highway, the dust quickly dying as they put distance between them and the blades. He glanced over his shoulder to see that the traffic had stopped. He darted across, the others following, then disappeared into the trees, abandoning their weapons as they headed back for their SUV, emptyhanded once again.

But alive.

"I've got eyes on them! Our nine o'clock!" rumbled Atlas through the comms. Dawson eased up on the controls, dropping them to the ground with a bounce as Atlas yanked open the rear door. "Get in! Get in!" the big man shouted.

Dawson finally spotted the professors rushing toward them through the settling dust. "Hurry up!" he shouted as he spotted the second group of gunmen recovering. He twisted around to see Mai climb in, Spock pulling her inside and shoving her into a seat. Tommy followed then Laura. A man he didn't recognize was next then finally Acton.

"Let's get the hell outta here!" yelled the professor as Atlas hauled the door shut.

Dawson powered back up and pulled up on the cyclic. They lifted off the ground and he angled them forward, racing toward the gunmen, causing them to scatter before passing over the police rushing toward the scene. He banked left and off the highway as he gained altitude, then set a course south.

He glanced back. "Is everybody okay?"

Acton stepped forward. "Yeah, but does anybody have a change of shorts?"

Niner grinned. "Small or extra-large?"

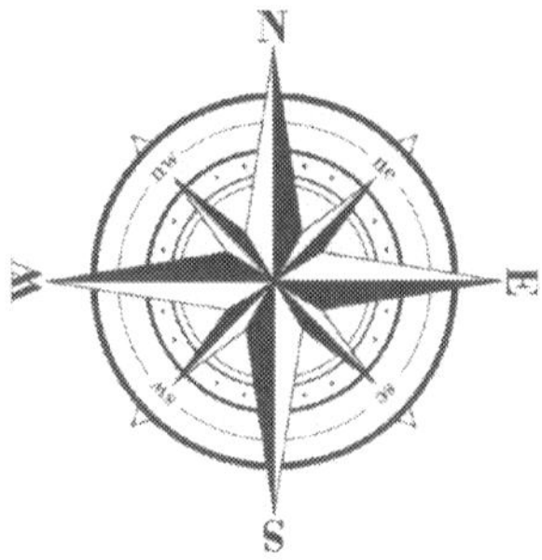

Giasson's Office

The Vatican

Giasson stood staring at the security monitors, watching as the crowds dissipated, the local imams having come through in the name of peace. There was a heavy police presence, but the feared violence had never come, which he thanked God for. A repeat of what had happened last time was his worst nightmare. So many had died including friends and colleagues. He had almost died that day, but cooler heads had prevailed today. As soon as the imams realized they were being manipulated, they ordered their congregations home, some of them even coming down to talk to the crowds, which did the trick.

The counter-protesters were hanging around, waiting to make sure they weren't being played, but he was confident the situation would be back to normal within an hour.

Rizzo poked his head into his office. "You're not going to believe this, but we've got a chopper inbound. They say they have the professors and their party on board."

"What?"

"Hey, I'm just delivering the message. They're requesting clearance to land at the helipad. What do you want to do? They're five minutes out."

"Let them land! Let them land!" Giasson bolted out of his chair then raced through the security office. He had been attempting to find out what was going on, but nobody knew except that it was chaos all the way up and down the A1, bodies apparently riddling a hundred-kilometer stretch. He had just heard from those in the second SUV that they had been attacked, but somebody had saved them. A group of civilians, heavily armed, had killed the terrorists attempting to get into their disabled vehicle.

Gun-toting vigilantes weren't something you saw in Italy. It just didn't happen, and it had him wondering who it could have possibly been. In the few minutes he had had to think about it, he could come to only one conclusion.

It had to be the Keepers of the One Truth.

And it appeared the Vatican owed them their thanks.

"Oh, thank God!" groaned Tommy as the helicopter that had saved them touched down within the massive walls of the Vatican.

Acton grinned. "Yep, that'd be the right person to be thanking, considering where we are." He unbuckled his lap belt as Dawson powered down the biggest civilian chopper Acton had ever been in. He had no idea how Mary had managed to arrange this, but she was getting a big bonus when he got home. Mai and Tommy had calmed down on the ride here, though they were still shaken. They all were. What had happened today was insane. Why some people took such an affront to words, he would never understand. They were just words. Disagree with them, debate them vehemently if you must, but you don't kill over words.

Atlas slid the door open then hopped out followed by Spock. The two Delta Force operators helped their passengers down. Dawson and Niner jumped out and Acton stared up at the late afternoon sun, enjoying the warmth of it on his face as he gave Laura a quick kiss. He shook the hands of the Delta operators, Laura giving them all hugs, Niner doing his customary bear hug, lifting her feet off the ground.

"We can't thank you guys enough," said Acton.

"You're just lucky we were on two days' leave and happened to spot you on TV. Otherwise, you'd be up shit's creek," said Dawson.

Acton grinned. "I'm sure we would've figured a way out."

Spock cocked an eyebrow. "That I would've liked to have seen."

Acton pulled the SIG Sauer handgun from his belt. "I did have this."

Giasson rushed up with half a dozen of his men as Acton handed the weapon back to Lombardi. Hugs, kisses, handshakes, and various other forms of relieved greetings were exchanged.

"What happened to the people in the second SUV?" asked Laura. "We saw them get taken out."

"They're fine. Some good Samaritans helped them."

Acton grunted. "I think we met those good Samaritans. They're the ones who engaged Tankov and his men."

Giasson shook his head. "I can't wait to hear the entire story, but neither can His Holiness. He wants to see you all."

Dawson stepped forward. "As much as I'd love to meet him, we were never here."

Giasson regarded the man. "Understood." He turned to one of the men with him. "Arrange a car and driver for them, and have them shown out discreetly. Take them wherever they want to go."

"Yes, sir."

More hugs and handshakes, and the four Delta warriors were led away. Giasson guided them to the pope's office, a place Acton and Laura had been before. The elderly pontiff rose from behind his desk, extending his hands toward them.

"Thank God you're all right. You are all right, are you not?" he asked, leaning over as he spotted Acton's bloody shirt.

"Just a scratch, Your Holiness. Nothing to worry about."

"Well, thank God for that. But before you leave, make sure one of our doctors sees you. In fact, make sure everyone gets checked over."

Giasson bowed. "Of course, Your Holiness. I'll see to it."

The pope approached them. "Do you have it?"

Acton produced the folio, holding it out with both hands. "It's inside here."

His Holiness didn't take it. "Is it genuine?"

"It's from the era, but whether Frederick II wrote it, there's no way to know."

His Holiness frowned. "A dangerous document at the time, and even more so in these times. Sharing it on social media might not have been wise."

Tommy shuffled uncomfortably, staring at his feet. Acton smiled at the young man. "It was my idea, Your Holiness. History shouldn't be hidden due to other people's ignorance and hate."

"I agree, but its existence is a threat to the Church. God only knows what those motivated by so much hate will do if they think we hold it within our walls." He took the folio and placed it on his desk then opened a drawer, producing a folded set of papers.

"What's that?" asked Laura.

"You are aware of the special place, shall we say, on the grounds. I checked the inventory and discovered an entry from Pope Gregory IX that showed four copies of the original treatise were stored there. I retrieved one of them."

Acton's eyes narrowed as he regarded the old man. He was referring to the Vault, an ancient repository under the Vatican known only to the sitting pope and a few trusted advisors. A location he and Laura had the unfortunate honor of searching several years ago. "What for?"

"Follow me." They left the office and walked down a hall then into a room. His Holiness stepped out onto the famous balcony, leaving them all confused. There was no crowd today, the grounds evacuated, but there were still thousands outside the gate. Somebody spotted him and shouted, and then the entire crowd turned to face him.

The pontiff turned to Tommy. "Young man, would you record this please, and make sure it gets distributed as widely as your earlier broadcast?"

Tommy's cheeks flushed, but he pulled out his phone and activated the camera. "You're on, sir—I mean, Your Holiness."

The old man smiled at him then held up the copy of the Treatise, producing a lighter from his robes. He leaned into the microphone. "For the sake of peace, I destroy this blasphemous document!" He flicked the lighter, the flame sparking, then held it to the corner of the ancient document, the dried pages bursting into flame, removing it, in the eyes of the public, from existence.

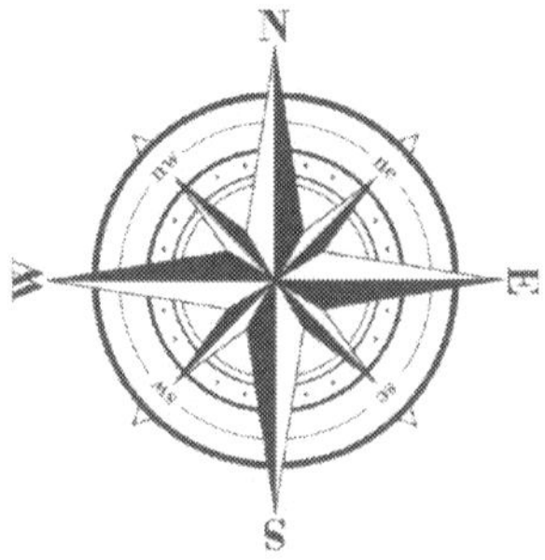

St. Thomas' Hospital

London, England

Reading bent over and stepped into his underwear, happy to be getting dressed, tired of the gown he had been in. Somebody groaned behind him.

"My God! What is it with you showing me your bollocks today?"

Reading hauled up his shorts then faced Michelle with a grin. "And you keep looking."

She gave him the stink-eye then turned to Spencer. "You could have warned me."

Spencer shrugged. "I didn't see you come in. I was already blinded by the sight."

"Sod off, the both of you!" Reading perched on the edge of the bed and pulled on his pants.

"So? What's the verdict?" asked Michelle.

"Just got cleared. No damage, apparently. I just need to take it easy for a few days, but I should be fine."

Michelle regarded him as he zipped up his fly. "So, no risk of a heart attack if I shock you with a little bit of news?"

Reading frowned. "No. Why? What's happened?"

She handed him his phone. "I forgot I had this in my purse, but when I saw the news and remembered, I thought it best you didn't see it."

Reading powered up the device. "Why? What's going on?"

"Your friends have been at it again."

"Jim and Laura?"

"Who else?"

He cursed as he checked his messages, scrolling through them and settling on the latest.

We're in Italy and heading home tonight. Care for some company?

He wagged the phone, staring at Michelle. "These are all messages about getting together. What aren't you telling me?"

Michelle handed over her phone, a BBC report already queued. He tapped play and watched the horror unfold. He handed it back to her, his head shaking, a decision made.

"Those two can't be left alone."

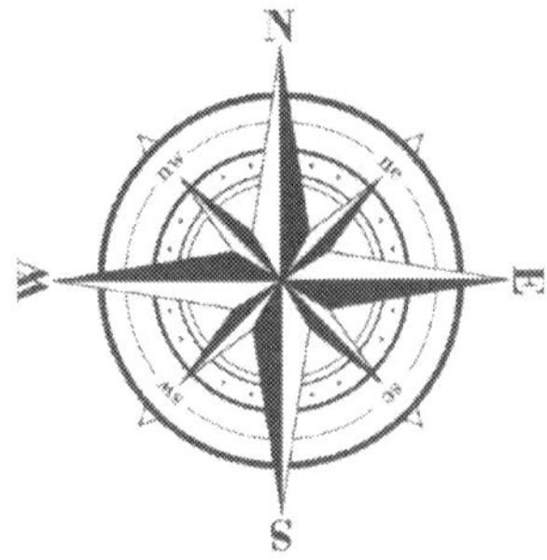

Two days short of Padua

AD 1239

Ricardo sat in the corner of what appeared to be an old root cellar. The laneway had indeed led to an abandoned farm, the walls of all the structures having long collapsed in upon themselves. He had stumbled upon an old cellar door and found his final refuge. It was as good a place as any to die. It was dry, he was out of the wind, and a sliver of sun came through the broken door overhead. His body was mostly numb now, the pain a mere throb. The bleeding had slowed now that he was stationary, but he was beyond saving, and unfortunately, it left him alone with his thoughts.

Why was he dying? What was it that he carried that merited death? What was in this document that had cost so much blood?

He was sworn to never look at it to preserve its secrecy, yet he was dying. He wouldn't last until nightfall. If anyone found him now, he was too weak to put up a fight and the document would fall into their hands. He would fail in his mission to deliver it, but he could still succeed in making certain it never fell into the wrong hands. He reached under his cloak. He retrieved the folio and let it fall in his lap, his chest heaving from the effort. He untied the strings holding it shut, then closed his eyes, resting his head against the cold wall of the cellar.

Please God, give me the strength to fulfill this one last task.

He opened the folio, shoving his thumb and forefinger inside, and pulled out the sheaf of papers it contained. Then frowned. How was he supposed to destroy this? He had no means of which to start a fire, and no strength to tear the pages. Yet he had to try. He flipped over the stack and lifted the first page toward his mouth with the aim of clenching it in his teeth then tearing it with his one good hand, when several words caught his eye, written in Latin.

Treatise of the Three Imposters.

He squinted.

A treatise? All these people had died because of an academic document? An angry pit formed in his stomach at the thought of his friend, Bartholomew, likely dead by now, along with his brothers, members of his order dead because of these "three imposters." Who were these three individuals, and why were they imposters?

He closed his eyes. He wasn't meant to see this. He had sworn an oath, yet the anger building inside gave him renewed strength and a determination to finally know what this was all about. He opened his eyes and continued to read what was a cover letter from His Holiness, informing the receiver that what was enclosed was this treatise. Ricardo gasped at who His Holiness claimed to be the author.

The Holy Roman Emperor himself, Frederick II.

And it left him puzzled. He continued reading the letter from His Holiness to the head of the Electoral College he had been tasked to deliver the folio to. It claimed the emperor was a heretic, and that the proof was this treatise penned in his own hand.

Ricardo's jaw dropped at the accusation. The Holy Roman Emperor a heretic? It was unfathomable. This was the leader of Christendom. How could he be a heretic? Ricardo set the cover letter aside and picked up the first page of the document and began to read, his Latin a little rusty, but as an educated nobleman, a language he understood well. And as he read the dry document, facts laid out without emotion, without adjectives to exaggerate the importance of the thoughts laid out in writing, his chest tightened.

A horror built up inside of him, his anger forgotten, replaced by despair and self-pity and confusion. Could this be true? The emperor was an educated man, an intelligent man, and if he felt this way, didn't there have to be at least a kernel of truth? Could his claim that Moses, Jesus, and Muhammad, the founders of the three great Abrahamic religions, were all imposters, lying to their flocks, be true? Could there be no God? Could everything he had devoted his life to be a lie?

Tears welled in his eyes as the words he read crushed his faith, casting doubt on everything in his final moments. He squeezed his eyes shut, unable to read any more of what he prayed was a blasphemous lie. He folded the pages back up and stuffed them back inside the folio. He was too weak to retie the string, so instead managed to wedge it back under his cloak where, if he were lucky, it would never be found.

For if there was a God in Heaven, surely He would not want these words to ever see the light of day, and would surely allow this old warrior, who had served Him well, to rest in peace. And should that not be possible and his final prayers were to fall on the deaf ears of a false god, then so be it. He didn't need a god to know the life he had led had been a good one, lived in service to his fellow man. He could die knowing that even if there were no Heaven, and after death there was simply nothingness, he would take his final breath knowing it had been a life well lived, and one in which he had no regrets.

He closed his eyes, settled his head against the wall, and said one final prayer to his Lord and Savior, refusing to allow the words of one man destroy a lifetime of faith.

THE END

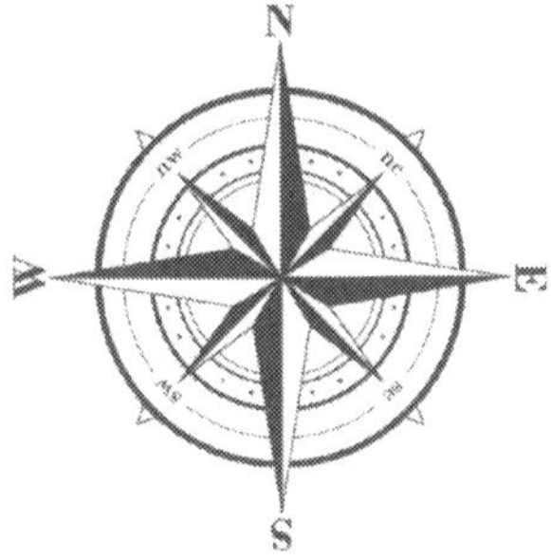

ACKNOWLEDGMENTS

As many of you know, I take things from my own life and put them in my books. This time is no different. Reading's SVT attack is much like mine, though I was fortunate enough that my daughter was home. But those injections, the conversations with the paramedics, were all pretty much as they happened with me.

Though I wasn't in my knickers.

And the scene at the hospital where someone died in the next room, happened to me years later, exactly as described. It went on for over fifteen minutes, and it had a similar effect on me as it did Reading. According to the doctor who came into my room a few minutes after the fight was lost, the man was my age with a history of heart problems.

Just like me.

I don't know how much life I have left in me, and I certainly don't know what comes next, but I, like Reading, pray that if there is something, I've led a good enough life to end up in a place where my loved ones are waiting for me, and the troubles and struggles of this world are left behind.

As usual, there are people to thank. My dad for all the research, Rick Messina for some Italian help, Brent Richards for some weapons info, Sheelagh Rogers for some British English help, and, as always, my wife, my daughter, my late mother who will always be an angel on my shoulder as I write, as well as my friends for their continued support, and my fantastic proofreading team!

To those who have not already done so, please visit my website at www.jrobertkennedy.com, then sign up for the Insider's Club to be notified of new book releases. Your email address will never be shared or sold.

Thank you once again for reading.

Made in the USA
Las Vegas, NV
30 March 2024